STRAY THREADS

by

Kenneth Amidon

Cover Design: Lindsey Ruane

ISBN: 978-1480131378

For my wife, Suellen

&

The Boys:

Christopher, Colin, Devin and Beckett

My thanks to:

Cindy Robinov and Ray VanBatenburg
who read endless drafts and gave me valuable
feedback and much needed encouragement.

Lindsey Ruane for her great designs.

Chris Amidon for his editing expertise.

And especially my wife, Suellen.
Without her patience, support, encouragement -
and great memory of the 1970s -
this book would not have been possible.

1

She lay on her back on the cobblestoned alleyway. The fetid stink of the nearby restaurant dumpster overpowered any smell from the splats of vomit coalescing near her left knee. A trickle of spittle glistened from the left corner of her mouth, trapping a few stray threads of blonde hair. Her grey Red Sox tee-shirt heaved in wobbly rhythm with her snores. Her jeans remained belted and un-violated. The rectangular outline of a box of cigarettes bulged her right pocket. Her right hand cradled her stomach, perhaps in some last ditch effort to soothe a boiling gut.

The young woman's left arm stretched out to her side, crooked up toward her head. Tim's eyes lingered on the hand. Once, he looked there for a ring, but now his eyes focused there because that hand belied the rest of her. Her long fingers rested poised like a ballerina's in perfect pirouette, determined and elegant. His eyes returned to her face and the smudge of tear-streaked makeup rubbed from her right eye. Tim shook his head, exhaled a hard breath, and bent to lift her.

The bartender at The Skipper's Key had called twenty minutes earlier.

"Hey, Timmy. It's Ray," he said. "Maggie came in. She's cocked. I think she needs a friend."

"Maggie drunk?" Tim said. "You sure?"

"C'mon, man, who knows drunks better than me?" Ray said. "She came in 'bout an hour ago. I'd bet my ass she'd put away a few before that. A couple of jokers conned her into flippin' down shots with them. Looked like a dare or a bet or something. All kinda weird, ya know? Very un-Maggie like. One of the morons musta hit on her. Whatever he said, Maggie's gasket popped, and she told the guy to stick it. Then she went an' dumped his brew on his crotch. Man, he got pissed. Didi jumped in and pulled her away to the other end of the bar. I gave the yahoos a freebie round to cool 'em down, as if moron number one needed it. Maggie'd already done a pretty good job at cooling his engi . . ."

"So Maggie's there now?" Tim said.

"Not exactly," Ray said. "She started crying, and Didi talked to her a bit, but Maggie wasn't saying what was wrong. Didi thought she babbled something about someone named Sharon, but Didi wasn't sure she heard it right. Then Didi went back to her tables and Maggie went to the head. I figured she was puking, which was probably the best for her. Five, ten minutes later Didi went in to check on her, and Maggie was gone. No one saw her leave."

"How long ago?" Tim said.

"'Bout ten, fifteen, maybe twenty minutes. Haven't a clue where she went."

"Ray, did you notice if she had any cigarettes with her?"

"Yeah," said Ray. "How'd you know that?"

"Lucky guess," Tim said. "I bet I know where she went. Thanks, Ray. I owe ya, man."

"No problem, Buddy."

In the almost two years they had lived together, Maggie and Tim spent a couple of evenings a week at The Skipper's Key, playing pool or darts and watching the '75 Red Sox win the pennant and lose the World Series. Maggie and Tim both smoked but wanted to quit. After cold turkey didn't work, Maggie came up with another idea.

"What we need to do is condition ourselves to hate cigarettes," she said.

"I already hate them," Tim said. "Until the cravings. Then I fall in love with them all over again. Same thing as I do every time I look at you."

"Are you equating me with a cigarette?" Maggie said, her head tipped, her eyes wide. "How flattering."

"No," Tim said. "I just mean I'm hooked on you. But you're definitely better than a cigarette. Although, now that you brought up the subject of butts, I think … you …" He flashed a contrite smile. "I think I should shut up."

"Good idea." Maggie rolled her eyes.

"So what's your plan?" Tim said.

"We need to associate cigarettes with something really nasty and disgusting, something that turns your stomach, so that when we think of lighting up, we make cigarettes even more disgusting than they are."

"Okay," Tim said. "How about we visualize me at a disco, wearing a powder blue leisure suit and gold chains, dancing to the hot sounds of 'Disco Duck?' Wouldn't that do it?"

Tim started moving his shoulders alternately up and down and pointing his arm and extended index finger in the air.

"C'mon, I'm serious," she said, smiling. "I read about this technique in a magazine. It works."

Tim nodded. "Sorry, go on. I promise to be serious."

"What I was thinking is we agree to smoke only in certain designated spots, only outside, and if possible, only in places so disgusting you want to barf."

"Sounds like an apartment I lived in once," Tim said. "Of course, it wasn't outside."

Maggie ignored him.

"I know a place where we can go from here that smells like rotted vegetables, rancid meat, and decomposing fish, where you're always worried a rat'll jump out and bite you."

"Sounds terrific," Tim said. "I can't wait to go there."

"Good," she said and rose up from the chair. "C'mon. I'll show you."

"Now?" Tim said. "But I haven't finished my beer."

"Don't worry," she said. "It won't take long. Ray will watch the beers for us. Right, Ray?"

"Absolutely," Ray said. He stood on the other side of the bar within earshot of the conversation. "I'll guard them with my life, Maggie."

Ray laughed as Tim give him a quick scowl.

"All right," Tim said. "Let's go."

Maggie grabbed his hand and led him outside. They crossed the street and headed south. A half block later she took a sharp right and pulled him into an alley.

"Where the heck you taking me?" Tim said.

"Over there," she said and nodded straight ahead toward the end of the alley and a three-stepped cement staircase leading to a service door. Above the door a weathered sign said – Portland Chowder House.

"Ah, your old employer," Tim said. "Frankly, it would be a lot more appetizing entering through the front door."

"We don't want appetizing, remember? We want disgusting."

"Oh, yeah. I forgot."

Maggie led him past the door to the rusty, yellow dumpster. She half-turned and sat down on the granite curb. Tim remained standing but still held her hand. He looked at the curb spot next to Maggie and twisted his head around surveying the ground around the dumpster.

"You're kidding, right?"

"I told you this was the idea," Maggie said. "We can only smoke in a place we don't want to come to. That discourages us from smoking."

"I'm worried a rat will come out and bite me," Tim said.

Maggie yanked him down next to her.

"Just sit down and give me a cigarette," she said.

Tim pulled a pack from his shirt pocket. He put two in his mouth, lit them and handed one to Maggie. They sat in silence for a few moments when Tim reached his arm around Maggie's shoulders. She pulled away.

"No, that's against the rules, too." She lifted his arm off.

The left side of his face scrunched up.

"Against the rules?"

"We're supposed to *hate* coming here. Remember?" she said. "That's the plan."

"Well, it's working," Tim said.

To Tim's surprise, the technique continued to work. Within a month both eased off cigarettes and stayed off for the most part. Maggie smoked one or two on those rare occasions when she drank more than her usual single beer.

Tim carried the unconscious Maggie from the alley's grunge. Maggie wrinkled her brow, cracked an eye, and mumbled. "...you're ... asshole ... all ... men ...ass ... holes..." was all he could make out.

"I love you, too," Tim said.

Maggie struggled to focus on the voice in the dim light. She recognized Tim, and her face softened a bit.

"Timmy?" she slurred. "Not you...I mean...th'other asshole."

"Thanks, Mags," Tim said. "I feel better now."

"No, I mean...um...sorry...I mean...other asshole is asshole...you're not asshole...where we going?"

"Home."

"Whose home?"

"Yours."

"Kay." She tried to put her left arm up around his neck, but it slid off as she slipped back toward unconsciousness.

At Maggie's apartment, Tim carried her straight to her bedroom and set her on her bed. He looked down on her considering what to do. He couldn't leave her like this. She needed a shower. He'd seen Maggie naked many times in the past, but undressing her semi-comatose body felt like a major violation.

Tim puzzled about Maggie to himself. *Maggie never gets drunk. Ever. What's going on here? What happened? And who's this Sharon person?*

Tim averted his eyes and sat at her feet at the bottom of the bed, catching his breath after carrying her up three flights of stairs.

"Glad I quit smoking," he said aloud.

Tim stood, and as he turned toward Maggie, he saw his face in the large mirror over her dresser. His dark brown eyes reflected back at him the hundreds of "what ifs" and "shouldas" embedded in his brain. He smiled at his own pathetic image and then shook his head and shrugged. *This isn't exactly how I envisioned our shower scene.*

"But will she respect me in the morning?" He said aloud and slipped off her sandals and jeans. He left her in her T-shirt and panties.

"Mags?" Tim said. "Maggie." Then louder. "Margaret."

"Don't call me her." She squeezed open an eye, saw him, and managed a sour, semi-perceptible smile.

"Sorry, Mags," he said. "We need to get you cleaned up, okay?"

Maggie closed her eye and shook her head. "Want sleep," she said and made a futile effort to roll away from him.

"C'mon," he said, grabbing her right elbow with his left arm, slipping his right under her waist, and pulling her up. "You need a shower."

She grunted and said, "I don't feel so good."

"I know. This will help."

Once standing, Tim lifted Maggie's arm around his neck and walked her toward the bathroom.

Too tiny to hold a tub, the bathroom sat wedged into the corner with a narrow shower stall and a swinging plexiglass shower door that hit the toilet when opened too far. Any thoughts he entertained of cleaning her up with him standing outside the shower soon disappeared. Even at its maximum opening, the shower door blocked him from effectively assisting her. He decided on a Plan B.

Tim eased Maggie into the shower and propped her up against the wall with his left arm. He kicked off his sneakers. He tried to strip off his jeans, but couldn't hold her up and do that at the same time. He shook his head, sighed, and pulled out his wallet, tossing it out the door toward the bed. He slid into the cramped shower with her.

"Stand up, Honey," he said. "We'll make this quick."

Maggie stood with her back towards the shower nozzle, leaning forward on Tim, her head against his chest, her arms up around his neck for support. He reached for the hot water handle then hesitated. *Oh, crap. Why didn't I think to run the water first? Ah, well, maybe she needs a jolt.*

"Uh, Maggie," he said. "Sorry, but this may feel, um, a bit cool for a moment."

He reached past her and turned the hot water knob all the way on. Even with Maggie blocking part of him from the water, it struck him like a thousand icicle darts. Maggie got the brunt of it. Her eyes popped open.

"Shit!" she screeched and lunged forward on him.

She would have sent both of them to the floor, if the shower stall were any bigger. But Tim regained his balance and managed to shift them around so he took the direct spray. *Holy crap! Colder than a Maine beach.*

"Hang on, Maggie. It'll get warm. Soon."

Maggie curled her shoulders in and shivered herself tightly against him. Despite the cold shower, Tim felt a quick jolt of remembered passion. Then Maggie's chest began to pulsate, and Tim knew what was coming. Even within the confined space of the straightjacket shower, Tim managed to twist Maggie away from him and around towards the drain. She heaved.

"Let it go, Honey," Tim said. "Let it all go."

He grabbed a fistful of the back of her wet T-shirt with his right hand, holding her like a ventriloquist's dummy, bent forward, head up against the shower wall. After her stomach emptied itself of its remaining contents, Maggie continued with dry heaves. Tim fought an overwhelming urge to follow suit but held it in. Maggie finished as warm water flowed.

Tim cleaned her off as well as he could, using the squeezable plastic bottle of shampoo as soap after the ovoid Dove bar squirted out of his hand. He couldn't bend down to pick it up.

The shower and the up-chuck revived Maggie enough so with Tim steering and supporting her, she staggered back to her bed.

"Needa lie down," she said and fell forward onto the bed. Tim didn't hesitate this time and stripped her of the wet shirt and panties, drying her as well as he could. He shifted her enough to pull down the covers.

He started to cover her up, but stopped for a

moment. He couldn't resist one quick look at her lying there. So helpless and frail. So perfect. He wished he could turn back the clock. He wished for another chance. *Someday, maybe.* He pulled the covers up under her chin, bent down, and kissed her lightly on the forehead.

"Good night, Fair Princess," he said, as he once did. He saw an almost-smile at the corner of her lips.

"Night," she whispered, mumbled something else and shifted into a fetal position. Her breathing steadied as it shifted to heavy sleep.

STRAY THREADS | 11

2

Tim rubbed the damp towel through his hair. In the main room he draped it around his neck and started unbuttoning his wet shirt with his left hand. He picked up the handset of Maggie's phone and tucked it between his shoulder and cheek. He dialed.

"Yeah, it's me," he said three rings later. "Everything's cool...yup...going to be a while...don't worry...yeah, I did...don't wait up...yeah, me, too." He hung up.

Tim retrieved a dry towel from the bathroom and stripped away his wet clothes. He wrapped one towel around his waist and hung his wet clothes to dry over the top of the closet door.

Maggie's tiny, two-room apartment doubled as home and studio. She furnished it with college holdovers, flea market acquisitions, and a few bargains from the Salvation Army Store. But few noticed the furniture.

Watercolor and oil paintings, charcoal drawings,

and scores of photographs covered the walls. Some of the watercolors hung mounted and framed, but most were taped or pinned up in clusters. A few casual sketches of people interspersed with oil painted seascapes of the Maine coast and cityscapes of Portland and Boston. Maggie paid her bills by designing advertising inserts for The Portland Times - a job, Tim believed, fell far beneath her talents. While he never claimed to be an expert, Tim knew Maggie's paintings rivaled anything he'd seen in the local galleries. When they lived together, he'd urged Maggie to quit her day job and devote her full efforts to painting. Maggie insisted she would someday. But not yet.

"Not until I get it right," she said. But she never explained what "getting it right" meant.

Maggie's easel stood at the far end of the main room, just to the right of the skylight, where it could catch the early morning sun. Cans of brushes and other tools of her trade lined the middle shelf of an old, now reborn bookcase Maggie rescued from a trash pile in front of an apartment building. Art books and photography compilations sat stacked on the upper shelves, while the bottom shelves held fifteen or so worn hardcover editions of classic novels. A three-foot stack of dog-eared paperbacks sat on the floor next to the bookcase.

Above the bookcase hung a two-level maple shelf with a set of 1901 editions of the complete works of Shakespeare, each play individually hardbound and in near perfect shape. This shrine Maggie dedicated not only to her favorite writer but to her college roommate and best friend, Annie. Annie inherited the volumes, but she gave them to Maggie a month before Annie died from complications of breast cancer, a few months before they were to graduate from Boston University. That was five years ago.

Tim slipped past the old cobbler's bench, which doubled as coffee table and foot rest, and plopped himself in the big comfortable green chair, his favorite. He flicked on the nearby floor lamp and reached for the magazine on the bench. He couldn't watch television. Maggie refused to own one.

"Not with a bang, but with a whimper," Maggie had said. "The end of civilization will come with a click. God will get fed up and simply push the 'power off' button."

Maggie called television the "moron's mind melter." Tim tried to point out some of the great things TV carried, but Maggie wouldn't buy it.

"Believe it or not," he said," some great movies and even Shakespeare show up on TV."

"If I want to see a film, I'll go to a movie theatre," she said. "If I want to see Shakespeare, I'll go to a regular theatre. I don't want to watch *Hamlet* interrupted by some guy selling toilet bowl cleaner."

"To pee or not to pee?" Tim said. "That is the question."

"Exactly!"

"Yet the Sox games on TV at The Key are okay?"

"Red Sox games are different," she said. "I don't own a car and Boston's too far away." Maggie was a woman of many passions, loyalties and a handful of compromising principles. "Besides, it's my way of staying connected to Boston."

Tim wrapped himself in her afghan. Maggie's scent – brush cleaner with a touch of lavender candle oil - surrounded him. He propped up his feet on the cobbler's bench and turned on the lamp.

The light illuminated Maggie's work-in-progress on her easel. The canvas held little paint beyond the grayish blue background wash, but Tim could see the spidery collection of charcoal lines she used to sketch out her subject. Too tired to get up from the chair, Tim struggled to decipher it. After a few moments of concentration he could make out what looked like mountains, and after a few short minutes, he knew the spot. A stab of sadness passed through him. *Sky Castle.* He thought. *My Waterloo.*

On a small table along the wall sat Maggie's stereo system. Like most of Maggie's belongings, it was nothing fancy, but she invested in two good speakers and a cassette player. Stretching toward it, Tim turned the volume knob down a few notches before he clicked the "On" dial in case some ear-popping song queued up.

Maggie possessed the most eclectic musical tastes of anyone Tim ever met. The chances of hearing Carlos Santana equaled the likelihood of hearing Mozart, Duke Ellington, or Patsy Cline. When the music started, Donovan sang "Colours." He left it on.

Next to the stereo's right speaker, Tim spotted a baseball sitting at the empty end of a plastic cassette tray. Maggie's "Rico Ball." He lifted it, tossed it up a couple of times, and turned it in his hand so he could see the inscription. He smiled remembering the night she got it. *A great catch!*

Maggie Hammond and Tim Roper met three and a half years ago as newly hired employees of the Cape Anne Mutual Insurance Company in Salem, Massachusetts. Both needed just-out-of-college-and-desperate-for-work-type-jobs and found them as claims adjusters in the city famous for hanging witches. Sharing the bottom end of the corporate totem pole and a passion for the hot pastrami at Herb's Delicatessen, they became friends by the end of their first week.

Among his long list of rules their boss, Mr. Griffin, warned them about was avoiding romantic relationships with co-workers. While not in the official Employee Guide, Tim theorized Mr. G. created this rule as he believed the devil infected the entire young generation of the nineteen sixties. Mr. G. took it as his sacred duty - passed down to him from both God and the Board of Directors - to keep drugs, sex, and rock and roll from the hallways of Cape Anne Mutual. Witchcraft wore many faces in Salem. Despite his attraction to his new co-worker, Tim needed the income and complied with Mr. G's rules.

At lunch one day Tim told Maggie about his plans to head into Boston to meet up that night with a couple of old UMass friends to take in a Sox game. The arrangements called for Tim to go from work to Kenmore Square by commuter train and subway. After the game, his buddies would drop him off back at his car in Salem, and he would drive home to his apartment in Gloucester. Maggie offered to save him train fare and time by giving him a ride to Boston. Her apartment sat six blocks from Kenmore in Boston's Back Bay.

Maggie and Tim found a parking spot on Marlborough Street. She knew a short cut to Kenmore and offered to walk him to his rendezvous point. They arrived earlier than planned, and Tim stationed himself at the designated spot. Maggie said she'd keep him company until his friends arrived.

A half hour past meeting time, his friends were still no-shows. Game time ticked closer, but Tim didn't care. Maggie engrossed him in her commentary on city life and why everyone should live in Boston for at least one year of his or her life.

"Everything you could ever wish for is here," she said. "Art, concerts, theatre, opera, great food, just about anything you can think of."

"Opera?" Tim said.

She flashed her crooked smile and rolled her eyes. "Opera is for those who have evolved past lip-synching Sha-Na-Na albums at college parties."

Tim once made the mistake of telling her about those parties at the old farmhouse near Amherst he and his buddies shared their senior year at UMass.

"Actually, I did go to an opera once at UMass," Tim said. "The best part was when they all stripped naked and sang. Except for the guys, of course."

"The guys didn't strip?"

"Yeah, they stripped," he said. "But that wasn't the best part."

"Don't tell me," Maggie said. "The 'opera' was *Hair*?"

"Yup."

"*Hair* is a musical, not an opera."

"Same thing. They sang a lot."

"No doubt it was written by Rossini or Puccini or Verdi?"

"Don't think so. I believe it was Yastrzemski or

something like that," Tim said. "Which reminds me. You forgot to mention the Red Sox. They're here in Boston."

"Yes," she acknowledged. "Boston has some sports teams, too."

"Some sports teams?" Tim said. "Yeah, I'd say they have *some* sports teams."

She glanced at her watch. "Your friends are late. Didn't the game start already? You'll miss the...uh...first half."

"First half?" Tim said. "You mean first *inning*."

"Oh, yeah, that's what I meant," Maggie said, a hint of a smile trying to break out. "The first inning."

"You don't get to a lot of baseball games, do you?"

"After a short-lived flirtation with a high school pitcher went sour, I stayed away from baseball games," Maggie said. "I didn't need reminders of him."

"Get out!" Tim said. "You've lived in Boston for over four years and never went to a Red Sox game?"

"Nope."

"Well, it's time you did," Tim said. "Okay...my so-called friends look like no-shows. Come to the game with me?"

"You're kidding," she said. "Now?"

"Now," he said. "I'll even buy you dinner. You haven't lived until you've dined on hotdogs and beer in Fenway Park. C'mon. If you don't have fun, I promise I will make all your first calls tomorrow. I'll take all your recorded statements and write them up for the files. I'll be your slave for a day."

"Be careful what you promise." Maggie looked Tim straight in the eye and smiled. "Okay," she said. "Let's go."

They started towards Fenway.

"By the way," she added. "How are you getting home without your friends?"

"I'll take the train back to Salem and walk to my car. The last run's at eleven."

They got good seats along the first base line. For someone who said she knew nothing about baseball, Maggie absorbed details like a sponge. Tim explained every nuance of the game.

"How come when the batter misses the ball, it's called a strike? Isn't striking something the same as hitting something? Having both hits and strikes is misleading. Shouldn't they call strikes, misses?"

"Probably," Tim said. "You should write a letter to the Commissioner suggesting that."

"Why is that guy called a shortstop? How come the guy with the ball doesn't have to tag the runner at first base, but when the runner goes to second base that guy does? Why do they call a strike a 'K'? Why not an 'S'?"

"An 'S' means either a sacrifice, if it's done by a hitter, or a save if by a pitcher," Tim said.

"Opposite meanings. Very confusing," she said. "Baseball sacrifices? That sounds very weird."

"It is," he said. "They do it quietly after the sixth inning. Behind that big wall in left field. Very bloody. It helps the home team get good voodoo though, so it's good for us. Hitters also steal things."

She smiled, shaking her head.

"Disgusting game. No wonder society is going down the toilet."

After the third inning Tim went down to the concession stand to grab a couple of beers. Leigh and Bruce, his would-be companions, stood there.

"What the hell happened?" Tim asked. "I waited over an hour for you guys to show."

"Yeah, we know," Bruce said. "We watched you from a bar window while we popped down a few."

"We assumed she was Maggie," said Leigh. "She's a fox. It took you long enough to ask her to the game."

"Are you shitting me?" Tim said. "You jerks didn't show on purpose?"

"We didn't exactly plan it that way, but when we see opportunity, we react," Bruce said. "Even if the opportunity is yours, not ours."

"We can make amends, if you want," said Leigh. "We can go back to your seat with you and tell Maggie you no longer need a babysitter. We'll take care of you, and she can go home."

"I'll even volunteer to walk her home," said Bruce. "She's way too good for you, anyways."

"You guys are assholes," Tim said. He paid for four beers, handed each of them one, and picked up the other two. "But I'm forever in your debt."

They raised their beers in toast, and Tim went back to his seat.

By the fifth inning and her second beer, Maggie became engrossed in the game. And she picked the right game. Four homeruns flew out, and Sox pitcher Diego Segui beat the Oakland A's Catfish Hunter, 10 to 9. That one game turned Maggie into a Red Sox fan. She would evolve to fanatic status the following year when the '75 Sox went to the World Series. But Maggie's biggest Fenway highlight on this night wasn't the win or the home runs. It came off a Rico Petrocelli pop foul in the sixth.

The ball arched high and headed down in the general direction of Maggie and Tim. Tim jumped up with the rest of the crowd. The ball came down two rows in front of them, deflected off the fingers of a beer impaired guy in a Boston College T-shirt, and came towards Tim. Tim made a stabbing catch of the ball and raised it victorious above his head, grinning to his cheering throng.

"That was so cool!" Maggie said.

Tim handed her the ball.

"Aren't you going to give it back?" she said.

"Nope. You get to keep it."

"Really?!" she said. "Then you need to sign it for me."

"Me?" he said. "You need Rico to sign it for you. He hit it."

"A foul ball?" she said. "You said foul balls were just bad hits that counted as strikes. That's not very impressive on his part. But your catch was impressive." She took a ballpoint from her pocketbook and handed it to Tim. "Sign it or I'll have a really bad time, and you will have to be my slave all day tomorrow."

Tim's imagination started to kick in, but the look on her face forced compliance. He signed it, *Tim the Man*.

Maggie took the ball back, smiled, and wrote something else on it. She showed him the ball. Under his name she had written, *A great catch!*

Mr. Griffin's fraternization rule fell a few hours later in the Back Bay.

Tim woke up in Maggie's chair. Pushing his hair back off his forehead, he looked around, trying to process where he was. The clock showed eleven-fifteen. He'd been asleep almost an hour. Standing, he rewrapped the towel and walked to the bedroom door.

Edging the door open, Tim listened for the cadence of her breathing. He peeked in. Maggie lay on her back, her face cocked toward the middle of the double bed. He smiled as he realized she was back in a pose similar to the one she had when he first came upon her earlier in the alley. *Ballerina hand.*

Back in the main room, Tim sat back down. *I guess she's over the worst. Tough day coming for her tomorrow. Might be a good idea to be gone when she gets up.*

While pondering, Tim noticed a new looking hardcover book on the small table beside him. He picked it up. *Looking for Mr. Goodbar.* He hadn't read it, but he remembered something about it being made into a movie. An envelope stuck out of the pages. Tim opened the cover to read the dust jacket, but when he flipped it to the back piece, the envelope fell out. As he tried to guesstimate where it fell from, he found a newspaper clipping stuck between two pages.

"Body in River Identified as a Reading Man" read the headline. The top left of the article identified the newspaper as the *Reading Ledger* and was dated two weeks ago. He knew Maggie grew up around Reading, Pennsylvania. He read on.

"A Pennsylvania State Police spokesman has confirmed that the body recovered yesterday in Alesbrook Township is that of thirty year old William Shannon of Reading." The article said Shannon was a graduate of Rethinger College and worked as a teacher at Pottlesburg High School. He unfolded the single crease. Shannon left a wife and two young children. The article did not mention the wife's or children's names and ended, "Cause of death has yet to be determined." But what it said at the bottom of the article caught his attention more than the story itself. Handwritten in blue ballpoint ink were the words, "Got your wish. Rot in Hell."

Tim inspected the envelope. *Hand addressed to Maggie. No return address. Postmarked a week ago in Reading. Nothing else in the envelope. Very weird. Maggie's "wish?" What the hell does that mean?*

Guilt eked into Tim's brain. *I shouldn't be reading this. Maggie's business is not my business anymore. If it ever was.* He glanced over at the bedroom door and put the envelope and the article back into the book. He set it back on the table. *She got her wish? Maggie wished someone dead? William Shannon. Shannon? Ray said Maggie told Didi something about a Sharon? Maybe Maggie said "Shannon?"*

Tim struggled to get the wet, clammy jeans pulled up his legs and over his butt. His oxford shirt went on easier, but he didn't button it. He rolled his wet undershorts and socks into a ball and stuffed them into his pocket. Pulling the door behind as he left, he tried the knob and pushed it to confirm security.

Goodnight, Fair Princess.

3

Tim climbed the back staircase to his third floor apartment. The door was unlocked.

"*Cheri!*" The female voice came from around the corner in the kitchen. "You have come home to me at last!"

"*Oui, ma petite,*" Tim said, as he entered the kitchen. He stopped, spread his arms, clicked his heels together, and bowed slightly. "*C'est moi.*"

Sophie sat at the kitchen table with an anatomy book in front of her, opened to a diagram of a human kidney. She held a cup of steamy tea in her right hand and a yellow highlighter in her left. On the chair next to her slept an orange tiger tomcat.

Sophie looked up, furled her brow, and did a slow examination of him standing there in his wet, disheveled clothes.

"Were you swimming?" she said.

"No," Tim said. "I got caught in a rainstorm."

"It has not rained in a week," she said.

"It's a long story," he said. "How about you make

me a cup of that tea, while I change and think up a believable story? Then I'll sit down and tell it to you."

"Go, but be quick," she said and looked towards her cat. "Pierre *et moi* are *tres curieaux*. We are cats, after all."

When Tim returned, a steamy mug sat across the table from Sophie. Next to the tea, a small plate with two slices of flatbread, each folded into triangles and holding some type of stuffing, awaited him.

"What're these? Some French thingies?" Tim said. "There's no snails or eyeballs or anything like that in this is there?" Someone once told Tim the French eat sheep eyeballs.

Sophie yellowed over a line in her book, and then lifted the highlighter about a half inch and moved it slowly to her right as she read the rest of the line. Sophie did not look up from her book.

"I am Canadian, not French," she said. "Canadians do not eat eyeballs."

"You sure?" Tim said, but he picked one up, smelled it, and bit into it. "Not bad. Unidentifiable...but not bad."

In stocking feet, Sophie would stand barely five feet tall. Her wavy auburn hair, parted gently on the left, framed her face, ending just below her ears. Sophie's straight, upturned nose supported a pair of horn-rimmed reading glasses. Her pursed lips lengthened her pointed chin.

Sophie looked up, lifted off her glasses, and left schoolmarm mode. Tim picked up the other bread triangle and bit into it.

"French Canadians do eat snails, however," she said. Tim stopped mid-chew and scowled at Sophie. He reached up as if he was going to spit it out in his hand. "But those are made from Maine clams."

Sophie put her glasses back on and set them low on her nose. Her large brown eyes stared at him.

"Okay, Timothy," she said, bringing back her best school teacher-ish manner. "What is your sad and pathetic story?"

"Well, it was like this," Tim said. "The dog ate my homework."

"And you jumped into the harbor to catch the dog, when he tried to escape?" she said, nodding. "Like I have not heard that excuse a hundred times before?"

"How about I had to go help this drunk in an alley?" Tim said.

"I have heard that one before, as well," she said. "One of your fellow inmates from The Key, I assume?"

"Yeah, I guess you could call her that."

"Her?" Sophie said. "Oh. A new chick, aye?"

"No," Tim said. "An old one."

Sophie smile faded, her eyes narrowed, and her smirk evaporated. Her face folded from mockery to concern.

"Marguerite?" she said.

Tim nodded.

"Marguerite was drunk in an alley?" Sophie said.

"Yeah, unconsciously drunk. Ray called before you came home and gave me the heads up. I found her in the alley where we used to go for smokes."

"Is she okay?" said Sophie.

"I took her home, cleaned her up a bit, and put her to bed," Tim said. "I dozed off in a chair, but checked her before I left. She'll feel like crap in the morning. But she'll survive."

"What is her problem?" Sophie said. "I did not think she drank that much."

"She doesn't. I don't know what her problem was. She was in no shape to talk. I'll call her tomorrow."

"You still have not told me why you were soaking wet." Sophie said.

"I took a shower with her," Tim said.

"Really?" Sophie said. "Next time I suggest you take off your clothes first."

Tim smiled and hit his forehead with his palm. "Damn. Why didn't I think of that?"

Tim met Sophie nine months ago while looking for an apartment after Maggie and he split up. The real estate lady showed him a third floor walk-up in an old Victorian town house, subdivided into six good-sized apartments. The two bedroom apartment fit his needs, but the day before, he saw another one he liked a lot better. As Miss Realtor-lady locked the apartment door, and just before Tim was about to tell her he was not interested in taking this apartment, he turned to the sound of footsteps coming up the stairs. He saw Sophie Daigneau for the first time.

Sophie smiled and nodded polite greetings. She held a large bag of groceries in her right hand and her keys and a suspended bag of potatoes in her left. As she unlocked the adjacent apartment door, the potato bag slipped from her hand to the porch floor. Tim closed the few steps between them, picked up the bag, and handed it to her after she nudged the door open.

"*Merci*," she said with a wide smile. "Thank you." She went in and closed the door behind her.

"I'll take the apartment," he told the realtor and moved in three days later.

Within days Tim, Sophie and her roommate, Kate, became quick friends. Sophie told Tim how she had grown up in a Catholic orphanage in Montreal and had moved to the United States with her older sister eight years ago at the age of fifteen. She was now in her third year as a nursing student and supported herself with a scholarship and by working part time as a nurse's aide.

Kate worked as a stewardess with a small regional airline. While Kate displayed a demure, professional front to the world, at home she was laugh-out-loud funny. The three of them spent many an evening sitting around Tim's kitchen table listening to Kate's over-dramatized portrayal of pompous passengers, stormy skies and bumpy landings. But three months after Tim took the apartment, Kate accepted an offer with Swiss Air. She would be based in Switzerland. Her departure was unexpected, but Kate gave Sophie a check for half of the next three months' rent to help Sophie get by until she found a new roommate.

Tim knew Sophie would struggle to afford the apartment on her tight, part time job. He debated jumping on the opportunity to invite Sophie to become his roommate, but he had not given up on Maggie and leaned toward doing nothing that might squash any possibilities of a reunion. Two weeks after Kate went off to Europe, Sophie knocked on his door.

"Timothy, how would you like a roommate?" she said, then quickly added. "I mean *apartment*-mate."

"Um...sure," he said. "And I knew what you meant."

"I would not be a lot of trouble," Sophie said.

"Honest. You know me. I just study and go to class and work. I will pay half your rent." She gave him that demure look of hers and batted those eyes, as if there was even a chance he'd refuse.

"Fine," Tim said. "When would you want to do this?"

"This morning I saw a sheet on the Student Center bulletin board from two graduate students looking for an apartment," she said. "I called them, and they agreed to take over my lease. They move in tomorrow afternoon at two o'clock. Kate's brother will pick up her furniture tomorrow morning at ten. I can move in here any time before two, after you have awoken and had your coffee. *C'est bien?*"

Tim wrinkled his brow and fought the urge to laugh.

"Let me get this straight," he said and began ticking off his fingers. "You already leased out your apartment. You made arrangements with Kate's brother to clean out her furniture - which is most of the furniture in your apartment. And you've scheduled the move for tomorrow by two o'clock - after I have my coffee, of course? And I assume you will need my massive, masculine strength to assist with the move. Did I actually have any real say in this?"

"Of course, you did," she said. "But I think you would not be able to resist my offer, *non?*"

"No, I could not," Tim said and laughed. "I was going to ask you if you were interested. But I didn't want to give you the wrong impression. And I...uh...I think this is a great idea."

Sophie looked him straight in the eye.

"Timothy, do not fear," she said. "We are friends just sharing an apartment. We are great friends, but only friends. I will make that very clear to Marguerite myself, if you want?"

"No, that's okay."

"*Tres bien*," she said. "Let us agree to some other rules. You are a much better cook than me, so you can do most of the cooking. And I am obviously a better cleaner than you. I will take all the cleaning chores. Deal?"

"Deal," Tim said. "What about the bathroom? You know there's only one."

"I will not clutter it up with all my girl supplies, and I promise to be considerate of time and not making you late for work," she said, crossing her heart. "We are on different schedules, so I will take my long, luxurious baths only when you are not around."

Sophie taking steamy baths in his bathtub was not something that would actually upset Tim, but something in her smile told him she already knew that.

"Okay," he said. "In return, I promise to leave the seat down."

"*Bon. Et la couverture?*"

"Yes, I will put the lid down, too."

4

The dark-haired woman opened her bureau drawer and pulled out a long sleeved, black pullover shirt and a pair of dark blue jeans. She set them on top of the black sneakers already in her suitcase. Opening the bottom drawer, she slipped her hand under the folded summer tops and stretchy pants and pulled out a manila envelope. She put it in her suitcase and covered it with another change of clothing.

She carried the suitcase outside to her blue Honda Accord, placed it in the back, and slammed the hatch shut. She returned to the kitchen and checked the backdoor. Locked. Picking up her pocketbook and the folded map, she returned to her car. In less than ten minutes she turned onto the highway and headed west.

***

Tim jumped awake when the phone next to his bed rang. He looked at the clock. *10:30.*

"Hello?" Tim said.

After a moment he heard a soft, "Hi, Timmy."

"Maggie?" he said. "You okay?"

"I've felt better," she said. "If I could remove the vice that's squeezing my brain out through my ear canals, it might help."

"Beef bouillon," he said. "It's one of the most important things I learned in my four years in college. Cures a hangover in no time."

"Beef bouillon? Ugh."

"And maybe an aspirin. I used them myself on those rare occasions when I imbibed a bit too much. Drink it like tea. It works. Just make sure you eat something with it."

"I'm never going to eat food again," she said. "Ever."

Tim suppressed a chuckle. "Start with dry toast. You'll be fine."

"Oh, Tim," Maggie said. "I'm so sorry. And I'm so embarrassed."

Tim heard the sniffle. His mind teemed with questions and curiosities about what caused Maggie to get drunk. He feared part of the problem may have something to do with him. He wanted to ask about Sharon or Shannon or whomever she brought up to Didi. He wanted to know about the note scratched underneath the newspaper column.

"Don't be sorry," he said. "And don't be embarrassed. You'll be a legend at The Key for dumping the guy's beer on his crotch. I bet Ray will name a drink after you. He could call it a MuggaMaggie."

"Oh, God," she said. "I can never go back there again."

"C'mon, Mags. I'm only kidding. I just want to hear you laugh."

"That won't be for at least a month," she said. "Maybe longer."

"Bouillon. You'll be fine in a few hours. I'll make you laugh."

"Timmy," she said, "I don't know how to thank you. Once again, you came to my rescue."

"I'm just glad Ray called me."

"Me, too."

"Mags, when and if you decide to eat food again, how 'bout I take you out to dinner?" he said. "Somewhere nice. You know that new place down near the old pier? It's supposed to be real good. We haven't been alone together for over a month. I just want to talk, you know, just about normal things, nothing else. Promise."

"I really don't think that would be possible," she said.

Tim's back stiffened.

"Maggie, I'm sorry," he said. "I'm not trying to take advantage of the situation. Honest. I just thought we could go out to dinner as old friends. Just friends. No ulterior motive. Really."

"Don't be sorry, Timmy," she said with a touch of lightness in her voice. "I wasn't worried about you taking advantage of me. I was worried about how you could take me out and pay for the meal when the check came at the restaurant."

"I'd probably use money," he said with no idea of what she was talking about.

"But you have no money," she said.

"I don't?" said Tim.

"No. Check your wallet."

Tim stood up and reached for the still damp jeans he had thrown over his desk chair. He checked his back pocket. No wallet.

"Uh, oh," he said.

"Guess what I found under the edge of my bed this morning."

"I bet it's a wallet," he said with faked defeat. "What a coincidence, two people losing wallets on the same night. I guess you'll have to pay for dinner?"

"Yes," she said. "I just came into some money."

"Not a lot of money, I'd bet," he said.

"Maybe you can come over around noon to get it?" she said. "I'll put the coffee on."

"Absolutely," he said. "That will give me time to take a shower."

"Another shower? You must be the cleanest person in Portland," she said. "I'll try your remedy and see you around noon. I'll need at least that much time to make myself semi-presentable."

"I'll be there."

"And Tim," she said. "Whatever happens in the future, I don't believe that we can ever be *just* friends."

An hour later, Tim pulled his car into an open parking spot across the street from Maggie's apartment. He shut off the ignition and looked at the dashboard clock. 11:45. *I don't want to be early*, he thought. *Give her time.*

He looked across the street to his old parking spot in the section marked "Residents Only." He wished he still qualified to use it. Six months after their fateful

Red Sox game three years ago, Tim convinced Maggie that Portland would be a great place to live. He sought and received a job offer from the Whitfield Casualty Company claims office in Portland and talked Maggie into moving in with him. She waited on tables for a couple of months until she got hired by the Portland Times.

Sitting there waiting for the clock to reach noon, Tim thought about his two years up here with Maggie. Everything felt so great. Until the Saturday that started as a jaunt to Maggie's and Tim's favorite place on Earth. That day cost him his parking spot...and so much more.

The Kancamagus Highway rolls through the southern edge of New Hampshire's White Mountains. The two lane road lies speckled with easy pull-offs and spectacular views for autumn leaf-peepers and wandering lovers. One pull-off near its highest point sports an open-sided, stone gazebo along a wall of granite rocks neatly arranged like a castle wall along the edge of a steep hill. The first time Maggie and Tim stopped there, they were awash with new love and spectacular mountain views. She named the Gazebo their "Sky Castle," and anointed them the "Sweet Prince" and "Fair Princess" of their realm.

The last time they went to their Sky Castle, almost a year ago, Maggie and Tim sat on the hood of his VW, leaning back against the windshield, their arms folded back supporting their heads. They stared out at familiar peaks.

"I'm pregnant," Maggie said.

Tim turned his head toward her, unsure he heard her right. Maggie looked straight ahead avoiding his stare.

"Pregnant?" he said.

"About six weeks."

"How...?" he said searching for words.

"The old fashioned way," she said. "Probably the time we..."

"No, no, that's not what I mean," he said. "I'm sorry. I'm just trying to absorb what you said."

Maggie told him she was about two weeks later than usual and felt different. She called her doctor and went in for a test.

"The doctor confirmed it three days ago."

"Is he sure?" Tim said.

"So he says," Maggie said. "But in any case, I am sure."

"Why didn't you tell me when you heard?"

"I don't know," she said. "I think I just needed to process it."

They sat there in silence for a few moments, staring at the green foliage stretching out before them.

"What are you going to do, Maggie?"

Maggie turned her head to face him. "What am *I* going to do?"

"I mean, what are *we* going to do?" Tim said.

"I don't know," Maggie said. "What do you think we should do?"

"Well, we have options," he said. "You should make the decision. I'll support you whatever you decide."

"Support me?" she said. "You mean like pay my share of the rent and the electric bill?"

"C'mon, Mags, you know what I mean," he said. "I

will go along with your wishes whatever you think is best."

"You mean like if I want to have an abortion, you'll go along with that? Of if I want to have our child and give it away to some stranger, you'll go along with that, too?"

Maggie turned her head away from him and looked up toward one of the peaks. Tim saw the slight shake of her head.

"Maggie," Tim said. "You know I love you. I just want you to be happy. I'll do anything to make you happy."

"Like marry me? You'll even go along with that?"

"Of course," he said. "I figured we would eventually get married."

"You figured?" she said. "Did you figure children in your calculations, as well?"

"Of course," he said. "Why are you acting like this?"

"Like what?"

"Like I'm not supporting you in this," Tim said. "I love you, and I want to do what's right."

"So you will marry me, if I ask you to?"

"Yes," he said. "I told you I would support your decision. I love you."

Maggie slid forward off the hood of the car to her feet. She walked to the passenger side.

"Okay," she said. "Let me think about it. I'll let you know what I decide." She opened the door and slid in. "Let's go. I want to be back in Portland before three. I have work to do."

Tim got into the driver's seat and inserted the key into the ignition. But before he turned on the car, he turned to Maggie and said, "Maggie, please look at me."

Maggie turned her head toward him. Tim saw the glint of moisture at the edges of her eyes. Her head was cocked a bit to the right, her lips a straight line, her eyebrow arched, waiting for him to speak.

"Maggie," Tim said. "I'm sorry. I love you with all my heart. Will you marry me?"

The tear welling under her eyes leaked and before its trail could reach the corner of her mouth, she wiped it with the back of her hand. She forced a weak smile and moved her left hand to cover his right one resting on the shifter.

"Sure, Tim," she said. "But not tonight. I'm too tired to think, and I don't feel that hot. Let's just go home."

Three days later, Maggie miscarried.

5

Tim climbed the stairs to Maggie's apartment. He knocked. Maggie opened the door, managed a weak smile, and stood aside for him to enter.

"Hi, Timmy," she said. She moved to him and wrapped both arms around his neck, pulling him against her, her right cheek pressing hard against his chest.

"Thank you, thank you, thank you. I am so sorry."

He felt the pulse of her sobs against him. Tim's arms enwrapped her.

"Maggie, please don't apologize." She squeezed harder against him. Tim held her and let her cry.

"It's okay, Maggie," he whispered. "It's okay."

He held her tight. In a few minutes her sobs subsided, and she sighed as she pulled her upper body away from him.

"Here I am thanking you and begging forgiveness and everything, and I am committing yet another sin," she said. "I invited you here for coffee, and I've failed to deliver."

"I was waiting for you to notice that," Tim said.

"Giving me a free shower is one thing, but stiffing me on the coffee promise the very next day is a major faux pas." He shook his head and let out a dramatic sigh. "Could I even stop at Dunkin Donuts? No. I have no money."

Maggie managed a smile, then leaned forward and gave him a quick kiss on his cheek.

"And don't try distracting me with your feminine wiles," Tim added, putting his hands up, palms toward her. "I came for brew, not woo."

She laughed this time, clasped his hand, and led him to the green chair he sat in the night before.

"See, I told you I could make you laugh."

"Sit," she said. "I'll fetch your coffee. Think of me as your slave for the day."

"Wow," Tim said. "A flashback."

"Just have low expectations. My head still feels like crap. I'm not catching any pop-ups today."

While Maggie poured two cups of coffee, Tim glanced at the table, where last night he found the book with the envelope and newspaper clipping. It was gone.

"Dark no sugar," Maggie said, handing him the cup in her right hand.

Tim took a sip.

"Perfect," he said. "Strong and hot, just like me."

"Yeah, right," she said.

"I meant to say, just like you," he said.

"Oh, yeah," she said. "My eyes are red and swollen. I can't keep my hand steady enough to put on any makeup. And my hair needs life support. But I guess I look a little better than the last time you saw me."

"That depends on how you look at it," Tim said.

Maggie shook her head. "You are incorrigible."

"Seriously, Maggie, you look fine."

Maggie sat on the cobbler's bench, facing Tim. She sipped her coffee.

"When Ray called you last night," Maggie said. "What did he say?"

"He said you got into a drinking contest with a couple of jerks," Tim said. "There was an argument and you poured a glass of beer on some guy's crotch. Didi broke it up. You slipped out shortly thereafter."

"How did you know where to find me?"

"I asked him if you had cigarettes on you."

Maggie nodded, impressed by his cleverness.

"He didn't say anything else?" Maggie asked.

"Well, he said he really didn't hear much of anything you said. You were a bit...'slurry.'"

"What did Didi say?"

"I didn't talk to Didi."

"Did Didi say anything to Ray?"

Tim hesitated.

"Didi thought you were angry at someone named Sharon."

Maggie stiffened a bit.

"Sharon?" she said. "I don't know anyone named Sharon."

"That's only what she thought you said," Tim said. "She said it could have been something else. Or someone else."

Maggie stared at Tim for a few moments.

"So how is Sophie?" Maggie said.

"She's doing fine," Tim said. "Study and work. Work and study. She's relentless."

Maggie nodded. "She'll burn herself out."

"Not Sophie," he said. "I think she actually went on

a date Thursday night. She told me she was going to study with one of her classmates, but the guy who came to pick her up did not look like a nursing student to me."

"Well, good for her," Maggie said. "I suppose he was tall, dark and handsome."

"Actually, he looked fairly normal," Tim said. "Closer to my age than Sophie's."

"Ah, an older man," Maggie said.

"Four years doesn't make him that much older," Tim said. "And I should remind you that I am only six months older than you. Be wary of any old age references."

Maggie smiled. "You should learn to never mention a woman's age."

"Sorry," he said. "What was I thinking?"

"So why do you think she didn't tell you she had a date?" Maggie said.

"Probably worried that I'd be jealous and would want to evict her," Tim said.

"Would you?"

"Would I evict her?" Tim said. "Of course not."

"No," Maggie said. "Would you be jealous?"

Tim hesitated for a moment.

"Yes," he said. "I'd be jealous of any guy who might marry half my rent money."

"Ah, I see," Maggie said and smiled. Tim grinned.

"Looks like you're feeling better," he said.

"I'm getting there," she said. "Thanks to you."

"Aw, shucks," he said, dipping his head and shoulders like a shy country boy. "It was nothing, Ma'am. Sometimes old Timbo actually can come through in the clutch."

As the last words came from his mouth, Tim regretted them. *What the heck is wrong with me?* His smile dropped, he closed his eyes, opened them and looked up at Maggie. Her smile had melted, her head tilted downward, her eyes looking away from him.

"Maggie," he said. "I'm sorry. I didn't mean any..."

"Tim," she said. "Don't worry. It's okay."

"Maggie, really, I...I wasn't..."

"Tim," she said louder and looked right at him. "I get it. Don't worry. I finally understand."

Tim didn't respond. Instead his forehead wrinkled and his head tipped.

"Understand what?" he said.

Maggie let out a deep breath and said, "I understand what happened at Sky Castle."

"You do? Then tell me. What happened?"

Maggie sighed, then took a deep breath and began.

"On that Wednesday, when I found out I was pregnant, I didn't know what to think or what to do. My first reaction was shock. I couldn't grasp the reality of the situation. It was like some dream, like both a nightmare you might read about in the gossip sheets and a fairy tale that always turned out perfect when the movie ended. I thought about creating a new life and closed my eyes and watched a little girl playing with dolls in our apartment and a little boy splashing his bare feet in the Swift River. I thought about the shame of telling my grandparents I was pregnant and the snide comments whispered by their neighbors about 'that girl who got herself knocked up.' I thought about abortion, but knew I couldn't do it. And I didn't know if I could carry a child and give it away when it was born.

"But most of all, I thought about you. I loved you and believed you loved me. I knew you would be a great father and pictured you teaching our son to fish or interrogating our daughter's prom date. My two years with you were two of the best of my life, and I wanted them to continue."

She paused to take another deep breath.

"Maggie, I..." Tim said.

"Please, Tim," she said, raising her hand in the *stop* position. "I came up with the idea of going to the mountains. I pictured the Fair Princess and her Sweet Prince sitting among the exotic beauty of their mountain realm, safe in their Sky Castle. At the perfect moment, the princess would turn to her prince and tell him of their future child. He, of course, would jump to his feet with glee, wave his sword wildly in the air, and carry her off on his steed to the Land of Happily Ever After."

"Mags," Tim said. "I'm sorry, I..."

"Stop." she said, raising her palm toward him.

"No, you didn't react the way I wanted. You didn't jump with glee or take me in your arms or carry me away to bliss. You didn't immediately kneel down and ask me to marry you. You didn't jump for joy. You looked shocked. You looked scared. You looked like a lost dog. And I reacted. I regretted those stupid fairy tales I concocted in my head. I withdrew from you. After I lost the baby, I blamed myself."

"Maggie ..."

"Tim, please let me finish," she said and took a few deep breaths. She stared at him.

"A few weeks later, when I told you I needed space and asked you to look for another place, I meant it." She paused, and Tim saw the welling of tears in her eyes. "And I am sorry for the way I treated you."

Maggie put her hands over her face and cried. Tim went to her and wrapped her again in his arms. She leaned against him, sobbing.

"Maggie, I cannot tell you how much I regret that day," Tim said. "I wish I could rewind the clock and do it over. I would do everything you dreamed of. I would..."

"No, you wouldn't, Timmy," Maggie said. "You'd do exactly the same thing. You did what this idiot brain of mine failed to understand then. I spent three days thinking about my pregnancy, three days adjusting to the shock, three days mulling realities, exploring possibilities, eliminating options. I spent three days building a fairy tale. I took three days to come to my solution and expected you to come to the same conclusion in three seconds.

"I know you all too well," she said. "Given that same situation, you would stumble around, grasping to comprehend the situation, knowing you had to respond to me, wanting to say the right thing to make me happy, but unable to get from point A to point Z without tripping over points B, C, D, and all the rest. You'd want to do the right thing, not just whatever it takes to shut me up. That is how you would do it. That's how the man I loved would do it. It just took me a long time to understand all that."

Tim held her and knew enough to say nothing. They sat there, she leaning on him, his left arm around her, resting on her shoulder, her hand reaching up grasping his. For three or four minutes they stayed that way. Tim broke the silence.

"I'm going to evict Sophie," he said. That got him an elbow to the ribs. "Ouch!"

"You are not going to evict Sophie," Maggie said with feigned horror. "Why would you do something like that?"

"Well, I was hoping you would rescind your answer to my question," he said.

"What question?" she said.

"The one where I asked you to marry me."

Maggie did not respond.

"Would it help if I get down on my knee this time?" he said.

After a long pause Maggie said, "Timmy, I can't marry you." She rose, took a few steps toward the kitchen area and stopped with her back to him. Tim watched her fold her arms in front of her.

"You can't?" Tim said. "Or you won't?"

"Both," she said. "I have too many issues."

"Issues?" he said. "What issues? Are they why you got drunk last night?"

"Yes."

"Issues with me?" he said.

"No," she said. "Issues with me."

"Will you talk with me about them?" he said.

"No."

"Why?"

"Because I just can't right now."

"When?"

"I don't know."

Tim hesitated for a moment and took a breath.

"Will you talk to me about William Shannon?"

The telephone rang. Maggie reached over and answered it, keeping her back to Tim.

"Hello?" she said. "Hey. Hi, Didi...Yeah, I'm okay now. Little shaky, but I'm getting there...I can't thank you enough...I am so embarrassed...I know, Tim told me...Yes, he's here right now...Yes, I know...I owe you, Didi, big time...Thank you...Yeah, I'll tell him...Bye."

Maggie hung up the phone and stood with her back still turned away. She said, "Didi said 'Hi,' and thinks you are one of the 'most fantabulous' guys she ever met. Her words, not mine."

"I was saved by the bell, I think," Tim said.

"That's up for debate," Maggie said.

"Maggie, all I want to do is help you. Please talk to me, tell me what's wrong. I know we can work it out."

Maggie turned and stared at Tim.

"So you were snooping through my personal stuff last night? Is that how you heard that name? Reading my mail? What else did your investigation uncover about me?"

"Wait a minute," he said. "First of all, I did not go 'snooping through your personal stuff,' last night...or ever, for that matter. And I cannot believe you'd think that. Other than bringing you home, cleaning you up, and getting you in bed – all of which was *very* personal, at least to me - the most personal I got was listening to your stereo and thumbing through *Waiting for Mr. Goodbar*, because I was curious about the book."

Maggie closed her eyes.

"When I flipped to the back cover of the book," Tim continued, "A folded piece of newsprint and an open envelope fell out. I picked them up and put the envelope back in the book around the area where I thought they were bookmarked. The headline on the article caught my eye, and I just started reading it. Sorry if that compromises my integrity. I realized the guy came from the same area of Pennsylvania you did. Before I flipped open the full page of the article, I just thought he was someone you knew from the old days, and a friend sent it to you to let you know the poor schmuck died. Yes, I saw the writing at the bottom. It was hard to miss. I guessed that somehow this was related to your out-of-character bender. I was not snooping, whatever you may think."

Maggie bowed her head, opened her eyes, and stared downward toward Tim's feet. She shook her head.

"My life is so frigging screwed up."

Tim wasn't sure how to react. He had pushed Maggie beyond what he intended. And she had pushed back. He knew he had to back off.

"I'm not a jerk," he said, "even if it's coming out that way."

"I know that," she said. She looked up, walked over to him, and put her arms around him. "C'mon. Let's get out of here. I need a walk."

6

The Accord pulled into the parking lot of the hotel, proceeded around to the back, and parked in a space near the corner where a row of tall arbor vitae formed the corner boundaries of the property. A white panel truck sat a few spaces away, between the Accord and the back of the hotel. The dark-haired woman opened the trunk and removed her suitcase.

The desk clerk looked up when she entered and stood up when he saw her. The dark-haired woman walked to him, read his name tag, and smiled.

"Hello, Henry," she said. "How are you today?"

"I'm fine, Ma'am," Henry said. "Can I help you?"

"Yes, please," she said. "I need a room for the next two nights."

"No problem, Ma'am," the young man said. "We're not even half full. It's been a slow couple of weeks since the graduations ended."

"Great," she said. "And please, you don't have to call me 'Ma,am.' It makes me feel old."

Henry smiled and opened his mouth as if to say something then stopped.

"You can call me 'Cindy,'" she said. "Cindy Peterson."

Henry smiled and nodded.

"Okay, Cindy," he said. "You need to fill out this card."

He slid the info card toward her and handed her a pen. The dark-haired woman began filling out the card. She reached the line asking for her vehicle information. She wrote "Ford" in the line asking for year, make and model.

"Dammit," she said. "I can't remember the plate number on the car. I've only had it a month. I should write it down. Ah, well. I'll walk around and get it."

She started to turn when Henry said, "Don't worry about that. We only ask for those to make sure the parking lot isn't being overridden by people parking here who aren't staying here. We're not close to full today. Nobody's going to tow you away."

"Thanks, Henry," she said. "You saved me a walk."

Henry smiled and said, "Are you putting this on your credit card?"

"No, I'll pay cash," she said.

Henry rang up the bill, and she paid him. Henry gave her the key and she walked to her room.

***

The smells of Portland harbor and the warmth of the late spring sun engulfed them. They walked side by side through the East Bayside neighborhood, past rows of older single and multi-family homes set close to the sidewalk and interspersed with shady maples and tight driveways. Blooming window boxes hung from second floor windows. They turned left at Atlantic Street and headed toward the waterfront. Neither spoke. When they stopped at a corner, waiting for a car to pass, Maggie reached over and took Tim's hand in hers. He squeezed.

At Fore Street, they crossed to the Eastern Promenade, a park lining the waterfront along Casco Bay.

"How's the head?" Tim said.

"Much better," Maggie said. "I'm starting to feel like a human again."

"Good," he said. "Maybe you'll change your position on never eating again for the rest of your life? I'll be getting hungry soon."

"There's a chance," she said. Maggie was about to say something else when the peel of a boat horn rang out. They looked to their right and saw the big ferry boat leaving its pier. It passed by them through the harbor on its way to Nova Scotia.

"I've got to get on that boat one of these days," Tim said. "I've never been to Nova Scotia or any other part of Canada for that matter. Pretty sad considering I have a Canadian roommate."

"I went to Montreal once when I was younger," Maggie said. "My Uncle Bill's company relocated him there for a short while. When I was twelve, my parents took us there on vacation. I thought it was so exotic, at least compared to Cummington. Then again, most everything is exotic compared to Cummington."

Maggie nudged him toward a bench.

"Come on, Timmy. Let's sit."

They sat looking out across island studded Casco Bay. The far shores of the bigger islands - dotted with trees, rocks and buildings - guided Maggie's eyes to wide channels leading to the Grand Banks and the cold Atlantic. Just to their right, on its tiny plate of rock, sat Fort Gorges still ready after two centuries protecting Portland from marauding British and Confederate warships.

The smells of fresh pine, wet seaweed and ferry exhaust rode the soft incoming breezes following the tide. The sounds of boat horns, fork lift motors, and cavorting seagulls harmonized in the rhythmic cacophony of the city's heart. The sun poured down on them, warming souls and healing wounds.

"I love this city," Maggie said. "Portland is real and its people are real. Portland is the most honest city I've ever seen. Someday I will paint all of it."

Tim squeezed her hand.

A grey and white seagull landed about six feet in front of them, dancing back and forth, surveying them.

"He's checking us out for French fries or hotdog rolls," Tim said. "They are the seagulls' natural food source up and down the New England coast."

"In my part of Pennsylvania, it was crows and pretzels," Maggie said. "With lots of mustard, of course."

"I don't get that mustard on pretzels thing," Tim said.

"In high school we ate them as lunch," Maggie said. "It was cheaper than the cafeteria food and tasted a lot better."

"We stuck to fluffernutters or bologna and cheese,"

Tim said.

The disappointed seagull flew off. Maggie sighed, leaned back on the bench and began to talk.

"The summer before my senior year in high school," Maggie said. "I took a workshop on set design at Rethinger College in Reading. Part of the workshop was to create a set for a production of *Much Ado About Nothing*. It became the first play by Shakespeare I ever read. I fell in love with him. And when I say fell in love, this was no light flirtation.

"In two weeks I read four of his plays. *King Lear. The Tempest. MacBeth.* And of course, *Romeo and Juliet.* I wanted to read everything Shakespeare wrote. I wanted to design sets and create Elizabethan costumes. Even more, I wanted to be a Shakespearian actress. I dreamed I was Juliet calling Romeo from the balcony or Miranda scolding Caliban.

"That fall, when Mr. Buffoni, our Drama Club advisor, told us he selected *As You Like It* for our senior play, I couldn't believe it. I read the whole play that night. Rosalind entranced me. She was smart. She was beautiful. By the time I finished reading it, I knew there could be no better Rosalind than I. I put everything I had into preparing for the part. I obsessed...and you know how I can obsess when I set my mind to it."

"I know all too well," said Tim.

"Two weeks before tryouts I went to the school auditorium and sat alone way up in the back corner, where I could see the whole expanse of stage, wings, and orchestra pit. I went through the play scene by scene, visualizing Rosalind, where she might stand and how she might move. I read Rosalind's lines and spoke them quietly, practicing their cadence. I *am* Rosalind, I told myself."

Then in her best Rosalind voice and with proper Elizabethan affectation, Maggie said, *"Well then, can one desire too much of a good thing?"*

Maggie stopped for a moment and then took a deep breath.

"I thought I was alone sitting there. But I heard what sounded like a girl's voice. I couldn't understand what she said or tell where it was coming from. I figured it was someone walking in the hall outside the auditorium.

"About thirty seconds later I heard it again, this time louder, but it was coming from above me not below me near the exit doors. I realized it came from the projection booth. I listened and heard a guy's voice responding to the girl. I stood to leave. The aisle took me closer to the side of the projection booth, and as I walked, I couldn't help but hear the conversation, or at least part of it.

"'Have you told anyone about all of this, you know, about you being pregnant?' the guy said.

Maggie stopped and stared out across the harbor. She pursed her lips and let out a long breath. Tim remained silent, letting her work through the thought. A half minute passed before she spoke.

"The girl said she hadn't told anyone," Maggie said. "But I could hear the sarcasm in her voice. 'Is that why you brought me in here?' I think she said. Then the guy said something like, 'If people find out about this stuff, I'll be screwed.'"

"'Speaking as someone who has been screwed most

of her life,' the girl said. 'My heart bleeds for you. But don't worry, I didn't tell anyone about our little secret.'

"'Our little secret?' the guy said.

"'That was a joke,' the girl said.

"'Please don't joke like that,' he said.

"I heard something crash," Maggie said. "Like a chair being pushed over. She yelled something I couldn't make out. I started down the steps, but then I heard the door to the projection booth open and slam shut. I stepped back so whoever came out would not see me. A girl ran down the aisle crying. I really didn't know the girl personally and can't even remember how I knew her name. All I knew was her name was Olivia Wood, and she was a sophomore.

"I thought about chasing after her to make sure she was okay, but I heard the door reopen, and I ducked back again. I expected to see some high school kid running after her. But when I saw him I froze."

Maggie put her head down and wiped the corner of her eye.

"Let me guess," Tim said. "William Shannon?"

Maggie nodded.

"He was her teacher?" Tim said.

"Yeah, well, actually, he was a student teacher," Maggie said. "More accurately, a college student interning in our high school. When the regular teacher who supervised him broke her leg in a car accident, the principal let him take over the class until the teacher came back."

"Either way," Tim said, "I assume there were rules against that sort of thing?"

"What sort of thing?" Maggie said.

"You know," he said, "fraternization with the

female students."

"I didn't say he was 'fraternizing' with Olivia Wood," she said.

"You implied it," he said.

"No, I didn't," Maggie said. "Olivia implied it."

"You sound like you are defending him," Tim said. "She was a sophomore. What's that? Fifteen, sixteen maybe?"

Maggie did not respond.

"He sounds like a scumbag," Tim said.

Maggie turned to Tim and looked him square in the eye.

"Maybe he was," she said. "But he was also my boyfriend."

7

"Your boyfriend?" Tim said. "You dated one of the teachers in your high school?"

"It's not what you think," Maggie said. "I didn't date one of the high school teachers."

"Didn't you just say he was your boyfriend?"

"Yes," she said. "But we didn't date while he was at Cummington."

Tim said nothing.

"I met Billy in July at the theatre workshop at Rethinger College. He was a college student taking a summer course in directing, as an assistant director for *Much Ado*. We hit it off. What can I say? Billy was handsome, smart and charming."

Tim didn't say anything. *Billy?* He fought the jealousy pulling at him hearing Maggie talk about another guy. *Give it a rest, idiot,* he told himself. *The guy's dead, for God's sake.*

"I know what you're thinking," Maggie said.

"I'm not thinking," Tim said. "I'm just listening."

"Okay, then," she said. "Just listen. When the

workshop was over, Billy and I started going out. Just before Labor Day, Billy told me he got his assignment for student teaching. He was going to my high school. I was excited at first, but when I looked at Billy shaking his head, I realized we couldn't continue a boyfriend-girlfriend relationship while he was teaching at my school. He said we could talk on the phone and maybe see each other for an occasional dinner date but not in public anywhere around Cummington.

"When school started we talked on the phone a couple of nights a week, but Billy always had a good reason why we couldn't meet somewhere. Maybe I should have picked up on that, but I just thought he was a bit paranoid. We avoided each other at school. When the thing in the auditorium happened, I went home in near tears. Had he cheated on me? Did he got her pregnant? I didn't know what to do. But Billy made it easy for me. That night, he called me.

"I can hear still his voice. 'Hi, Margaret. How's my sweetheart tonight?'

"'Your sweetheart?' I said. 'Your sweetheart feels like a betrayed piece of dog shit.' And those were the exact words."

"I told him what I heard and saw in the auditorium that afternoon. I called him a liar and a two-timer. I accused him of seducing Olivia. I told him Olivia was only fifteen, and he could - and should - be locked up for statutory rape. And I think my frustration grew even worse, when he didn't say a word during my diatribe. When I finally took a long breath, he spoke.

"'Margaret," Billy said. 'Now do you want to hear the truth?'

"'I just told you the truth,' I said. 'I heard it this

afternoon.'

"He asked me to hear him out. Part of me wanted to slam the phone down, but something inside me wouldn't let me. Timmy, I so wanted this not to be true. So I listened.

"Billy told me Olivia was one of his sophomore English class students. As he did with all his students, he read and evaluated all the essays being passed in by their students. He told me Olivia's essays stood out because of the high quality of her writing. But he also told me he saw something strange about her subject matter. Her first essay had something to do with the 'murder' of her dog when it got run over by a car or something like that. He told me he saw 'a darkness' in what she wrote, a despair that went beyond the loss of her dog. He said it was creepy.

"He said Olivia's second essay scared him even more than the first. The assignment was to write about a 'unique and life altering experience.' She wrote about committing suicide. He said it wasn't like some desperate, emotional cry for help. It was detached and analytical, so matter-of-fact, so casual, very strange. His first thought was to run to the guidance counselor for help, and he admitted to me that in retrospect, that probably would have been the smart thing to do. But he kept re-reading the essay, and the more he read it, the more unsure he was whether Olivia was writing this as a plea for help or as a stupid joke, a parody or something like that, just to get him going. He told me she was talented enough to pull it off."

Maggie stopped for a moment and shook her head.

"Billy said he decided to approach Olivia on his own, hoping his young age might help Olivia open up to him. Frankly, I think his idealism and naiveté convinced him he could either save her from suicide or tutor her into fame as a great writer. He said he talked to Olivia after class and told her about how good her writing ability was and how he thought she had the ability to become a professional writer. He said he could help her and asked if she wanted him to work with her one-on-one after school a couple of days a week."

Maggie paused for a moment and looked at Tim. Tim didn't say anything.

"Yeah, I know, I know," Maggie said. "At least I know now. But I was barely seventeen when all this happened. I believed a lot of things I wanted to believe."

Tim shrugged and nodded.

"Billy said he got Olivia talking about herself. When he brought up her essay about committing suicide, Olivia smirked. She said she wrote it as a joke. She said she'd never do anything like that. Never.

"Billy told me their sessions went well until the day she came in with tears in her eyes. She told him she just found out she was pregnant."

"They must have had a very good relationship," Tim said, "for her to tell him something like that."

"I know, Tim, I know," Maggie said. Tim saw Maggie's jaw tightening. "And I know what you're thinking, but I didn't see him as the father of her baby. He just wasn't the type."

Tim shrugged and managed to keep his mouth shut. *The type?* He thought. *Every guy is the type.*

"Billy said Olivia wouldn't tell him who the father was," Maggie said. "She never said anything to him about having a boyfriend. She never mentioned any close friends. Billy assumed he was the only one she could talk to about this whole thing."

Tim spread his arms and furled his brow, as if to speak. Maggie stared at him waiting. Tim caught his words before they passed through his lips, shook his head slowly, dropped his arms, and looked back to the harbor. Maggie went on.

"Olivia told him she didn't want a baby. She said she could never marry the man who did this to her. She also said just when her life looked like it was going to change for the better, this happens, and no one really cares. At least that's what Billy told me.

"Billy told her he would help her. She said she wanted an abortion. He told her they were illegal, but he would call someone who might be able to help her. He told me he knew a pregnancy counselor in Philadelphia a friend of his once talked to."

"A friend?" Tim said. Tim could see Maggie's lips tightening.

"It wasn't me," Maggie said, "if that's what you're thinking." She turned away from Tim and crossed her arms.

"I'm sorry, Maggie," Tim said. "I'm really sorry. I was not thinking it was you. I just think this guy may...I just think he had too many of his bases covered."

Maggie's shoulders eased a little. "I know. I was stupid to believe him."

Tim reached over and put his hand on the rounded corner of her shoulder. He squeezed it gently but said nothing. Maggie continued.

"Billy told me he spent the entire night thinking about what he should do. Getting involved in this type of thing could end his teaching career. He should go to the guidance counselors, but now he was afraid of what they might think about him. He told me he decided it was time for him to separate himself from Olivia and her issues.

"So he asked her to meet him in the projection booth where they could get absolute privacy. When he got there, she was waiting. He told her she should tell her father about her pregnancy.

"'Tell my father?' she said. 'Tell my father?' Billy said she spit the words. He said she swore and kicked over a chair, and that's when she stormed out."

Maggie stopped talking and tipped her head back feeling the heat of the Portland sun. Tim saw the wetness of her eye.

"You believed him?" Tim said.

"I don't know," said Maggie, resignation in her voice. "I asked myself that question many times over the past nine years. Most of what he said fit into what I heard. But maybe I just wanted to believe him."

"Love is grand, ain't it?" Tim said. Maggie nodded and looked up, watching the gull fly up and over them. After it passed, she lowered her head and looked at Tim.

"I do know one thing," she said turning toward Tim. "You are very different from him."

"Please tell me you are not referring to his 'smart and charming' parts," Tim said, trying to lighten the mood. "I'll concede 'handsome,'"

Maggie relaxed a bit and smiled. "You are all three," she said and reached out her hand.

"C'mon, let's walk some more," she said. "Maybe we can find a hot dog vendor or something."

"Shh," Tim said. "That seagull might hear you."

Maggie and Tim walked along the packed gravel path holding hands.

"By the end of our phone call," Maggie said, "all Billy seemed to worry about was not getting himself in trouble with the school. I asked him what would happen to Olivia. He said it was not his problem."

Maggie shook her head.

"I guess I should have just walked away from him then and there," Maggie said and shook her head slowly. "But I couldn't stop thinking about Olivia. And you know me, Tim. I just can't keep my nose out of other people's business."

"The Fair Princess always protects the down-trodden," Tim said.

Maggie smiled. "And her Sweet Prince protects her," she said.

"The following Monday morning, Miss Bodden returned from her disability, and I saw her walking toward me from the faculty parking lot with a cast on her right leg from the knee down. One of the sophomore boys carried her book bag," Maggie said.

"All the kids loved Miss Bodden. The boys were entranced by her beauty and her blue Mustang convertible - before she cracked it up, of course. The girls just wanted to be like her. We all trusted her. Of all the teachers in the school, I thought she might be the one best able to help Olivia."

"At lunch I sat with my usual group of friends. All we talked about was *As You Like It* tryouts, my desire to become Rosalind and my best friend Patty's desire to play Rosalind's cousin, Celia. But as we were talking and laughing and arguing about who would play whom, I looked over and saw Olivia sitting alone at a table away from most of the other kids.

"It was so sad, Tim," Maggie said. "She picked at her salad. She never looked up. I could only imagine what was going through her mind. I wanted to go talk to her. But I was afraid. Part of me said it was none of my business. And I hate to admit it, but I think part of me just wanted her to fade away, to keep her as far away from Billy as possible."

Maggie stopped walking and held onto Tim's hand. They faced each other. Tim saw the tiredness in Maggie's eyes. She stared at him.

"I feel like such a terrible human being," Maggie said.

"Don't be absurd," Tim said and moved toward her. He put his arms around her. "You're the best person I have ever met."

"You obviously don't get around a lot," Maggie said and hugged him. "But thanks for lying."

"I wasn't lying."

Maggie turned, and they resumed their walk.

"I could not get Olivia out of my head. Pregnant. Fifteen. No apparent friends. No boyfriend. Mother dead. Her father...who knows?" Maggie sighed.

"When I woke up the next morning, I knew what I had to do," Maggie continued. "I waited for Miss Bodden at the edge of the faculty lot with my sketch pad out, pretending I was working on a sketch of the school. When I saw Miss Bodden climbing out of the white rental car, I began putting my pad away, timing it to match Miss Bodden's crutch-assisted march from the car.

"When she reached me I offered to help her carry her bag. Before we reached the school, I decided to ask her if I could talk to her about something. "

"Without revealing the names of either of the people involved," Maggie said. "I told her about the conversation I overheard in the auditorium. I told her I see the girl in school, and she looks withdrawn and keeps to herself. I don't know her well enough to go and talk to her, but I would feel guilty, if I just did nothing. I asked Miss Bodden what did she think I should do? She just stared at me."

"She probably thought you were the one who was pregnant," Tim said.

"You're right," Maggie said. "That's exactly what she thought. I reassured her it wasn't me."

"'I think you have three choices,' Miss Bodden said. 'You can ignore it. You can talk to the girl and offer your help. Or you can tell someone else who may be in a better position to help. All three choices have their upsides and downsides, but I would strongly advise against ignoring this.'"

"I thought about it for a moment and asked Miss Bodden, if she would be willing to help the girl. She said she would. I asked if this would get the girl in trouble. She told me that she would keep this in confidence. Her job would be to help the girl in whatever way made sense. So I told her it was Olivia."

"You did the right thing," Tim said.

"You know, Tim," Maggie said. "It was kind of strange, though. She didn't seem surprised when I told her it was Olivia. She didn't raise a brow or question me much about her. The only question she asked me was, 'Do you know who the father is?'"

"I told her I didn't, and she asked me if I was sure," Maggie said. "I said I did not see the boy who was in the projection booth with Olivia and did not recognize his voice. She said that was okay and just let her know if I heard anything about him. Miss Bodden told me that I had done the right thing and not to tell anyone else.

"I thought I was done with it. Miss Bodden would talk to Olivia and help her make arrangements for whatever she was going to do. Billy could stay out of it, as long as Olivia kept her mouth shut. I believed I'd done my job. But the truth was what I had actually done was transfer my job, my responsibilities, and my guilt to Miss Bodden. It was her problem now. All I had to do was keep my mouth shut and wait for the end of the semester. Billy and I would get back together. Life would be good again."

"Why do I think," Tim said, "somehow this didn't all work out that way?"

"You are the perceptive one," Maggie said. "Oh, yeah. It all blew up in my face."

8

"After school the next day," Maggie told Tim, "I went to my locker. There were five or six other kids in the hallway at the time. As I lifted the latch and started to open the locker, someone came up behind me and slammed it closed. I turned and saw Olivia.

"You wouldn't believe what she called me," Maggie said. "She called me a fucking bitch and said I had a big fucking mouth!" Maggie's eyes were wide, her arms spread from her side, her palms up. Her cheeks blushed.

"I didn't know what to say. I tried to say I was trying to help her, but she wasn't listening to anything. She just kept yelling and swearing at me. The other kids stared at us. A few others came around the corner of the next hall. I figured one of them would find a teacher. I didn't know what to do, except get out of the corridor. I moved toward a nearby music practice room, went in, and she followed me, berating me all the way.

"'I don't fucking care if I get thrown out,' she said. 'I'm leaving this fucking place anyways. I'm getting out of this fucking school, this fucking town, this fucking state.'"

"Wow," said Tim. "She's sounds like quite the nutcase."

"She definitely was angry," Maggie said. "Besides yelling, there was something she did that I didn't think too much about at the time. But as I thought about the whole scene later, it struck me as odd."

"What's that?" Tim said.

"When she was yelling about leaving the school and the state and all that stuff, she stood at the open door with her hand on the knob. As soon as she said that stuff, she shut the door. I kind of had the feeling she wanted to broadcast that she was leaving the school but did not want to broadcast what she said to me after she shut it."

"What did she say?" Tim said.

"She said that because I told Miss Bodden she was pregnant, she had no choice.

"'Of course you have a choice,' I said. 'Miss Bodden will help you, and I'm sure your father would help you, too.'

"'My father is a psycho,' Olivia said. 'I'm getting away from him, too. If Miss Super Teacher wanted to help me, why did she tell my father?'

"'She told your father?' I said.

"'Don't play stupid,' Olivia said. 'You knew she was going to tell my father when you told her.'

"'That's not true,' I said. 'She promised not to speak with anyone about it but you.'

"'That's not what she told Mr. Shannon,' Olivia said. 'Oh, sorry. That's 'Billy' to you.'"

"I couldn't believe it," Maggie said to Tim. "Miss

Bodden not only betrayed Olivia, she betrayed me. Okay, I understand the father thing. She probably had some legal reason as a teacher. But Billy? Why would she talk with him? Why didn't she tell me she was going to tell him?"

"Something doesn't sound right," Tim said. "Maybe Miss Bodden was trying to protect Shannon? Maybe he really was the father of the baby? Then again, how would Olivia know that you were Shannon's girlfriend? Did anyone else at school know about that?"

"Patty knew," Maggie said. "But I would trust her with my life. She would not tell."

"Okay," Tim said, his voice sounding skeptical. "But something was going on. Did Olivia say anything else to you?"

"Not really," Maggie said then added. "Oh, yes. There was one thing she said when I told her I was sorry, before she turned and stomped out of the room."

"What was that?" Tim said.

"She told me to just stay the fuck out of her life."

Maggie and Tim walked for a hundred yards or so. Neither spoke until Tim broke the silence.

"So did you?"

"Did I what?"

"Did you stay the...did you stay out of her life?"

"I never saw her again," Maggie said. "I did see Miss Bodden, however."

"That must have been interesting," Tim said.

"Depends on what you mean by interesting," Maggie said. "After Olivia left me, I sat in the music room for a while, catching my breath and calming myself down. I cried. Then I got mad."

"I found Miss Bodden still in her room packing the latest round of assignments into her bag. 'You promised me you would tell no one what I told you,' I said.

"'Margaret,' she said. 'You didn't tell me she wanted an abortion. Abortions are illegal. And Olivia is a minor.'

"'I told you what I heard,' I said. 'I told you she mentioned an abortion.'

"Miss Bodden hesitated for a few seconds then she said, 'Margaret, because of the legal situation now, I am not allowed to discuss anything with a student about the private business of another student.'

"'What about Mr. Shannon?' I fired back. 'You talked to him.'

"'I cannot discuss this matter with you,' Miss Bodden said. 'It is no longer your business. I suggest you forget about all of it.'

"Miss Bodden limped by me and walked out of the classroom. I just stood there and stared.

"Olivia never showed up in school again," Maggie said to Tim. "There was a great deal of speculation as to where and why she went. A lot of people thought I knew what was going on since the kids who witnessed her verbal attack on me made sure that factoid got around. But I just kept denying I knew anything and hardly knew who Olivia was. I told people that after we talked in the practice room she realized she had the wrong person."

"No one knew where she went?" Tim said.

"Not that I knew of," Maggie said. "Rumor had it that her father showed up at the school and told the principal Olivia had moved to Colorado to live with her aunt. Miss Bodden probably told the principal or the guidance counselor, and they figured Olivia's departure was done to cover up her condition. Who knows? But there were no cops snooping around or anything. We figured that was what happened."

"What about Shannon?" Tim said. "Did you two get back together?"

"Yes," Maggie said. "For about sixty seconds when he called me that night."

"So what was his story? If I can ask?"

"He actually didn't have a story," Maggie said. "Or more accurately, he never had the chance to offer a story. I answered the phone and began a monologue covering every iota of the negative side of the emotional spectrum, ending with 'do not ever phone me, speak to me, or look at me ever again, as long as we both shall live, you son of a bitch.'"

"Whoa, Maggie!" Tim said and clapped his hands. "The sleeping giant awakens. I'm proud of you!"

"Just don't ever piss me off."

"I'm forewarned," he said.

"Two weeks after that conversation, Billy finished his internship, and was gone. I never saw him again. I avoided Miss Bodden and managed never to speak with her. I focused on getting into BU and not flunking trigonometry."

"I take it you passed," Tim said.

"Yeah, but I only got a B."

"And I thought you were smart."

"You think I'm smart even after hearing my story?" Maggie said.

"Yes, I do," Tim said. "But you left out one important thing I need to know."

Tim stopped and looked at Maggie. He bowed before her, his left leg reaching straight behind him, his right cocked at the knee, his arms outspread after making a sweeping move with his right hand like he was removing a hat. Maggie's puzzled look dissolved to a laugh when she got it.

"And yes, my Sweet Prince," she said with a curtsy. "I was - and they say so even to this very day - the fairest and most eloquent Rosalind ever to grace the stage of Cummington, Pennsylvania. And as Rosalind said, 'My way was, and still is, to conjure you.'"

They laughed, but as they walked, a silence passed over them as each retired to their own thoughts.

"Hungry?"

"Believe it or not, I am," Maggie said. "I almost feel human."

"How 'bout we take a walk back up Congress Street," Tim said. "I know a place where we can pick up something light and safe for your stomach."

Maggie looked at him.

"This place wouldn't also have their menu written in chalk on a blackboard hanging from the television set playing a Red Sox game due to start in about forty-five minutes and has a new drink called a MuggaMaggie?"

"Ah," Tim said. "You've heard of the place?"

"Yes, and they've heard of me," Maggie said. "I told you I can't show my face there ever again."

"Aren't you curious about your new drink?"

"No. I told you. I'm never drinking alcohol ever again."

"Okay, then," Tim said. "They have milk."

Maggie shook her head. "You don't give up, do you? But I guess I do owe Ray an apology and a thank you. I'll go, but one question."

"What's the question?"

"Who's pitching?"

"Reggie Cleveland against Mike Torres."

"Yankees?" Maggie said. "Okay, I'll go. I just hope they don't laugh at me."

"I'll make it clear," Tim said. "No Maggie jokes."

They walked to Eastern Promenade Boulevard, waited for a safe gap in the traffic, held hands, and jogged across the street to the bottom of Congress Street.

"Timmy," Maggie said, as they walked up the hill, her voice getting serious again. "On Wednesday I received the newspaper article. I don't know who sent it. Olivia was the only one who came to mind. Maybe Miss Bodden. Definitely not Patty. They were the only ones I knew of who could make any connection between me and Billy. But it didn't seem to make sense either way. It bugged me for those two days, and I finally decided it must have been Olivia.

"Friday morning I called Patty. I figured maybe I could find out if Olivia had shown up back in town. Patty keeps me posted on what's happening in Cummington. I didn't tell her about the note, but I told her someone sent me an article from the Reading paper. I told her it said Billy Shannon was found dead in the Schuylkill. I was just curious if they had figured out what happened yet. Patty told me she had heard nothing new since that article.

"We chatted for a while, and I worked the conversation back to our senior year. I asked about some of the people we knew and finally said, 'Patty, remember that sophomore girl who took off just before Christmas? You know, the one who tried to pick a fight with me? I was wondering if anyone ever heard from her. Is she back in Cummington?'"

"Olivia Wood?' Patty said. 'Funny you should ask that. About three, maybe four weeks ago, we heard she committed suicide. Can you believe it?'

"Tim, that floored me," Maggie said. "My heart broke. My first thought was that Olivia's escape from Cummington didn't save her. But the kicker came when Patty told me Olivia killed herself only a few months after she left Cummington. That was nine years ago. No one in Cummington knew until recently."

Tears welled in Maggie's eyes. Her hand shook, and Tim reached for it. He pulled Maggie to the low brick wall in front of one of the old Victorian houses lining the street. They sat. Maggie turned to Tim and buried her face in his shoulder. Tim cradled her in his arms.

"I killed her, Timmy," she said. "I killed her."

"Maggie," Tim said. "What are you talking about? You didn't kill her. She killed herself."

"I drove her to it. I betrayed a trust. I told on her and washed my hands of the mess. I drove her out of town. I drove her to kill herself."

Tim squeezed hard.

"You did the right thing, Maggie," he said. "She needed help, and you got her help. You went to the person you believed was the best one to help her. You put yourself on the line by doing that. If Miss Bodden handled it wrong, she'll have to live with that. But you did what a compassionate person would do. You saw a desperate girl you could have ignored, and you tried to help. And damn it, Maggie, you were a seventeen year old high school kid. How many kids in that situation wouldn't take that opportunity to broadcast to the entire high school what you overheard in the auditorium?"

"Except that I was in love with one of the culprits," Maggie said. "How pure were my motives?"

"Motives don't always have to be pure as long as actions are good," Tim said.

They were quiet for a few moments.

"I worked at home in my studio yesterday, but I spent all day playing everything back and forth in my head," Maggie said. "Why did Olivia do it? Was Billy's recent death related to Olivia? Who sent me the newspaper article? Miss Bodden? Did one of the other kids in the high school somehow know about me and Billy? Billy got married. Was it his wife who sent it? None of my answers made any sense."

"Maggie, anything could have happened over nine years," Tim said. "Who knows what could have caused her to kill herself?"

Maggie sighed, shook her head, and looked away toward the bay.

"By late afternoon Thursday, I was beside myself. I needed to get away. I needed to shut my brain off. I needed a friend."

Tim withheld comment.

"On Thursday some of the girls at the paper talked about going out for drinks after work on Friday. At the time I planned on spending the evening on my painting. I told them I wasn't up for a wild night of drinking with the girls. But by the time I got home from work on Friday, I decided I needed one.

"I got dressed and headed to The Seaside where we

usually gathered. I had a drink and waited. They hadn't arrived by the time I finished it, so I headed up the street to the Captain's Tavern, another of our meeting spots. I had another drink, then another. You know me, Tim. I was already way beyond my limit. By seven o'clock the girls from the paper were still no-shows. I figured they decided to try something new this time. I had no way to contact them.

"Then some guy sat next to me and paid for my drink. I could see where he was heading. I told him I was waiting for my boyfriend to pick me up, and I just saw his car through the front window. I picked up my drink and downed all that was left. I walked out and headed to a place where I knew I could find a friend. And the rest, as they say, is history."

"Wish I was there," Tim said.

"Me, too," said Maggie.

"Well, I'm here now," he said.

9

"Hey, Maggie!" Ray said, when he turned from the far end of the bar to see Tim and her sitting down. Ray walked toward them, a short bartender's apron wrapped around his skinny waist. "How ya doin'?"

"I've felt better," she said. "Ray, thank you for last night."

"Geez," he said. "It's not often I hear those words coming from a beautiful young woman."

Tim laughed. Maggie shook her head, rolled her eyes, and smiled.

"Seriously, Maggie," Ray said. "Nothin' to thank me for. All part of the service. Besides, Didi looked after ya, not me. Thank her. She'll be in soon."

"Well, thank you both."

"No problem," he said. "Whatcha want? A little hair of the dog?"

"Ugh," she said. "Right now I'm a confirmed dog hater."

Tim turned from Maggie to Ray and said, "We'll

have two Muggamaggies."

"Two what?" Ray said, his forehead wrinkling, his left eyebrow raised.

Maggie put her forehead down on her hands, her elbows resting on the bar. Her head slowly turned back and forth in denial. Tim laughed.

"Club soda with lime," he said. "All around."

"I thought you said 'No Maggie jokes?'" Maggie said.

"I meant no one except *me* would make any Maggie jokes," Tim said. "I thought you understood that."

Maggie gave him a scowl and shook her head.

Ray brought the two glasses. Tim started to pull out his wallet, but Ray waved him off and turned to wait on three guys who just came in.

"Let's grab a booth," Tim said. Maggie nodded, and they carried their drinks to the corner booth, where they could both talk in privacy while watching the game.

"Maggie, I do get it," Tim said. "I understand how upsetting the news about Olivia was. I'd probably freak out if it happened to me."

He sipped his soda.

"But I don't believe any of it is your fault. You don't even know what pushed Olivia over the edge. It could have been something that happened later. Maybe she had an abortion, had second thoughts, and the guilt ate away at her? Maybe she had the kid and gave it up and felt guilt about doing that? Maybe it was issues with the baby's father? Or her own father? Maybe her father...never mind. Maybe she just couldn't take it anymore? People take their own lives for reasons that the rest of us can never fathom. We'll never know why she did it. We don't even know if she actually did it."

Maggie looked up at that comment.

"What do you mean?"

"You said Patty 'heard' that Olivia killed herself," Tim said. "She didn't say she saw it in the paper or heard it from Olivia's family or from a cop or anyone with inside knowledge. It's really nothing more than a rumor."

Maggie thought for a moment and said, "I suppose that's true. It is only a rumor. But it had to start somewhere. And there had to be a reason. Why would someone even bring it up eight, nine years later?"

"It could be anything," Tim said. "Gossip can infest small towns. Someone might be trying to prove some stupid bet or maybe there was a suicide in the paper and one of your old Cummington classmates says how he or she always thought Olivia killed herself. You know as well as I do how rumors build and spread and get more dramatic the more they're told. Olivia might have tripped on a crack in the sidewalk and cut her knee once, and people said she did it as a first attempt at suicide. People blow things up so much, it becomes news-worthy, regardless of truth."

"You could be right," Maggie said, nodding. "But that doesn't make me feel any less guilty."

"C'mon, Maggie," Tim said. "Stop beating yourself up. I know you. You wouldn't hurt a fly. You need to let it go. Maggie, no one is responsible for another person's choice to commit suicide."

"Tim," she said. "I can't let it go. I can't get it out of my mind."

"The one who should feel guilty is Miss Bodden," Tim said. "She's the betrayer. She betrayed both of you."

"And I picked her," Maggie said.

Tim rolled his eyes, let out a deep sigh, shaking his head.

"Maybe you should just go down to visit Patty, and while you're there, go in and talk with Miss Bodden? That might help."

"Miss Bodden is no longer in Cummington," Maggie said. "I went down there, what was it, three, four years ago for a reunion, and someone said she left the school. Apparently it was short notice. During the summer right after we graduated. No one at the reunion knew where she went."

"Another unexplained disappearance?" Tim said. "What is it with that place? Maybe the cops should get involved. Someone should investigate her. "

"Believe me," Maggie said. "Cummington was a lot more boring than it sounds."

"Why don't you call her on the phone? She probably still lives in the area."

Maggie hesitated for a moment and shook her head.

"There's nothing she could say to me that would make me feel any better."

"How do you know that?" Tim said. "What are you going to do? Spend the rest of your life in a depression?"

"You know, Tim," Maggie said, "I don't know how I'm going to spend the rest of my life. I don't know how I'll feel tomorrow or next week or next year. I don't know what happened to Olivia. I don't know what happened to Billy. I just know I feel guilty, more guilty than I've ever felt in my life."

"Yeah, I know, Maggie," Tim said. He sighed. "I'm not trying to be an ass. I just want to help you." Tim reached across to table and touched the back of her hand. She turned her hand upward and grasped his.

"I know," she said.

"So now that we're here," Tim said and decided to change the subject. "What d'ya want to eat? Hotdogs, beans and brown bread is the special."

"I think I'll pass on that," she said. "You know what? I think I'd like a cobb salad. Bernie makes a good one."

"Okay, but I'm having the dogs and beans," he said. "Drink?"

"Club soda's good," she said.

Tim nodded and walked to the bar to place the order with Ray. He came back with a draft beer and another club soda with lime.

"Figured I may as well have one."

"Enjoy," Maggie said.

Tim took a long sip and then let out a long "eeehhh" and smiled. "So how's work going?" he said. "You guys busy?"

"Yeah, somewhat," Maggie said. "We are officially in tourist season, and there's usually a rush before the fourth. Nothing I can't handle. How 'bout you?"

"I'm on a claims training mission next week. Heading south."

"Wow," she said. "Exotic trip?"

"Oh, yeah," he said. "You can't believe how exotic Piscataway, New Jersey is in mid-June. Beats a sunny day at Old Orchard Beach any day." He laughed and made a gesture with his hand as if wanting to choke himself. "Actually, Piscataway isn't all that bad," he said. "A long drive, but there's some nice people and some good restaurants. And I'm on an expense account."

"Why don't you fly?"

"Nah, I like driving. By the time I get through the airports and rent a car, I may as well drive. I'll leave early Monday, get there just after lunch, and set up. Class all day Tuesday. Drive back Wednesday. "Cept Jack warned me they may have a side trip for me in one of the other offices. That may delay me until Thursday."

"Long trip," Maggie said.

"Wanna come?"

She laughed. "I wish. But Jill's out all week."

"Too bad," Tim said. "You don't know what you're missing."

Maggie smiled and raised her eyebrows. "Raincheck?"

Time raised his glass and tipped it in mock toast toward her. "Anytime."

Ray signaled the food was ready, and Tim went and picked it up.

"Game's coming on," he said when he returned.

They ate and watched the game amid the cheers of the other Skipper's Key patrons. Boston jumped to a six to two lead after four innings. Didi arrived and talked with Maggie for ten to fifteen minutes at the booth. Tim moved to the bar, grabbed another beer, and chatted with Ray until Didi went on duty. He met her back at the booth.

"You look exhausted, Mags," he said.

"It's been a long few days," she said with a half smile. "I need sleep."

Tim raised his beer glass and chugged the remaining ounces. He placed it on the table and said,

"C'mon, I'll walk you home."

They walked up Congress and turned down Beckett Street toward her apartment. He walked her up the steps to the doors of the building. Before Maggie unlocked the door, she turned to Tim.

"Thank you, Timmy," she said. "Thank you for last night. Thank you for today. Thank you for listening. Thank you for just being you."

Maggie reached up, put her arms around him and kissed him fully on the lips.

"Can we talk again tomorrow?" she said.

"My day is yours," he said. "Want to go for a ride? Nowhere special, just a day in the country."

"Sounds fantastic," she said. "I want to paint a bit in the morning. How about you come and get me around eleven or so?"

"Perfect."

"But right now I need to go to sleep. Your shining armor is blinding me."

"Then sleep, Fair Princess," Tim said.

"As should you, Sweet Prince."

Tim lifted her hand, kissed it and turned down the stairs.

Maggie smiled and unlocked the front door.

"One more thing, Fair Princess," Tim said from the bottom of the stairs. "Should my lady need assistance with her shower, please know that I have experience in those matters. You know my number."

Maggie laughed. "You will be among the first I shall call."

"*Among* the first?" Tim said.

Maggie displayed her best royal wave and shut the door.

***

Eight miles from her hotel, the dark-haired woman pulled into the supermarket lot and parked at the far end of the last row that had cars. The front of her car pointed toward the entrance of the market. She turned off the motor, shut off the headlights, and picked up the manila envelope from the seat beside her. In her dark shirt and navy jeans, she walked to the rear of the car, opened the trunk, and retrieved the flathead screw driver. She removed a license plate from the manila envelope.

It took her less than forty-five seconds to remove the two loose screws holding her red on white license plate and replace it with the yellow on blue plate with the Liberty Bell in the middle of the line of numbers. She placed the old plate in the envelope and stood up. She surveyed the building and the parking lot. No one.

She reached up under the lip of the trunk and flicked off the small switch she'd spliced into the wire carrying power to the license plate light. The newly added Penn State decal sat proudly across the top of her rear window, drawing attention toward it. The Massachusetts inspection sticker on the corner of her windshield receded behind a coating of powdery dirt she had sprinkled on top of a thin layer of Vaseline along the outer edges of the glass before she left. Not perfect, but it would blur the sticker.

Five minutes later the blue Honda turned onto a dark, tree-lined, dirt driveway and switched from headlights to parking lights. The car made its way through two turns and stopped in front of a detached, two-car garage. She switched off the parking lights and looked out the side window at the grey ranch house visible in the dim moonlight.

A tire iron and flashlight in hand, the dark-haired woman stepped out. She grabbed a wooden milk crate from a stack next to the garage and carried it around the far corner of the house. She returned a minute later for two more. After stacking the crates below a side window, she climbed them and forced the tire iron into the crack where the sash met the sill. She pushed down with all her weight and the aging wood gave way. Shattered glass rained down around her. She cleaned shards and splinters from the sill, removed what she could of the broken sash, and slipped through the black opening.

The woman pulled the flashlight from the back pocket of the dark jeans and flashed it around the room. She knew where to look and what to look for and moved to the corner of the iron bed where it was closest to the wall. She sat on the floor - her back to the bed, her feet on the wall - and pushed. The bed moved. She kneeled and moved to the corner. The edge of the moldy green, wall-to-wall carpet slid out from under the white baseboard. She folded it back and used her fingers to lift out an unattached, ten inch square of plywood sub-flooring, and removed from beneath it an old cigar box, held closed with a stretched rubber band. She tried to slide the elastic off the box, but it snapped when she started to move it. She flipped up the lid, looked in and smiled. She closed the lid, replaced the floor board and rug, and stood to leave.

She stepped out the window onto the milk crates with her right leg, but as she pulled her left leg through, she felt the cracking of wood beneath her weight. Losing her balance, she lunged away from the house and caught the back of her left calf on a broken piece of glass still imbedded in the sash. Her jeans ripped, and she felt the parting skin of the sharp cut on her leg. When she hit the ground, the cigar box slipped from her hand, dumping half its contents on the ground. "Shit!" she said and picked up the spilled contents and returned it to the box.

She got to her feet, picked up her tire iron, and returned to her car. Placing the tire iron in the trunk, she removed a slightly soiled golf towel and tied it around her leg, covering the cut. At the end of the driveway, she turned left. A hundred yards before the next house, she switched from parking lights to full headlights.

10

"So where we going?" Maggie said, as Tim steered them onto Route 1 out of Portland and headed north.

"I thought we'd just take a ride up the coast a bit. I was thinking Camden area. Let's just relax and enjoy the afternoon."

"I couldn't think of anything better," Maggie said. "But are you sure you want to drive that far? You have a long trip ahead of you tomorrow."

"I'm fine. This will be my practice run."

They passed through Yarmouth and Falmouth, up past Freeport. After Brunswick, Route 1 became more of a highway. When they crossed the Kennebec River, Maggie stared at the gigantic Bath Iron Works with its sprouting cranes and dry docks that gave birth to so many of the Navy's ships.

"This is incredible," Maggie said, leaning on her arms and staring out the window. "Look how big that place is. And the river is just sparkling."

Tim smiled.

"I was thinking about what you were trying to tell me last night," Maggie said, turning forward in the seat.

"About what?" Tim said.

"Maybe the information I'm getting is not accurate," she said. "Maybe Olivia didn't kill herself. Maybe she had the baby. Maybe she found a good guy, settled down, and lives in a house in the burbs of Colorado or California or wherever she went. Maybe Billy just tripped and fell in the Schuykill. Maybe. Maybe. Maybe. I just don't know."

"Call Patty," Tim said. "Take some time off and go visit her for a few days. See some of your old friends. You need to find out what really happened."

"Yeah, maybe," she said, laughing at her overuse of the word. "Maybe you can go with me?"

"Sounds great," Tim said. "I've never been to that part of Pennsylvania. I'd like to see the Amish farms and those little Pepperidge farm buggies."

"It is beautiful, especially in spring," said Maggie. "I admit there's no more wonderful a place to be than New England in the fall, but southern Pennsylvania in the spring is right up there."

"I hear there's a town down there called Intercourse. That's definitely a place high on my list of places to visit," Tim said.

"It's not far from a place called Virginville," Maggie said with a laugh. "You want to go there, too?"

"Actually," he said, "what I'd like to do is go to a Saturday afternoon football game between their two high schools. I can only imagine the cheers – and the cheerleaders – from each side."

"I bet I know which side of the field you'd be sitting on," Maggie said.

"Go Big I!"

A Portland station played sixties rock, and Tim hummed harmony with The Temptations.

"If I go back down there any time soon," Maggie said, "I'd want to talk with Olivia's father. I've never met him, and I haven't heard much about him, but he probably knows what's going on. I don't know if I should try to find Miss Bodden. I really don't want to talk to her. But if anyone knows what happened to Olivia, she might. She's probably married by now. I don't even know her new name."

"If she was as good a teacher as you said she was, I'm sure she's still teaching somewhere. We can find it out at the library easy enough."

"If she's there," said Maggie. "She wasn't a native Pennsylvanian. She went to Bryn Mawr for her Masters, but I remember she once said in class she was from New England."

"Where in New England?" Tim said.

"I don't remember," Maggie said. "Connecticut, maybe? Massachusetts? She came from money."

"Why do you say that?"

"For one thing, she always dressed really well," Maggie said. "Her clothes were not cheap. And she drove a brand new Mustang convertible. I don't know what teachers make, but she drove the coolest car in the faculty parking lot."

"Maybe she had a rich boyfriend," Tim said.

"Could be. I don't know. She just felt rich to me."

They followed Route 1 through Wiscasset and crossed over another bridge toward Damariscotta. Tim glanced over at Maggie, watching her blonde hair fluttering in the wind from the open front window. Her right arm rested on the door, supporting her head. Her eyes were closed, but a hint of a smile showed at the corner of her lip. *My God, she is the most beautiful person I have ever seen,* Tim thought. *I've got to help her get past this guilt thing. But first we need to find out what actually did happen.*

As he drove, the theme song to the movie *M.A.S.H. - Suicide is Painless* - popped into his head. *Painless to whom?* he thought. *Painless to whom?*

They drove into Damariscotta and parked along the main drag. Tim steered Maggie toward a small restaurant called "Sallie's Salads."

"I stopped here once, and it was pretty good," Tim said. "Hungry?"

"A salad would be great," Maggie said.

They ordered their salads to go and walked down a block to the waterfront area. They found an empty bench near a small marina and sat.

"Is every town in Maine on a river?" Maggie said.

"No," Tim said. "Some are on the ocean. The rest are on lakes."

They finished their salads, and Tim collected the trash and walked it to the can. When he returned, he sat and said, "Tell me about Olivia's father."

"I didn't know him," Maggie said. "From what little Olivia said, they were definitely not close. One of my friends said he saw her father show up in school after Olivia left, probably when he told the principal she went to Colorado. The kid said he definitely didn't look like Olivia's father."

"What does that mean?" Tim asked.

"I think what he meant was that he looked kind of sketchy. Olivia wasn't the coolest person in the school, but for the most part, she dressed like the rest of us. From what the kid said, Olivia's dad probably didn't belong to the country club," Maggie said. "Then again, neither did my Dad."

"I can't envision you father being sketchy," Tim said.

"No, I didn't mean it that way," Maggie said with a laugh. "He just wasn't the golfing or country club type. He's more interested in his paintings and his collection of circus paraphernalia than hitting a ball in a hole."

"That's right," Tim said. "You father was a circus historian."

"Only as a hobby," Maggie said. "We probably had the largest library of books about the circus in the country. Most of my high school essays related to circus themes."

"That's cool," Tim said. "I bet you went to the circus a lot as a kid."

"You can never imagine," she said. "Remind me when we get back to call him."

"Call him?"

"It's Father's Day," she said.

Tim nodded but stayed silent.

"You really miss your father, Timmy. Don't you?"

"That I do," he said. "I can't believe it's been seven years."

Maggie grasped his hand and squeezed it.

"He'd be very proud of you, Tim."

Tim stared out over the water.

"For being a claims supervisor?" he said.

"No," she said. "For being a good man."

Tim looked at Maggie and nodded.

"Thank you," he said.

They sat in silence for a while, watching the passing boats. Tim spoke first.

"Maggie, I lied to you."

Maggie looked at him, her forehead wrinkled in puzzlement.

"You lied to me about what?"

"About my dad."

"What did you lie about?"

"About how he died," Tim said. "I told you his heart gave out. That was my cop out half truth. His heart didn't give out physically, it gave out emotionally. He killed himself."

"Oh, my God, Timmy," Maggie said. She turned to Tim and stretched both arms around him. She hugged him. "Oh, my God."

When she released him, he cleared his throat and put his arm over her shoulder. After a few moments, he spoke.

"You know my parents split up when I was ten. You know my mother moved us to the city. You also know my father remarried. He struggled to keep his small engine repair shop going, but even with the music gigs he played at night, he was in financial disaster. It was made worse by trying to support a young family and have some type of relationship with my sister and me. When his second wife filed for divorce, he moved into his shop."

Tim stopped for a moment and brushed the hair back from his face.

"He started drinking, but that didn't help. One

night, he went out to his pickup truck with a bottle of peach brandy, and a vacuum cleaner hose. He stuck one end of the hose up through a rust hole in the back of the truck cab. The other end he put over the tail pipe. He got in the truck, started it, and began working on the peach brandy. A few hours later a cop found him."

Tim took a deep breath and wiped the back of his hand across his eyes. Maggie squeezed him tight, ignoring the tears streaking down the sides of her face.

"I was a sophomore in college," Tim said. "My friends at school knew what happened. They all came to the funeral and got me through it. But after I graduated I never told anyone else how he died. Not even you. I'm sorry. I should have at least told you."

"It's okay, Timmy," Maggie said. "I really do understand."

"At first I told myself I wouldn't say anything because I was ashamed of my father for killing himself. I didn't want friends to think my father had been a weak man, a man who abandoned his family and took the 'easy way out' when life got tough. But that really wasn't it.

"I wasn't ashamed of my father, I was ashamed of myself. My brain conjured up all those moments in the last years of his life. He needed me, and I wasn't there. He lost his first family and was losing his second. He was being pushed out of the lives of his children, and me, the oldest and only one close to being a full-fledged adult, I was not there for him."

"Oh, Timmy," Maggie said.

Tim did not give her a chance to speak.

"One Sunday he was driving me back to Amherst when he told me he had an opportunity to start his business over in Florida. An old army buddy of his said he would back him financially. He said he didn't want to leave us kids, but if things went well, after a year or two he'd come back. He said it was his only alternative. He asked me to take a semester off from college and go with him. He told me how good an opportunity it would be for both of us."

Tim stopped and breathed in hard. He let it out, waited a moment and went on.

"What did I say? I laughed. I said I couldn't leave school. I had a great group of friends. I had good grades. I had a girlfriend.

"A month to the day before he died, we attended a family funeral together. As we followed the train of cars from the cemetery, he said to me, 'You know what people always think about at a time like this?'

"I looked at him and shook my head."

"'I wonder who's next?'"

I think he was telling me who would be next. But I just wasn't listening."

11

The traffic heading south on Route 1 moved slower than their earlier drive north. McCartney sang *Let It Be* on the radio. Tim nodded in time with the music and focused on the stop and go traffic caused by the signal a hundred yards ahead. Maggie rested her arm on the rolled down passenger's window, pondering the granite wall cut-out created to build Route 1. The light changed. Tim accelerated.

Maggie reached out at the wind rushing by the car. She cupped her hand, pointed it forward and surfed the rushing air as she once did when she was a kid riding through the Pennsylvania countryside with her Dad.

"Timmy," she said. "I'm sorry about your Dad."

"I know," Tim said. He looked over at her and gave her a weak smile.

"I think I understand why you didn't say anything before, but I appreciate you telling me now. That must have been hard."

"Yeah, it was." Tim said. "But it's time. I can't

pretend anymore."

Maggie nodded.

"And it helps me with Olivia and Billy," Maggie said. "I know my problems are not the same as those you had. You are helping me put mine in perspective."

"Maggie, I didn't tell you about my dad because I wanted to help you with your problem. I told you to help me with *my* problem."

"I thought I *was* your problem," she said smiling.

Tim laughed.

"That's a good point," he said. "I'd forgotten about that."

"Actually," Maggie said. "I'm only pretending to be your problem. That whole incident Friday night was just a ruse to get you to open up a bit. You're so quiet and laid back. I figured I could bring you out of your shell a bit."

"That was a good plan," he said. "It worked."

"See," she said. "I'm smarter than you think."

"If you are so smart, why didn't you tell me to let the hot water run in the shower before we got in."

"I already have that written down on my reminder list. I'll remember next time."

"Next time?"

"If I need a next time."

Tim nodded. They rode for a few minutes before Maggie spoke again.

"Timmy, tell me about your Dad."

"Tell you what? The good things or the bad?"

"Tell me whatever you want to tell me."

Tim thought for a moment.

"I guess any story about my Dad starts with music. I told you he was a musician, right?"

"Yes," Maggie said. "He played bass."

"They call it 'stand-up bass' nowadays," Tim said. "But he always called it a bass fiddle. He played mostly swing, jazz, you know, the big band stuff, and some country music, or more appropriately, cowboy music. Gene Autry and Roy Rogers were huge when we were kids. Rock and roll was a no-no.

"My mom took me to some of his band's performances, and all I remember is staring at my Dad watching him pound that bass. You could feel the vibrations from it pulsing through your brain and your spine, your whole body. I remember seeing him after he played. His hands were calloused, and often so sore, he could barely close them. And sometimes they even bled. But he didn't care. Music *was* his blood.

"But my Dad's best music came on Christmas Eve. We'd go to my grandparent's house. You've been there, and you know how the street's a dead end and had those older homes all along it, something like East Bayside?"

Maggie nodded, smiled at Tim telling his story. She felt the moistness of a tear.

"That street was like the United Nations. The families would go from house to house, dropping off cookies and tasting lasagna at the Manzini's, gowumpkis at the Kostelnik's, or some other things I still haven't identified at the Gagnon's. But my grandparents' house was the best. That was where the musicians gathered.

"My Dad brought his bass, the old French Canadian guy next door – Pepe something or other - brought his fiddle, and a few others showed up with an accordion, a clarinet, and one even brought a banjo. They played everything from Christmas music to jazz to folk to just about anything you could think of. It was unpracticed. They probably hit some wrong notes. But it was music you could not only hear, you could see it in the smiles, you could smell it in the meat pies and baked cinnamon, you could feel it puncturing your soul.

"Sometimes my Dad would pull over a stool, stand me up on it, and show me how to use my left hand to press down the strings and my right to pluck the rhythm. I'm sure my playing sucked, but if it did, no one told me. I swore I would someday learn to play that bass. I wanted that feel. I wanted that love." Tim paused for a moment. "That's how I remember my Dad."

"You didn't learn to play the bass?" Maggie asked.

"No," Tim said. "By the time I was old enough to learn an instrument, I wanted to be in a marching band. I picked trombone. You can imagine how awkward it might be marching down the street with a bass fiddle."

"Yes, I can imagine," Maggie said. "You should buy a bass fiddle and learn to play it."

"I have a bass fiddle," Tim said. "It's the same one I played on Christmas Eve. It's been in my mother's attic for seven years. I brought it home from the back of his shop the night before we buried him."

"You're kidding me?" she said. "Why haven't you learned to play it?"

"I don't know. I guess I think of it as a shrine to my father."

"Letting his passion collect dust in an attic is no shrine," Maggie said. "A shrine would be you standing in the middle of a band with your left fingers pressing the strings and your right hand plucking rhythm with a big smile on your face."

Tim could feel the emotion surging to his eyes. He turned to Maggie.

"Hey, wait a minute," he said. "Who's supposed to be saving whom here?"

Maggie laughed.

"Believe me, Timmy. Every word you say is saving me."

He paused and continued.

"There are a lot of stories I could tell about me and my Dad. I could make you laugh. I could make you cry. The stories got sadder as time passed. I hit my midteens around the time my father remarried. I adjusted to city life and high school, all their pressures and distractions."

"Distractions like girls?" Maggie said.

"Yes, like girls," Tim said. "Did I ever tell you about Sandy..."

"Never mind Sandy," Maggie said, paused for a moment, and added, "Sandy goes against my grain."

Her eyes widened as did her mouth in a smile.

"How's that, Tim? I just made a stupid joke."

"That's great. It shows me I'm rubbing off on you."

They worked their way down Route 1 toward Portland. In Brunswick they stopped for some fried clams and a beer.

"It's six," Maggie said from across the table. "I have to get you home soon. You have a long day tomorrow."

"I'm fine," Tim said. "Once I get on the highway, I just go into cruise mode. I listen to talk radio. I have all my stations lined up as I go."

"Just be careful," she said.

"Who me?" he said. "I'll come back safe and sound. Trust me."

"Okay, I trust you," she said.

"Are you sure?" he said.

"Sure of what?"

"Sure that you trust me."

"Of course," she said. "Why are you asking me that?"

"I'm asking you if you trust me to help you."

She looked at him, her head cocked, her left brow wrinkled.

"Why'd you ask me that?"

"No reason in particular," he said. "I just want to make sure we are on the same page, and I am not sticking my nose in where it doesn't belong."

"I trust what you do is in my best interests. I trust you with my heart. I'm just not ready to trust myself with my heart. I need to take things slowly. "

"I'm a patient man," he said. "As long as you know how I feel about you,"

"I do."

"Finally!" he said. "You said it!"

"Said what?"

"I do."

Maggie shook her head. "You are so bad."

**

The dark-haired woman closed the book, laid it across her lap and rested her folded hands across it. She stared up at the ceiling and tried to digest some of what she read. A smile nudged the corners of her mouth. She swung her legs over the edge of the bed and sat up, being careful not to disturb the taped gauze around her wound. She picked up the five photographs from the bed stand and cast a lingering look at each one before inserting them into the book.

"First things first," she said aloud. She stood, picked up the room key, and left.

Thirty minutes later she pulled up in front of an apartment building and walked around to the back porch. She reached into her pocketbook and removed a small envelope, opened the bendable metal fastener, and tipped it. A key fell out into her right hand. She opened the door and walked in.

The small, one bedroom apartment was empty of furniture or personal objects except for a small leather briefcase and a heavy paper shopping bag filled with what looked from across the room to be picture frames. She walked to the bag and lifted it to the kitchen counter. She pulled out one of the frames and stared at the photograph. Tears filled her eyes. She put it back in the bag and set it down next to the back door. The briefcase weighed more than she expected. She lifted it onto the counter and opened it.

Wedged in the middle of a half dozen manila folders filled with paper was a loose-leaf binder. The dark-haired woman opened it and saw a title page. "Yellow Petals in Moonlight: A Play in Three Acts, by W. Shannon." She shook her head slowly as she smiled, put her hand to her mouth, and said, "My God, Billy, you finished it."

12

Tim hit Hartford before the end of the morning rush hour. Traffic slowed. He turned up the radio and searched for a sports talk show. Over the weekend, the Red Sox swept three games from the Yankees by a combined score of 30 to 9. He expected there would be someone on the radio here in Hartford glorying in that fact, but he found nothing. He flicked over to a rock station, landed in the middle of a Barry Manilow song, and moved the dial upward. He found Natalie Cole singing, *I've Got Love on My Mind*. He left it on. Not only was Natalie in his class at UMass, Tim did have love on his mind.

Through Connecticut he thought about Maggie. He wanted her to be happy. He wanted her with him. After this past weekend, he believed they would get back together. But he had to figure her out first.

Maggie was a jigsaw puzzle with all its sculpted pieces lying out there, face up on the table, a mix of colors and patterns so diverse and contrasting, you believe someone mixed up the puzzle pieces from a bunch of different boxes. You swear to yourself this will never fit together, but somehow it does. And when you see the sweeping beauty of the fully constructed picture, you say to yourself, *I have found a masterpiece.*

Tim thought about the past two days and his discussions with Maggie. While he believed it a legitimate possibility Olivia may be alive, he knew the guilt that eats the hearts of suicide survivors. He also knew rumors start as a tiny mist of speculation, coalesce as droplets seeping from mouths to ears, to settling in brains as icy facts. But the fact of Olivia's death was not his worry, however tragic it may turn out to be. His worry was Maggie and the newspaper column with its scribbled note at the bottom.

How did Shannon die? If Olivia did kill herself, were her death and Shannon's related? That didn't make sense to him if they were in fact almost nine years apart. Did Shannon lie to Maggie about his relationship with Olivia? Or was that just bullshit?

"You got your wish. Rot in Hell." Was it just someone's awful idea of a verbal lashing rooted in grief at a perceived rival? Or was it a threat? Tim feared the latter. *I have to make a decision,* he thought.

Tim reached the Tappen Zee Bridge and crossed the Hudson River. In fifteen minutes he turned onto the Garden State Parkway and passed into New Jersey. Tim tuned in a New York City sports station to rest his brain from his thoughts. He spent this last hour of driving, reveling in the whining coming out of New York fans.

Tim's two hour afternoon seminar in the Piscataway office went well. He felt confident about tomorrow's

STRAY THREADS | 103

double header sessions. That night he relaxed over dinner with a couple of claims guys he knew. Tim fought off the fog of his long drive until he couldn't keep his eyes open. He returned to his room at the hotel and slept.

Tuesday morning's class went well, and after lunch he found himself with an hour to kill before he started his afternoon session. His boss hadn't called about going to another office tomorrow. He shut the door to the conference room and dialed Jack's direct line.

"Hello?"

"Hey, Jack. It's Tim."

"Hi, Tim. How's the seminar going?"

"Pretty good. They've been very receptive. I sense there's a great thirst for *The Art and Science of Workers Compensation Medical Case Management* here in New Jersey. Some of these people are asking when the movie is coming out."

Jack laughed.

"You may have to move down there just to keep up with demand."

"Shoot me," Tim said. "My heart is in Portland."

"Yeah, I know she is," Jack said.

"I meant my heart is in the Portland Claims office," Tim said. "I'm loyal to my homeland."

"So if they gave you a huge raise to move, you wouldn't consider it?"

"Absolutely not," Tim said, paused, and added. "How much we talking?"

They both laughed.

"So what about another office?" Tim said. "Am I supposed to go there tomorrow?"

"I haven't heard anything. Just skip it and drive

back."

Tim hesitated a moment.

"Jack, I was wondering if I might make a little 'sales call' to another office while I'm down in this area. I could call, get a manager or supervisor, and just say I was in the area, and maybe I could stop in for an hour. I'd tell them I wanted to show off our new Comp seminar. Maybe get them to buy into the concept. If we could get this thing going, Home Office will probably give us the go to expand the program."

"Sounds interesting," Jack said. "What are you trying to do, start your own training business?"

"Yeah, right," Tim said. "Didn't I just tell you I am loyal to you and Portland Claims? But I wouldn't mind doing this type of thing as a sideline for a while."

"And who would replace you here?" Jack said.

"Sandra."

"She could do it," Jack said. "Look, you're down there. Give it a shot. What office are you thinking of?"

"King of Prussia."

"Pennsylvania? You're adding a lot of drive time."

"I don't mind," Tim said. "I've heard southern Pennsylvania is beautiful in the spring."

"Well, then go for it."

"Great." Tim said. "I'll see you Friday."

"Good luck, Tim."

After his last session, Tim bought take out Chinese and ate in his hotel room. He turned on the local news to check the weather. Continued good weather tomorrow. Rain coming in on Thursday continuing through the weekend. Perfect.

He debated calling Maggie. If he did, should he tell her what he was thinking about doing tomorrow? She said she trusted him, but trust is not carte blanche freedom. Was it the right thing to do? He wanted to do the right thing, the smart thing. But whatever he did, he would do it for Maggie. He dialed.

"Hello?" Maggie said.

"Hey, Maggie. It's Tim."

"Timmy. How's Joisey?"

"Still here. How are you doing?"

"I'm actually feeling pretty good," she said. "Don't worry, I won't be lying next to some dirty, stinky dumpster somewhere?"

"I know. I just like to hear the sound of your voice."

"It's mutual," she said. "Hold on a sec."

Tim heard her speak to someone. "That's okay. Just pour it in the pan."

She came back on. "Sorry."

"I didn't realize you had company," he said, feeling a slight rise of jealousy. "You need to go?"

"No, of course not," she said. "Say 'hello.'"

Tim was about to say, "To whom?" when another voice came on the line.

"Hello, Timothy."

It took him a moment to process. "Sophie?"

"*Oui, mon Cherie*," Sophie said.

"What are you doing at Maggie's?"

"I am about to have dinner," she said. "Marguerite invited me."

"Really?" he said. "That's cool."

"Marguerite and I are becoming *bon amies*," she said. "By the time you return, we will each know everything there is to know about you."

"Oh, God, spare me."

"I may evict you and have Marguerite as a roommate."

"My name's on the lease."

"Do you honestly believe you stand up to both of us at the same time?" He could almost see those eyes lighting up through the 300 mile phone cord.

"Are you coming home tomorrow?"

"No, Thursday night," he said.

"Okay. Behave yourself. Here's Marguerite."

"Don't worry, Timmy," Maggie said. "She's kidding. I won't tell her *everything* I know about you. Did you say you were coming home tomorrow night?"

"No," he said. "I have to visit another office."

"Too bad. Where?"

"Oh, it's not too far from here, a little farther south," he said. "So what are you guys having for dinner? I bet it's better than the Chinese I just ate."

"We're having sheep eyeballs and snails," she said. "I'm learning how to make them for you."

"You two getting together is like my worst nightmare," he said.

Maggie laughed.

"I wish we'd gotten together sooner. I love talking with her. She's great."

"I know."

"Well, Timmy. It looks like dinner's ready. Thanks for checking on me. Don't work too hard."

"I promise," he said. "Enjoy the evening. And Maggie, don't believe anything Sophie says about me. She lies."

"So do I," she said. "Au revoir." She hung up.

***

The Honda slowed as it rode the exit ramp off the Taconic Parkway and turned east onto Interstate 90. Twelve miles later, the Honda passed the large green "Welcome to Massachusetts" sign with its big pilgrim hat with an arrow through it, the symbol of the Massachusetts Turnpike. She slowed for the toll booth.

The dark-haired woman accepted a ticket from the man in the booth and headed east on the Pike. Ten miles later she pulled into the rest area and went inside, first to the Ladies Room, and then to a telephone.

"I'm in Mass...on the Pike...in Lee, I think. Yes, the first rest stop...How're the boys?...Yes...Miss them, too...I'm not sure, but I'm going home first...Yes, I have the package, and it looks like it was intact...instructions were perfect...This will nail the...Nope, no problems."

She listened to the voice on the other end for about thirty seconds then went on.

"I stopped there, too...Everything's gone, just the bag and the briefcase they mentioned...All his papers, and you wouldn't believe it...he finished the play.. No, it's done...Not yet."

They spoke for a few more minutes and hung up. The dark-haired woman bought a coffee and returned to her car. She pulled out of the rest stop and continued eastward.

13

At 8:30 Wednesday morning, Tim sat in a coffee shop in suit and tie, a mile away from the King of Prussia office. At 8:45 he went outside to a pay phone, called the office, and got switched to the claims manager. His pitch worked and the claims manager agreed to meet with him at 9:15. By 10:00 Tim had convinced the claims manager to schedule him back for a presentation. Fifteen minutes later, he was back on the road heading west. He entered Cummington around eleven.

Tim's first stop was the public library. He found the research room and pulled the telephone book for the extended Reading area. He looked up 'Bodden' and found two addresses. One was for a 'K. Bodden' in Reading and the other for a 'James Bodden' in Barnard, a town that bordered both the City of Reading and Cummington. Tim copied both addresses.

Under 'Wood' he found fifteen listings. None of them listed Cummington as an address. Tim pulled an atlas from the shelves and looked up each town listing a 'Wood.' Three of them lived in towns bordering Cummington. Tim wrote down those addresses and returned the books to their locations.

Before leaving the library, Tim walked up to the front desk. A forty-ish woman in a grey suit sat with a stack of books, ticking them off a computer printout. Tim looked to his right, down the stacks, and saw a young woman, about nineteen or twenty years old, putting books from her three-tiered book cart back on the shelves. Of average height with shoulder-length, curly brown hair, the girl wore a short, blue skirt and an unbuttoned plaid shirt tied over a yellow tube top. Tim walked down the stack, lingered like he was scanning the titles, and walked over to her.

"Excuse me," Tim said.

She looked up at Tim and smiled.

"Oh, Hi," she said. "Can I help you with something?"

"Yeah," Tim said with a smile. "I'm a grad student at Villanova, and I'm working on my thesis about the history of Berks County. I'm doing research on the rise of the public school systems, their relationships with the Amish people, and why their students eat pretzels with mustard for lunch."

The girl nodded her head and looked at him like she had no clue what he was talking about.

"You're looking for books about local history here?" she said. "This is the cookbook aisle."

"No, I'm sorry," Tim said and laughed. "I was just kidding. Could you tell me how to find Cummington High School? I spoke on the phone to their librarian, Mrs...uh...Miss..."

"Donnelly?" the girl said. "Mrs. Donnelly's the librarian."

"That's it," Tim said. "Donnelly. She has a book she said would help me. I need to go borrow it. I had directions to the school, but I think I left them back in my apartment."

"Cummington High's about a mile and a half from here," the girl said. "Just follow Pearl Street down to the third light and take a right. Follow it to the top of the hill. Take a left on Grand Street. Cummington High is right there at the top of the hill."

"Great. Thanks," Tim said. "I heard it's a great school."

"It is," she said. "And I know, because I went there."

"Oh, really?" Tim said. "My mother's cousin lived around here, and I think her daughter went to Cummington. The families have been out of touch for so long. What the heck was her name? Um...I want to say it was Silvia or something like that. I never saw them much, and I'm awful with names."

"I didn't know any Silvias," the girl said, shaking her head. "When did she go there?"

"Jeez, I don't know. I think she was a year or two younger than me," Tim said. "I graduated in...Wood! That was their last name. Wood."

The girl stared at him. "Olivia?"

"Olivia, yes," he said. "You know her?"

"Not really," she said. "But I heard about her. She was a year ahead of me. I know she lived in Aldenburg. That's still in the Cummington school district."

"What did you hear about her?" Tim said. "I hope it was good."

The girl didn't say anything. She looked at Tim straight-faced.

"Nothing, except that she moved. I don't know where."

"Well, if I get this paper done earlier, maybe I'll take a little ride and see if they're still there. Do you know what street they lived on?"

The girl shook her head. "I just heard they moved."

"Okay. Thanks."

In the car Tim went through the "Wood" names and addresses he'd written down. None of them lived in Aldenburg.

Cummington High School straddled a hill surrounded by blossoming residential communities. As Tim pulled in the driveway, he looked down over the northern slope. Tiered levels cut into the long hillside and held tennis courts, a track-encircled football field with a black-painted panther on the scoreboard, a number of baseball-softball fields, and the eastern side of a new looking junior high school. *Wow,* Tim thought. *This is definitely nothing like the old South High School I went to.*

The school building itself was modern and multi-tiered in its own right. Tim parked in the visitors area of the near empty parking lot and walked toward the south-facing main entrance. He entered the door and stopped to survey the lobby.

The glass walled Administrative Office sat on the corner of a wide hallway and the top of an open, down stairwell. Through the glass Tim saw a tall man wearing a business suit and carrying a briefcase exit the corner office inside the main area. The man stopped at a file cabinet, opened the top drawer, and pulled out a file.

The man walked to the front desk where the only other person in the big office stood - a bespeckled, overweight woman in her late fifties, dressed in a flowery, yellow summer dress. Tim scanned the walls around him, saw what he looked for, and moved toward it, still keeping his eyes on the pair. The man and woman laughed at whatever was said, and the man moved to the large glass door and the hallway.

The men's room door closed behind Tim. He moved to the sink and stood there, touching his hair as if fixing it in the mirror. He waited long enough for the man - who he believed was the principal - to leave the building and get to the parking area.

As he opened the door to the Administration Office, Tim glanced over at the nameplate on the principal's door. *John Gleason.* He walked to the counter and smiled at the lady behind it.

"How are you?" he said. Tim held up the business card in his hand, part of his index finger covering his name and address. He left the company name visible.

"I'm Will Carlson from Whitfield Casualty in Philadelphia. I'd like to speak with Mr. Gleason. Just for a couple of minutes. I called him last week and asked if I could stop in on Tuesday, but I had to cancel. Trying to juggle work and a week-old baby. What I wouldn't give for even four hours of uninterrupted sleep." Tim exaggerated a sigh, while smiling, shaking his head slowly, and sliding the business card back into his jacket pocket.

The woman smiled and said, "Oh, that's so nice. A new baby. I sure know how babies can be. My daughter has two boys. Matthew is three and Christopher's one. They are a handful. But I told her she's just getting payback for how she was when I had her. What goes around comes around, I always say."

"Yeah, I think that's what my Mom is saying about me," Tim said. "But it's worth it. I've got all those Little League games and Boy Scout camping trips and all that stuff to look forward to."

"Well, I'm sure you will be a great father," she said. "And I'm sorry, Mr. uh . . ."

"Just call me Will," Tim said. "As the people in my office say, if there's a Will, there's a way."

They both laughed.

"Will, I'm sorry, but Mr. Gleason just left not five minutes before you came. I'm surprised you didn't pass him in the parking lot."

"Is he a tall guy, graying hair?" Tim motioned with his free hand with a sweep over his head. "I think I may have seen him as I was getting out of my car. Darn."

"He won't be back today," she said. "School got out last Thursday. He's gone for the next week."

"Oh, that's not good. I don't have that kind of time," Tim said. "We have a case going to trial, and I needed some information he may be able to help me with. Now I wish I didn't stay home yesterday to help my wife with the baby. Darn it. I should have come here."

"No, you did the right thing staying home with your wife," the woman said. "Maybe I can help?"

"Well, maybe," Tim said. "It's about a teacher who used to work here. She was a witness to an accident that happened nine years ago. She said she would testify when the trial came, but I went to her apartment, and she's moved. I don't know how to get hold of her."

"Well, I'm not supposed to give out any information about employees or past employees of the school system," she said. "I could get in trouble."

"Oh, Jeez," Tim said. "I don't want to get you in trouble. I'll try to work it out somehow. Maybe I can go to Mr. Gleason's home and ask him there, you know, before he leaves on vacation?"

The woman's eyes looked at Tim, then away, then back, her left hand going to her face, pulling on her lower lip. She sighed and looked straight at Tim.

"What's the teacher's name?" she said.

"Bodden," Tim said. "She taught English here about nine years ago."

"Sarah Bodden?" the woman said. "Yes. I remember her. She was so pretty and really smart. The kids all missed her when she left. She was a good teacher."

"That's what I heard," Tim said. "I was still in college then, but my boss was the lead investigator at the time. He said she was very willing to help us."

"Hold on a minute," she said. She walked to a file cabinet, pulled open the top drawer, and removed a file. She carried it back to the front desk and opened it.

"You want to know where she lives now?"

"Yes. That would be great. But I don't want to get you in any trouble."

"Well, she said she wanted to help you. So I guess she'd want me to help you find her, right?"

Tim smiled and shrugged his shoulders.

The woman looked through the file, frowned and shook her head.

"The last address I have here was eight years ago,"

the woman said. "It's some place in Vermont called Densmore. Never heard of it."

"Probably one of those places where they make maple syrup," Tim said.

"There's no street address, just an 'in care of' and a post office box," the woman said. "So I guess I can't give you the address after all." She smiled. "I won't get in trouble."

Tim smiled broadly and thanked her. He turned and headed to the door. As he pulled the brass handle, the woman said, "Oh, Will." Tim turned. "Maybe her brother Adrian can help you. I think he might live up there, too." She smiled and gave him a wink. "And you take good care of that baby."

He returned her smile with a matching one of his own.

As he walked to his car, a pang of guilt moved from the back to the front of his brain. *I shouldn't be lying to these people. I'm always such a pain in the ass to people with my preaching about honesty and values and doing the right thing. Here I am playing like I'm Sam Spade in a bad movie. I guess I didn't really hurt anyone, and none of them will know. And dammit, I'm doing it for Maggie. Still...*

Back in his car Tim pulled out a business card, and wrote: *Adrian Bodden, Densmore, VT.*

14

Tim started the car, but just as he reached for the shifter to put it in gear, he froze.

"What an idiot," he said and shook his head. He put the car in gear and left the school parking lot, retracing his route to the library. He went back in, didn't see the girl he talked to before, and walked to the front desk.

"Excuse me," he whispered to the librarian. "Do you keep old telephone books, you know, after the new ones come?"

"Of course," the woman said. "Upstairs, take a right to the third aisle. They're along there at the far left end."

"Thank you," Tim said and climbed the stairs.

He found the phone book marked *1967-68* and opened it to the last part. He thumbed through a couple of pages, found the one he wanted, and moved his index finger done the page.

"Bingo," he said. "Frank L. Wood."

Tim wrote the name, address and phone number on the back of the sheet the school clerk gave him. He dropped the phone book on the return table and went down to the main desk.

"Excuse me again," he said to the librarian, who looked up.

"How do I get to Aldenburg," he said. "How far is it?"

"Not far," she said. "Twenty minutes or so depending on where you're going once you get there."

"I'm looking for Hillsdale Street."

"I know where that is," she said. "Take a left out of the parking lot. Follow the road for about four miles. You'll come to a split. Bear to the right. In about two or three miles you'll come to Blossom Street. Take a left and follow it to the end. It forms the base of a 'T' intersection. The street where it ends is Hillsdale Street."

"Thanks," he said and left.

Once Tim turned onto Blossom Street, it became like driving through a maze. Tall stalks of corn formed walls along both sides of the street, and the sharp, ninety degree corners begged a caution he wasn't prepared for or used to. At the end of Blossom, he stared at the sign.

Right or left on Hillsdale? The address he pulled from the old phone book said 18052 Hillsdale Street. He peeked around the corn, hoping to see a nearby mailbox or house with a street number attached. He saw no signs of human habitation. He turned right.

After a half mile or so, the street began rising out of

the cornfields into a wooded area. Tim passed a house numbered 17034 and then another marked 17092. He watched for houses on his left. He passed an unpaved road, which could have been a driveway going up into the woods, but he kept driving and passed a house marked 19044 on his right. He three point turned around and headed back for the unpaved driveway.

The driveway went in about fifty feet, took a sharp turn to the right, snaking its way up to an open area with a grey ranch house and a two-car detached garage. Tim saw no vehicles. Small branches and fallen leaves littered the driveway and front steps. *Nobody lives here. I bet this is it.*

Tim shut off the motor and got out. He walked to the garage and peeked in the window. No cars, nothing that looks like someone has been in there recently. Leaning up along the side of the garage stood two stacks of weathered, wooden milk crates. On the front door a sign hung, and Tim walked up the stairs to read it.

"Property of the Commonwealth of Pennsylvania" it read. "No Trespassing Under Criminal Penalties." A large silver padlock was affixed to the door above the knob.

Tim walked around to the rear of the house. A mildewed, leaf strewn picnic table sat about ten yards from the steps of a small back porch. A sign similar to the one on the front door hung on the back door above another silver padlock. Bolted to the shingles just to the side of the porch, a rusting pulley wheel hung off a large, rusted steel hook. Tim looked back to the trees about fifty feet behind the house and saw another pulley bolted to a tree. A rotting clothesline hung from it to the ground below. Behind it, what looked like an overgrown trail cut between the trees.

Tim walked forward and turned to complete his circle around the building. In front of what he guessed was one of the bedroom windows, sat three milk crates, two lying neatly beneath the window, the other broken and off to the side. Shards of window glass littered them, and Tim could see how thieves or vandals entered. He looked through the opening into what appeared to be an abandoned house. He saw dark red spots on the ivory trim paint of the sill. Tim had looked at enough accident scenes in his job to know dried blood when he saw it. He followed the trail of spots up to a piece of glass sticking out where the full pane used to be. *Crime doesn't pay.* He considered entering the building himself but thought better of it.

Peering through the broken window, he saw a bed with an uncovered mattress, a dresser, and an end table beside the bed. A worn, green wall-to-wall carpet, mottled with grey splotches he assumed was mildew, covered the floor. The room contained no personal objects. The walls were empty of everything but a few nails or nail holes in the upper center of rectangles once protected from sunlight. He noted the bed was askew as if pushed away from the side wall.

Tim looked down at the milk crates and saw one of them was caved in, presumably from one of the burglars. Dried blood spotted one of the bottom crates. When his eyes followed the drips to the ground, they caught the white glint of sunlight reflecting off something caught between the two crates. He bent down and pulled out a four inch by three inch black and white photograph. It was faded and held a layer of dust and dirt. He brushed it lightly, but stopped, worried he'd scratch it. He could make out it was a picture of a female from the top of her thighs up. A dark smudge of dried blood covered part of the woman's face.

Tim heard movement above him and thought it came from the window of the house. He stood and stepped back, stretching up, looking in the window. He saw nothing. Movement in the corner of his eye made him look up above the window to the corner of the roof. A crow rested on the metal rain gutter. The bird surveyed Tim, cocking its black head so each of his eyes could get a good look, then it cawed a 'nevermore' and flew off. Tim slipped the photo in his pocket and decided to leave.

In the car he looked at his watch. Two o'clock. He was hungry. He turned right out of the driveway and retraced his route down Hillsdale to Blossom and back to the main drag. He turned left in the direction he believed was the center of town. In a small strip mall he saw a sign for an eatery named "A.J.'s" and pulled in.

Only a few people occupied the booths. Two pairs of older people sat around tables at the far side of the room near the restroom signs. The waitress was a tall, pink-uniformed blonde with stringy hair and an apparent need to chew gum while she spoke. He ordered the A.J. Burger Plate Special and a coffee. Tim stretched his legs and closed his eyes. He was tired. It had been a long few days.

He thought about what he learned today. Miss Bodden's first name is Sarah. She moved to, or at least left a forwarding address to Densmore, Vermont. He believed Densmore was on the New Hampshire side of Vermont in the general vicinity of White River

Junction. Dartmouth College was not far away. He knew Bodden was rich, pretty and smart. *I bet she went to Dartmouth.*

Tim knew neither Olivia nor her father lived at their house in Aldenburg. For some reason, the cops locked it up. Why would they do that? Foreclosure? But wouldn't the signs then be posted by the bank not the state? Is it a crime scene? Did Olivia hang herself there? Probably not. That house has been sitting there like that for a long time. Patty's information would have been a lot clearer, if something like that happened this close to Cummington. *I need to find Frank Wood. Is he dead? Did he just take off? Did he commit a crime? I need to find out more.*

Tim sat up straight. He remembered the snapshot and pulled it from his shirt pocket. He set it on the table in front of him, reached across and pulled the clean, cloth napkin from under the extra silverware set. He dipped one corner into his water glass and wiped it across the photograph, being careful not to use too much water or scratch it with the gritty dust.

He lifted the snapshot in his hand and stared at it. The woman had medium shaded hair, pulled back in a ponytail. She wore a light-colored tunic, a dark skirt, and a white sling on her left shoulder. Her eyes were partially shaded and difficult to see. She did not smile.

He heard movement behind him and turned to see the waitress. She hesitated, staring at him for a moment, then quickly smiled and moved to set down his order. Tim laid the snapshot face down on the table. He looked at the giant burger and the stack of fries.

"Wow," he said to the waitress. "I could live off of this for the next week."

The waitress smiled.

"The house specialty," she said. "Come back after five and this place will be packed, especially on the weekends when the kids hang here. They love these things."

"That's great," Tim said. "Good for tips. I bet." He looked at her, smiled and raised his eyebrows.

She smiled, popped a bubble, and gave him a quick wink.

"Amen," she said and walked toward the cash register.

The burger tasted as good as it looked. The hand-cut French fries had just enough salt. The coffee was strong. Tim ate. He looked at the facedown snapshot and saw some handwriting on the back, upper left corner. He read it. *Dr. Martin - October 17, 1961 - Dislocation.*

Tim flipped the picture over and examined it, like he was analyzing a workers compensation claim. He couldn't tell whether the woman's arm was broken or dislocated. He'd take the writing on the back at face value. The way the shadows darkened her eyes made him believe the camera angle was below the woman. Was she taking it herself, holding the camera with an outstretched arm? He doubted that - she looked to be too far away from the camera, and if the lens was wide angle, it would have distorted much of the outside aspects of the picture. Maybe it was set on a table? Or maybe the photographer was sitting or simply very short? He stared at the eyes. One of them looked almost like she was winking, but that belied the rest of her face. The waitress interrupted his examination with the pot of coffee and refilled his cup.

"Can I ask you a question?" Tim said.

"Depends on the question," she said, looking at Tim like he might be hitting on her.

"Did you ever hear of a guy named Frank Wood?"

Her head turned, and she looked directly at Tim. She hesitated, and then she cocked her head like she was trying to remember something.

"I think he used to live around here," Tim added.

"Don't know him," she said. "Sorry."

Shrugging her shoulders, she went to the far table with the coffee pot.

Tim finished the burger. He picked at the fries as he sipped coffee. He looked over at the cash register and saw a phone book on the shelf underneath the register. He waited for a waitress to go there and ring up a payment. He walked over and asked her permission to borrow the book. She smiled and nodded.

He found the listing for William Shannon in Reading. He wrote the address and phone number and returned the book. Back in the booth he picked up his coffee cup. He saw a tall, red-headed man dressed in white, with a greasy apron around his waist, walking toward him. The man, obviously one of the cooks, stopped at Tim's table and looked down at Tim. Tim didn't know what to do or say, so he smiled.

"You looking for Frank Wood?" the man said.

"Uh, yeah," Tim said. "I heard he lives around here, but I couldn't find him."

"You his friend?"

"Oh, God, no," Tim said. "I've never met the guy. I work for an insurance company. It's about an old claim we have."

"What kind of claim?" the man said. "Fraud

involved?"

Tim thought for a moment and said, "Well, I'm not supposed to discuss that with anyone but him."

"Well, it doesn't matter anyways," the man said. "He's in jail."

"In jail?" Tim said.

"Some cops carted him off two maybe three years ago," the man said. "Probably for fraud. Wood was a scumbag, a pathological liar, and a con man."

"Wow," said Tim. "Maybe it's just as well I didn't find him."

"You're lucky," the cook said. "Okay. Sorry to bother you. Hope you enjoyed the burger."

"It was great." Tim said. "They don't make them like that up my way."

"I know, I invented it," the cook said. "Where you from?"

"Ma..., uh, Massachusetts," Tim said. "Born and raised."

"That's funny," the cook said.

"Funny?"

"Yeah. The cops who came for him were from Massachusetts," the cook said. "I saw their license plates when they came in to arrest him."

"They arrested him here?"

"Yeah," the cook said. "Wood and his brother - and sometimes his brother's idiot son - used to come here for breakfast a few times a week."

"They get arrested, too?"

"No," the cook said. "His brother didn't show up that day. The son neither."

"What was his brother's name?" Tim said. "Maybe he can help me find him?"

"Don't remember. Maybe Tommy? Tony? Timmy? Something like that. I haven't seen him since."

"What about his son?"

"He used to come in once in a while," the cook said and shook his head. "I think he had the hots for one of the waitresses. No more though. Don't know his name. Frank and his brother called him 'Junior.'"

The cook turned and started to walk away.

"One thing," Tim said. "Didn't Wood have a young daughter? She still live around here?"

The cook stared at Tim.

"I heard she killed herself," the cook said. "Poor kid didn't have a chance. Especially after her mother ran off."

"Her mother ran off?" Tim said. "I thought she got killed in a car accident."

"Naw," the cook said. "Just took off one day, and I think no one ever heard from her again." He turned and left.

Tim finished his coffee and went looking for a motel.

15

The dark-haired woman put the play script on her bureau and began sorting through the manila files. The first folder contained an annotated copy of "The Egg and I," a play once popular on the high school circuit. The next was a collection of essays Shannon wrote for a college course in expository writing.

As she separated the folders into piles on the bed, she came across a folder marked "Students/Bodden." She opened it. Inside were various essays, which appeared to be written by students. Most of the essays were photostats of graded papers. William Shannon's fluid penmanship was evident. One appeared to be an original, entitled, "Doggone" by Olivia Wood. The dark-haired woman placed it separately on her bureau with the script.

The last folder she pulled from the case contained a small collection of carefully cut newspaper articles, two handwritten letters, three typewritten sheets of paper, and five receipts from a pawn shop called

Rodney's. She moved to her desk chair, turned on the light, and began to examine the materials in the file.

A half hour later she leaned back in the chair, pulled out a pack of cigarettes from her purse, and lit up. She removed a sheet of paper from the file with her left hand, rereading it through the swirling smoke cloud, illuminated by the desk lamp's light. A smile grew, her eyes widened.

"Holy shit," she said. "He found it. Bill friggin' found it."

***

The morning ride to Reading put Tim in the middle of rush hour. He stopped to top off his gas tank before he got into the city, and while the attendant was pouring the gas, he walked next door to a variety store and came back with a street map of the city. He paid the attendant for the gas, pulled away from the pump, and stopped in the side area to look at the map. He found the street he wanted, marked it on the map, and headed down Route 422 toward downtown.

Reading looked a lot like Portland to Tim, with about the same number of people, buildings and streets. No seaport, of course, but Reading had the Schuykill River. A big pagoda stared down from the side of a small mountain. Weird.

He followed Penn Street and turned when he saw the street he'd mapped. He pulled over once to make sure he was on the right track, confirmed he was, and hooked a right according to his map route. He wound his way to his destination. He found a parking spot about twenty feet from a "Residents Only" parking sign and decided to take the chance on a ticket. *I won't be long.*

Tim walked, looking for Shannon's house number. He found the red brick apartment building and climbed the steps. He searched the names printed above the horizontal row of doorbell buttons. Five of the six buttons had names. None of the names said "Shannon." The one with the missing name was apartment 1A.

Tim tried to turn the knob to enter the common hallway, but found it locked. He cupped his hands around his eyes and pressed them and his face against the window pane in the middle of the door. He could see the door to the apartment on his left and made out what looked like "1B" in brass figures attached to it. He turned to his right and walked to the side of the porch, where the paned front window of apartment 1A allowed a partial view inside. There were no curtains.

His view showed an empty front room with a door next to the opposite corner and a short hallway leading to what looked like a kitchen area. The apartment appeared empty of furniture and residents, clean and ready to rent.

The small size of the apartment surprised Tim. The newspaper article said Shannon left a wife and two young boys. Tim found it hard to believe a family of four could live in this tiny apartment. He knew teachers weren't the highest paid workers, but you'd think Shannon could afford something bigger than this.

Tim turned when he heard the sound of someone climbing the stairs behind him. A heavy, middle-aged woman, in a black dress bedecked with a white and yellow daisy print, huffed her way up the stairs. Her left hand held onto the left rail, while her crooked right arm cradled a brown Pomeranian. The dog looked at Tim and growled. The woman baby-talked it into hushing up.

"Don't worry," she said. "He doesn't bite."

"I'm not worried," Tim said with a smile. "Can I pat him?"

"Sure." She lifted her arm and turned her right side toward Tim. Tim reached out and scratched between the dog's pointed ears. The dog lifted his head to extend the scratching to under its chin.

"What's his name?" Tim said.

"Hercules," the woman said.

"Hercules?" Tim said with a growing smile.

"It makes him feel tough."

Tim laughed and continued to scratch.

"I'm thinking of getting an apartment around here," Tim said. "It looks like 1A is empty?"

"Yes," she said. "The guy that used to live there died some weeks ago. I think he drowned in the river or something. I really didn't know him. He moved in about a year ago. The paper said he was a teacher."

"I thought his wife and kids would still be living here," Tim said. "Did they move out right after he died?"

"His wife?" she said. "I don't think he had a wife. I know the newspaper said he had a wife and kids, but I think it was a mistake. I never saw them. Maybe he was divorced or something He was pretty quiet and kept to himself."

The woman hesitated for a moment, shrugged her shoulders, and went on.

"I think he had a girlfriend, though. Very pretty girl. Dark brown hair. She drove one of those foreign cars. A blue one. She came here every few weeks or so and stayed overnight. She didn't wear a wedding ring or anything." The woman blushed and hiked her grip on Hercules. "Maybe she was his sister or something. I don't know."

"You don't know her name, do you?" Tim said. "In case I wanted to ask her a question about the apartment."

"No. Like I said, I really didn't know him very well."

"Okay," Tim said. "Well, thanks for the info."

He gave the dog a quick rub between the ears. "See ya, Hercules."

On the way back to the car, Tim shook his head. *What's going on? Shannon must have been separated or divorced, but probably just separated. Wouldn't the paper say he 'leaves his two sons...' without mentioning the wife, if he was divorced? Maybe, maybe not. It was a news article not an obituary. But still, this seems odd.*

"Oh well," he said out loud. "I'm tired. I'm lonely. I'm going home."

Tim found Route 222 and headed north.

In Kutztown he saw a large farm stand coming up on his side of the road. He pulled in and came out a few minutes later with a bag and a smile.

"Next stop Portland," he said and turned onto the highway.

16

"Hello?"

"Hey, Mags."

"You back?"

"I'm home. How ya doing?"

"I'm doing well, Timmy. You and Sophie helped me a lot. Thanks."

"No thanks necessary," he said. "I have something for you. I bought you a present."

"A present? From New Jersey? What for?"

"Because I'm 'fantabulous,' like Didi said. But don't get too excited. It won't make you rich or be something you hand down to future generations."

"So when will I get it?"

"In about fifteen minutes, if you want."

"I'll be waiting with bated breath."

When Tim came in he carried a brown shopping bag with two heavy paper handles. He set it down on the counter, and Maggie came to him, put her arms around him and hugged. While pulling back, she gave him a quick kiss on the cheek.

"A present!" she said rubbing her palms together in front of her. "I'm so excited."

"Let me caution you about building high expectations," he said. Tim opened the bag, reached in and pulled out a smaller white bag with the top folded over to seal it. He handed it to Maggie.

She opened it and looked in. A broad smile covered her face, and she started laughing.

"A pretzel! Just like the ones we had in Pennsylvania."

She looked up. Tim held up a jar of Pennsylvania Dutch mustard.

"Oh. My God!" Maggie said. "Manna from Heaven for us lost souls wandering in the desert."

"How you have suffered living on lobster and drawn butter," Tim said. "And there's five more in the bag."

She laughed and took the jar from Tim to look at the label. She leaned forward and kissed him on the cheek. She opened the jar, set it on the counter, and broke off a piece of the soft, Pennsylvania Dutch pretzel. She handed it to Tim and broke off another for herself. With her right hand Maggie held up the pretzel. She picked up the mustard jar with her left and held them both in front of her.

"This is the proper way to do it," Maggie said. "You take the pretzel..." She lifted it slightly toward Tim and nodded. "Then you dip it into the mustard." She lifted the mustard jar, dipped the pretzel, withdrew the mustard coated dough, and put it in her mouth. Her eyes closed in feigned ecstasy, chewing it.

"Mmmm," She said.

"Now that's hot," Tim said.

"It's spicy, but I wouldn't call it hot," Maggie said.

"I wasn't talking about the mustard," Tim said.

"Now you try it," Maggie said, ignoring his comment.

Tim casually dipped his pretzel into the jar Maggie held out to him. He plopped it in his mouth and chewed it, his head rocking, his eyes looking up, contemplating.

"It tastes like a pretzel with mustard on it," he said.

Maggie tore off another piece, dunked it and put it in her mouth. She interrupted her chew to say, "How did you ever find these in New Jersey?"

"I didn't buy them in New Jersey," Tim said. "I bought them in Pennsylvania."

Maggie suspended her chewing and stared at Tim. She swallowed.

"You went to Pennsylvania?"

"Yes. I slept there last night," he said. "In Cummington."

Maggie looked at him like she didn't quite understand what he was saying. She put the mustard jar on the counter and sat down on one of the two stools.

"Why were you in Cummington?"

Tim sat on the other stool.

"I had to see the claims manager at our King of Prussia office yesterday morning," Tim said. "I took the opportunity to go to Cummington and do a little investigating."

"Investigating?" she said, her eyes narrowing. "What does that mean?"

"It means I wanted to see what I could find out about what happened."

"What happened with me?"

"Sorta," Tim said. He leaned forward toward her. "I wanted to see if I could find out what happened to Olivia and Shannon."

"Why didn't you tell me you were going to do something like that?" she said. "Before you did it? That's something that should involve me, wouldn't you think? On Sunday, you asked me if I trusted you. Isn't this pushing my trust just a bit?"

"I didn't decide to do this for sure until Tuesday afternoon," Tim said. "I didn't want to put any more stress on you. I thought about telling you. In fact, when I called Tuesday night, I would have told you. But when I knew Sophie was here, I decided you sounded too happy to ruin your evening. Maggie, I did this for you."

Maggie stared at him.

"So did you find out anything with your 'investigation?'" She wiggled the index and middle fingers of both hands indicating quotes.

"A little," he said. "I learned Olivia's father's name is 'Frank' and lived in Aldenburg. I went to the house and found it padlocked with a sign on it saying it's the property of the state. No one lives there, and it doesn't look like anyone has for a while. Someone broke in through a bedroom window. Recently. There was blood on the sill which probably would have washed off when it rained."

"I guess you did do an investigation," Maggie said. "I take it you saw no sign that Olivia had been there?"

"Nothing. Unless she's the one who broke in. I considered going in through the open window," Tom said. "But I thought better of it and left. No one saw me there. Except a crow."

"A crow?"

"A joke," he said and waved a hand dismissing his comment.

"So that doesn't tell us much about Olivia," Maggie said.

"Well, I went into a local diner for a late lunch," Tim said.

"A.J.'s?" Maggie said. "Great burgers."

"Yup. Excellent burgers. I ended up talking to A.J. himself, in fact."

"Really? Maggie said. "How'd you manage that?"

"I told him I was investigating an insurance claim," Tim said. "I asked him about Frank Wood, and he said the guy was a jerk and a con man. He said Frank was arrested and carted off. He didn't know what for or where, but he told me something interesting. The cops who took him away were Massachusetts State Troopers."

"Really?"

"So whatever law he broke," Tim said, "it was in Massachusetts. I'll need to check that out."

"How are you going to do that?" Maggie said.

"C'mon, you were a claims adjuster for a short while," he said with a grin. "Public records are public."

"Good point," Maggie said nodding her head.

"One other thing," Tim said. "Didn't you tell me Olivia told Shannon her mother died by getting hit by a car when she was in first grade?"

"Yes," she said. "That's what he told me, at least."

"Well, let's assume he was telling you the truth," Tim said. "A.J. told me the mother just took off from the family and never returned."

"Olivia was lying?" Maggie said. "Maybe she was

ashamed her mother took off? Or maybe her father lied to her about it?"

"Maybe," Tim said. "But it's something to think about."

Maggie nodded.

"And I also found this," Tim said. He pulled the snapshot he'd found outside the window at the Wood residence. He handed it to Maggie.

Maggie looked at it, but showed no recognition of the subject in the photo. She looked up at Tim, her forehead wrinkled in puzzlement.

"Who's this?" she said.

"I was hoping you would know that," Tim said. "I found it outside the broken window."

"At Olivia's?"

"Yes," Tim said. "Her mother?"

"I never met her mother," Maggie said. "The picture's not the greatest. It could be someone who looks like Olivia but only in a general way."

Tim nodded.

"Look at it and tell me what else you notice."

Maggie stared at it. She didn't see anything that stood out. She looked up at Tim and shook her head.

"She wasn't exactly smiling."

"True. But look at her left eye," Tim said. "Does it look swollen to you?"

Maggie looked again.

"Could be," she said. "It's kind of dark, hard to see."

"I know," Tim said. "But I spent a lot of time looking at it. I think it's swollen. Flip it over."

Maggie turned the snapshot over and read the words.

"Who's Dr. Martin?"

"Don't know," Tim said. "But what I'm thinking is whoever this was, she was documenting her injuries. This was not taken for fun."

"She does look grumpy." Maggie said.

"Also notice how she seems to be looking down at the camera, like she had put it on a table to hold it for her. The camera may have been one with a timer."

Maggie looked again at the picture. After staring at it for a minute or so, she looked up.

"I don't think this was on a table," she said.

"You don't?" Tim said. "But see how it's pointing up? It's not head on."

"I can see that," she said. "But also look at the background. It's not level. If this was on a table, the picture would likely be level with the background. This has a tip."

She handed Tim the photo. He examined it and looked up.

"You're right," he said. "I never noticed that before. How'd you notice that?"

Maggie smiled at him.

I'm a designer," she said. "I notice things like that."

Tim nodded.

"I think this picture was taken by a person," Maggie said. "A sitting person. Or short person."

"Olivia?" Tim said.

Maggie nodded.

"I bet this is her mother," she said.

"Good work," he said.

"Likewise," she said. "So what does all this mean?"

"I wonder how she dislocated her arm," Tim said. "Mix this with the things Olivia said, and it sounds like her father may be even worse than we thought."

"That's what I'm thinking," Maggie said. She sighed and let her eyes drift away from Tim.

Tim could see the sadness returning to her eyes. He knew Maggie. He knew this information would bring her guilt back to the surface. She'd blame herself for not doing more for Olivia.

"I also got Shannon's address in Reading from the phone book and stopped there this morning before I left," Tim said. "It was a small apartment in the city. I could see through the window. The apartment was empty. Maggie, it was too small a place for four people, especially with two of them kids. A neighbor confirmed she never saw kids there."

"That's strange," Maggie said. "I guess he was separated or divorced."

"That's what I'm thinking," Tim said. "It also tells me three other things. First, the Police investigation into his cause of death must have been completed. Otherwise, the cops would have the apartment taped off. When I looked into the lobby, there was no signs that was done. Second, if there was any question of foul play, the neighbor would have seen signs of a criminal investigation in the apartment building. She saw nothing like that."

Maggie nodded. "Makes sense. What's three?"

"Third, someone cleaned out his apartment, and they did it pretty quickly," Tim said. "While I suppose it's possible, I get this feeling that with the timeframes involved, this doesn't pass my stink test."

"You know, Timmy," Maggie said. "I'm impressed. You should be a private eye or something like that. You're good."

"I am something like that, remember?" Tim said and smiled. "I'm a claims guy. And people think we're just a bunch of English majors who couldn't get real jobs when they got out of college."

"You're funny," she said.

"I also found out Miss Bodden's first name and where they forwarded her mail when she left your high school," Tim said.

"How did you do that?" said Maggie. "Now I'm really impressed."

"At your high school," he said.

"You went to Cummington High School?"

"I did," he said. "I promised a very nice older lady in the Administration Office, I would not reveal my source, but Miss Bodden's first name is 'Sarah' and 'Densmore, Vermont' popped up as her forwarding address."

"Densmore, Vermont?" Maggie said. "Now that you say that, I bet there's a big lake there. I remember Miss Bodden talking about a lake in Vermont where her family lived or owned or whatever. I remember the name Densmore."

"Good. Confirmation," Tim said. "That brings up an important question?"

"What's the question?" Maggie said.

"Want to take a ride this weekend?"

17

Twenty minutes out of Portland, Tim steered the VW onto Route 25 and into the rolling hills and small towns of rural New England. The grey sky looked darker to the southwest showing the weather front the TV guy predicted.

"Maybe we should've waited until tomorrow," Tim said. "I think we're heading into it." He nodded ahead and to his left.

Maggie looked over at Tim.

"The Post Office is closed on Sundays," she said. "Besides, there's nothing like an early summer rain. And I can drive, if you want? You've been behind that wheel all week."

Tim looked over at her and smiled.

"No big deal," he said. "I like driving, especially through here. Reminds me of when I was a kid and those few vacations when my mom and dad were still together. We either headed to the White Mountains or Hampton Beach. For some reason, New Hampshire was always *numero uno* on the family vacation list."

"Not Cape Cod, huh?" Maggie said.

"For some reason it was always Hampton for the ocean," Tim said. "We'd stay at *Mrs. Coomb's Cabins*, a small group of two room cabins a short walk from the beach."

Maggie smiled and closed her eyes.

"Our Hampton Beach was the Jersey coast," she said. "Ocean City."

"I heard Ocean City is a dry town," Tim said. "Not my idea of vacationland."

"I was a kid," Maggie said. "What did I care?"

"Yeah, but now?"

"Same thing." Maggie said. "I told you. I'm never drinking alcohol again."

"That's right. I forgot," Tim said. "How about a coffee then?"

"That would be great," she said. "In fact, I'll buy. I think it's my turn."

"That's what I like about you, Mags," Tim said. "You're a woman who knows the value of the phrase, 'Dutch treat.'"

"Well, thank you, Timmy," she said. "Your turn will be to buy lunch."

They skirted to the north of Lake Winnipesaukee, New Hampshire's largest lake. In Center Harbor they stopped for coffee and stretched their legs along the path to the lakefront. Tim pointed south toward a group of islands.

"I used to camp out here," Tim said. "When we were in college, Leigh's parents owned a cabin over there on Bear Island, and a group of us would come up at the end of summer for a few days before we went back to school."

"It's beautiful here," Maggie said. "I'd like to come back and paint it."

"Good idea," Tim said. "Maybe I'll tag along."

Maggie smiled and nodded but held her stare across the lake.

Beyond the island and to the west, the wall of dark clouds expanded.

"I think we better move it along," Tim said, gesturing with his coffee-cupped hand. "Big rain's a-coming."

Maggie nodded, and they turned to walk back to the car.

"My turn to drive," she said.

"God help us," Tim said, following her. "It'll be dark before we see Vermont."

Maggie looked back at him over her shoulder and stuck out her tongue.

A half hour later they passed through Plymouth, just below the southern edge of the White Mountains. The rain began with a few sprinkles on the windshield, but within minutes it became torrential. Their progress slowed.

The winding road narrowed, with forest close to the pavement on both sides. The wind began in earnest. Trees swayed. Leaves followed horizontal flight paths in front of them. Maggie steered around small, fallen branches. Water filled eroded gullies along the pavement's edge. They slowed to a crawl.

"I think we need to pull over," Maggie said, her voice edgy, her eyes focused through the up-tempo wipers splashing sheets of water to both sides of the car. "I can barely see."

"Yeah, I know, Mags," Tim said. His eyes focused out the right corner of the windshield. "You need to stay away from the edge of the road. It's all mud and water. Just stay slow and focus ahead. I'll look for somewhere to pull over."

"Kay, Tim," she said. "I'm just afraid some hot shot'll come zipping up from behind, if I go any slower."

"I know, Mags. Don't worry. We'll be okay."

They rode like this for ten more minutes before Tim saw what looked like an abandoned produce stand ahead on the left side of the road.

"I think there may be a pull off up ahead on your left," he said.

Maggie nodded. "Yeah, I see it."

"Be ready to turn, but not until we get close enough to see the ground in the parking area. We don't want to drive into deep mud."

Tim strained to see the pull off. When he saw the surface, he said, "Crushed rock. Good. Turn just beyond that white signpost. I'll watch for oncoming."

Maggie nodded, her eyes focused on the road.

"You're clear," he said a few moments later.

Maggie turned the wheel and pulled into the empty lot. She stopped the car, shifted into neutral and pulled up the handbrake. She left the motor and wipers on.

"The Eagle has landed," she said and let out a deep breath, her body drooping in relief.

"Nice job, Sulu," Tim said. He reached his left arm around her shoulders and gave her a hug and a kiss on her right cheek. As he started to pull his head away,

Maggie turned to him and reached her left arm around his neck. She pulled him to her and kissed him hard on the lips. Tim did not resist.

Maggie let her head turn forward and rested it on Tim's shoulder. They sat, his arm around her shoulder, her head on his chest, looking at the rhythmic splash of water through the steamy windshield, punctuated by the staccato sound of rain pellets on the roof.

Maggie broke the silence.

"Timmy," she said. "If you could be anywhere in the world right now, where would it be?"

Tim did not hesitate.

"I think it would be hard to think of someplace I'd rather be than sitting here in the rain in the middle of Podunk, New Hampshire, with my arm around you."

Maggie smiled and gently nudged her elbow into his side, "No, really?"

"Yes, really," he said. "But you tell me, where would you be? No, wait. Let me guess. You'd be living in Paris in a luxurious studio apartment with a big skylight, surrounded by canvas and paint. You'd have a season pass to the Louvre and live on croissants and sheep eyeballs."

Maggie chuckled.

"Close," she said. "But wrong." She paused for a moment. "I think I would be on an unplanned first date, sitting along the first base line at Fenway Park with this cute guy I worked with. He would teach me all about baseball and stuff. He'd catch a ball and sign his name to it and give it to me. It would turn out to be the best date I ever had in my entire life."

"That's cool," Tim said. "I had a date like that once, too. Except it was a cute girl, not a guy, of course."

Maggie smiled. "Of course," she said.

"Yeah," Tim said, paused a moment as if remembering a great moment. "She was a sophomore at Smith College, and boy, was she hot, and we went..." An elbow to his ribs interrupted him.

Maggie shook her head in mock anger.

"You are a creep," she said. She started laughing. Tim squeezed her to him.

"We can go to a Sox game anytime you want," Tim said. "It sounds like your question is more about turning back the clock than going to a game."

"Yeah, I guess it is in a way," she said. "Wouldn't you like to turn back the clock and edit out some of those regretful parts of your life and try again?"

"Sometimes," he said. "But I'm glad I can't."

"Not even those embarrassing moments that pop up in your memory every once in a while," Maggie said. "And while they happened a long time ago, you feel that hot flush of embarrassment flowing through you and wish you could go back and fix them?"

"You mean like when I ratted out my best friend to the teacher in fourth grade? Or when I laughed with the other guys at the poor kid who couldn't hit the ball in Little League? Or when I stood up Donna Elias after I asked her to a dance?"

"Yeah, stuff like that."

"I have a long list of apologies like that in my head," Tim said. "And there are worse things than those. The list grows every week. I will apologize to all of them before I die."

"Seriously?" she said. "If I did that, I'd be spending a good chunk of the rest of my life apologizing."

"I doubt that. You're too nice," Tim said. "I'll never

see most of the people I've wronged in my life. But there are other ways to apologize besides writing a letter, making a phone call, or taking out an ad in the newspaper. I think the best thing you can do is learn from those mistakes. I think you can use them to make yourself a better person. The person you wronged in 1969 will never know anything about this type of apology, and he or she will probably think you are a jerk for the rest of his or her life. There's nothing you can do about that. But your apologies to them are that you will try not to repeat your thoughtlessness to other people you meet, that you will do your best to make someone else's life better and happier. If we all did that, we'd all be happier."

Maggie looked up at Tim.

"Am I your letter of apology to Donna Elias?"

"No," Tim said. "You are someone's letter of apology to me, someone who must have done me something so rude, so hideous, so evil, they needed to send the perfect apology letter. I can't for the life of me remember what it was anyone did to me that bad, no matter how hard I try. So I worry all the time that you simply may have been delivered to the wrong address, and I don't deserve you. I'm worried they'll realize their mistake, track me down with dogs, and take you back."

Maggie laughed.

"You deserve more than me, Timmy. You deserve the perfect woman."

"I don't want the perfect woman," Tim said. "I want you."

Maggie pulled back away from Tim and looked at him, her mouth open.

"You don't think I'm perfect?" she said.

"Nope," he said.

"I'm shocked," she said, a smile pushing at the corners of her mouth. "You always said I was perfect?"

"No, I didn't," Tim said. "I said you were perfect for me. That's different."

"How's that different?"

"Men are attracted to those perfect women, the ones they see in magazines or movies, the ones with perfect bodies and flawless skin. The perfect woman's hair is always styled just so and her nails manicured. She wears a bikini on the beach and a long flowing gown to the ball. And she looks just as sexy in both. Everyone stares at her. She makes dinner when you come home from work and makes love for dessert."

"You're right," Maggie said. "I'm not perfect. I'd rather you make me dinner."

"Men are attracted by a woman's perfection," Tim said. "But we fall in love with her imperfections. We love what makes one woman different from all the rest. Perfection is imperfect. Perfection is sameness. Perfection leaves no room for exploration and discovery. Perfection is Stepford Wives. Perfection is boring."

"So what are my imperfections?" Maggie said, her head tilting away from him, her eyebrow cocked up in either anticipation or threat.

"With you, 'imperfections' isn't really the right word," Tim said. "'Unique attributes' is more accurate."

"Nice try."

"Okay, I guess I'd have to start with the first thing I noticed when I met you," he said. "It was the way you pulled up the left side of your mouth a bit when you smiled, like one side of your brain knew something the other did not, something funny your right brain would not share with your left, never mind the rest of the world. Yeah, like that. Your crooked smile."

He nodded at her and looked down at her mouth.

"I love it when we go to the movies, and you manage to cry at the dumbest things."

"What are you talking about?" she said. "*Bambi* was very sad."

"I'm not talking about *Bambi*," Tim said. "You cried for the shark in *Jaws*."

"Well, he was only doing what he was born to do," she said.

"I love it how you transform from this graceful, lissome ballerina into a total klutz without warning."

"Now wait a minute," Maggie said. "A rogue wave caused the kayak to tip."

"The lake was calm as glass," Tim said. "And I was referring to the pick-up hockey game in Salem."

"That was my first time being a goalie," she said with a demure smile.

"But most of all, I love watching you paint," Tim said. "Your eyes focus in, analyzing every millimeter of canvas, every speck of paint. You're like a conductor leading his orchestra through Vivaldi. Your brushes flow like perfect batons in the air. You hold the blue brush in your mouth like a pirate's blade, while you touch up with the green, then you switch back with a crescendo in blue. Your hand brushes away a hanging wisp of yellow hair and smudges a stroke of orange across your cheek. But you don't notice. You don't care. You stare. You analyze. You feel. You go back with the green or the red or the purple. You stare again. And then I see it. Your eyes widen. That peeking curve of a smile begins to form, and I know you have found what you wanted. I don't need to see the canvas to know, I have just witnessed creation."

Maggie stared at Tim. Tim saw the wetness forming in the corner of her eyes.

"You, my sweetheart," Maggie said, "are the one who is perfect."

18

The center of Densmore, Vermont lay squeezed along a narrow strip of land bordered by the Connecticut River on the east and an interstate highway on the west. On the other side of the interstate sat Lake Brenda, and its dominating resort, the Lake Brenda Inn. Route 5 split the town and acted as Main Street.

Tim sat behind the wheel when they crossed the Connecticut River to the center of town. He pulled into a gas station and parked near the phone booth. Maggie went into the Ladies Room, while he went to the booth and searched the directory for the name "Bodden." To his surprise he found nothing. He walked back to the car and pulled over to the pump.

The attendant was in his early twenties and wore a blue mechanic's uniform. He wiped his hands on an oily rag as he approached. Tim saw the name "John" on the patch above his left pocket. Tim stepped out of the car as the attendant approached. They exchanged nods, and Tim said, "Fill it, please." The attendant nodded and went about his business.

Tim leaned against the car and looked at the attendant.

"You guys got the rain, too, I see," he said. "We got clobbered on the way here. Had to pull over for about forty-five minutes."

"Yeah," the attendant said. "A lot of people had to stop. Couldn't see to drive." He nodded his head and kept nodding it as if to underscore the truth he was telling.

Tim saw Maggie walking toward them from the side of the building. He watched the attendant check her out.

"Hey, John, maybe you can help us," Tim said. "My sister here is trying to find an old friend of hers she met in school. Her name was Bodden, Sarah Bodden. You know her?"

John looked at him and shook his head. "Don't know her." John turned back toward Maggie.

Maggie nodded and smiled a hello at the attendant. He returned the nod and grinned.

"Any luck?" she said to Tim.

"No," he said. "Nothing in the phone book. John, here, doesn't know her either." He smiled and nodded at the attendant.

"Check the oil?" John said.

"No, we're good. Thanks," Tim said. "How much I owe you?"

"Seven dollars and fifty cents."

Tim paid him the money.

"John," Maggie said. "Is there a town library around here?"

John nodded and pointed.

"Up Main Street. On the left."

"Thanks," she said.

"The rain screwed us up," Tim said to Maggie as the drove on. "The Post Office closed a half hour ago. This could be a wasted trip. Dammit."

"I wouldn't call it wasted," Maggie said. "We'll make the most of it."

"There's the sign for the library," Tim said. "Let's see if they're open. Maybe we can find something there."

"Sounds good."

"Hungry?"

"Yes," she said. "But let's do the library first."

As they waited to turn left into the library, Maggie spotted the *Densmore Diner* sign across the street.

"I think I see where we're having lunch," she said. "Nothing like a diner for Saturday afternoon comfort food."

In the library they split assignments. Maggie went looking at old phone books while Tim went to the town records. They ended in the same section and stacked their books on the table.

"Should I start looking in last year's phone book?" Maggie said. "Or should I start in 1968 and work forward?"

"Go backwards," Tim said. "You'd have to check them out for changes anyway."

Maggie nodded and grabbed the top book. Tim spread his hard bound books in front of him and reached for the real estate transactions for 1976. He found nothing. He searched for voting info and found nothing there. He went to the preceding year. Nothing. Maggie found the first clue.

"Here we go," she said. "Adrian Bodden, 525 Brigham Hill Road, Densmore."

"Good," Tim said. "When was that?"

Maggie flipped over the phone book and looked at the cover.

"Nineteen seventy," she said. "Nothing after that. And no other Boddens."

"Well, that certainly cools down the trail," Tim said.

"Are you looking for Adrian Bodden?"

The voice came from behind Tim, from around the corner of the stack. Tim turned and saw a petite, older woman, dressed in casual slacks and a pink blouse, with a pair of eyeglasses hanging off her neck on a strap.

"Adrian passed away about seven or eight years ago," she said. "It was relief to his family, I think. I know it was a relief to him. Cancer. He was in a great deal of distress. It was very sad. He was a good man."

Tim stood and offered his hand to the woman.

"Hi, I'm Tim," he said. "And this is Maggie. We're pleased to meet you."

Maggie stepped forward, smiled and offered her hand to the woman.

"I'm Mary Louise," the woman said. "Very nice to meet you both."

"Maggie went to school with Adrian's sister," Tim said. "We were out for a drive and Maggie saw the 'Entering Densmore' sign. She remembered Sarah lived here. We thought we would stop in and say 'Hello.'"

"That's nice," Mary Louise said with a smile. "I bet she'd love to see you, but she really didn't live here very long. She sold the farm and moved back home after Adrian passed."

"Home?" Maggie said.

"Yes," Mary Louise said. "She came here from Pennsylvania."

"Do you know where in Pennsylvania?" Tim said.

"I don't remember," the woman said. She grimaced and looked up, struggling to remember. "I think she said it was somewhere between Pittsburgh and Philadelphia. Somewhere near a river."

"Are there any other relatives of hers around here we could talk to?" Tim asked.

"Not any more," Mary Louise said. "At one time there were a lot of aunts and uncles and cousins in the area. I think some of her family lives near Boston, but the only ones in Densmore were Adrian and Sarah. They were the only children, and Sarah really lived in Pennsylvania most of the time, and I think she moved back there. Or maybe not. And there was her son, of course."

"Her son?" Maggie said.

"Oh, yes," She said. "He was so cute, a little peanut with a big smile."

"When did she go back to Pennsylvania?" Tim said, but as the words were coming out of his mouth, he saw Mary Louise look past him toward the door. Tim turned and saw a woman about her age at the front door of the library.

"Oh, there's Viola," Mary Louise said. "I have to run. We're going down to Hanover." She looked at Maggie as she moved past. "Shopping." She smiled and winked as she said the word.

Maggie and Tim watched as Mary Louise got to the

door, picked up her handbag from a chair, and walked through. Just as the door was about to shut, Mary Louise stopped it, and stuck her head back in.

"And if you see Sarah," she said. "Please tell her that Mary Louise Shannon sends her love." She turned and the door shut.

Tim stared at Maggie, and Maggie back at Tim.

"Shannon?" Maggie said.

Tim moved to the door, went through it, and saw the two women walking down the sidewalk to the car. Two other women sat in the car and through the open windows the chatter began. Tim walked down the steps and got to the car as Mary Louise was siding into the passenger seat. He reached out his hand to give her something to hold onto as she sat down. Tim shut the door for her.

"You said your name was 'Shannon?'" Tim said through the open window.

"Yes," Mary Louise said as the car motor started. She laughed. "But we are not related," she said as Viola pulled from the curb and turned south.

Back in the library Tim slid into his chair. He looked at Maggie.

"She said they weren't related," he said.

"To Billy?"

Tim thought for a moment.

"I don't know."

"How would she know Billy Shannon?" Maggie said.

"Maybe he came here? Maybe he heard Sarah talk about him? I don't know."

"Maybe Adrian knew him or something?" Maggie said.

"Wait a minute," Tim said. He rifled down through his short stack of books, opened one to the index, and ran his finger down a page. He found what he was looking for and turned to a page in the middle of the book. His finger moved down the page and stopped.

"Here we go," he said. "January 28, 1969. Sarah Elizabeth Bodden married William Chester Shannon."

"Miss Bodden and Billy got married?" Maggie said, her mouth dropping in disbelief.

***

The dark-haired woman read the letter she wrote one more time. She knew this would get her in trouble. maybe even land her in jail. She looked at the stack of paper in front of her and sighed. She signed the letter, laid it on the stack, and slipped them all into the oversized, white envelope. She closed it and fastened the small brass clasp. She reached for her pack of cigarettes, removed one, and lit it with the stainless steel cigarette lighter engraved with her mother's name. Sitting back in the chair, she took a long drag, and ran the fingers of her free hand through her dark hair.

She thought about what all this meant. The ruined lives. The lost children. The trail of sadness and despair. She thought about what she could have done and what she should have done those years ago when she had the chance. But this was the time, this was the opportunity. Maybe she couldn't make things right, but she could deliver vengeance.

She rose from her chair and mashed the butt in the ashtray. She lifted the manila envelope and carried it to the corrugated box on the bed. She placed the envelope in the box on top of the cigar box, closed the flaps, and sealed them with thick plastic tape.

Tomorrow, she thought, tomorrow the avenging angel flies.

19

When Tim reached the landing, he saw the light inside and knew Sophie beat him home.

"*Bonjour, Sophie*," he said as he entered. "*Je suis revenue*. I'm home."

"Hello, Timothy." Her voice came from the living room.

Sophie sat in front of the television, her feet resting on the footstool. She wore her nurse's aide uniform. An almost empty glass of red wine and a small collection of crumpled tissues sat on the end table next to her. Even from the side angle, Tim saw the redness of her eyes. He thought for a moment and decided to let her bring up the issue.

"So, you do watch TV?" he said.

"What TV?" Sophie said. She shook her head and turned to face him.

"Timothy, can I ask you a question?"

"You just did," he said. "But you can ask me another one."

"At what do you think I would be better?" she said.

"Selling used cars or driving a bus?"

"Tough day?" Tim said.

"Terrible."

"School or Work?"

"Work," Sophie said. "I held a woman's hand and watched her die."

"Jeez, Sophie. I'm really sorry," Tim said. "Edna?"

"Yes," Sophie said. "Emphysema. It is so unfair. She never smoked a day in her life. I watched her slowly cough herself to death for the past four months." Sophie closed her eyes and shook her head.

"Very sad. Fifty-four years old. Her only son killed in Vietnam. Husband dead from a heart attack. No family. Only two friends. She's an orphan. Like me."

Tim saw the tears well at the corner of Sophie's eyes. He wanted to say something, but he saw her head shake, her elbows held tight against her side, her hands reaching up, pulling in like she was trying to grasp her next words from the air before her. She took a tissue from the box on the table next to her, wiped her nose, and balled the tissue in her hand.

"Some days," Sophie said. "Some days she looked so bad, I didn't think she would live through the end of my shift. The next day I'd come in, and she would be sitting and talking like she was going to get up, pull out her oxygen tube, and skip down the street."

Sophie managed a weak smile and looked over at Tim.

"The thing is, Timothy, I loved being with her as much as she loved being with me. I told her about Montreal. I told her about my big sister, and how we would walk along the river and watch the huge ships and elegant sailboats."

"I'm really sorry, Sophie," Tim said. He walked to Sophie, knelt and hugged her. Sophie squeezed him, let go her tears and cried. After a minute or so, Sophie eased the tight pressure on Tim's neck. He held her until the sobs subsided. Neither spoke. He pulled his head back and released her.

"I think I need some wine," he said. "And can I borrow a tissue?"

Sophie looked at Tim with her swollen red eyes and managed a weak smile. She reached for the tissue box and offered it to Tim.

"You do not need to borrow one," she said. "Keep it. I do not want it back."

Tim nodded toward Sophie's wine glass.

"Need a refill?"

Sophie nodded. Tim walked to the kitchen and returned with a half full wine glass and the wine bottle. He refilled Sophie's glass and sat down on the couch.

On television the Waltons said their "goodnights" before a teaser for *Hawaii Five-O*. Tim sipped his wine and watched a hula dancer's hips wriggle across the screen. Sophie spoke first.

"Timothy," she said. "Do you think I can do this?"

"Do what?" Tim said.

"Be a good nurse." She turned her head toward Tim.

"You're kidding, right?" Tim said, and then began ticking off on his fingers as he spoke. "You're smart. You're dedicated, you're honest, you're passionate. You're *com*passionate. You're not easily intimidated. You're not afraid to say you're wrong. And you will never give up. My God, Sophie, you are everything a nurse should be. Your patients will love you. Clara

Barton would be jealous of you." He hesitated a moment and continued.

"I've only known you for less than a year, but I see it in you. I see it all the time. Jesus, Sophie, you grew up in an orphanage, you moved to a new country, you learned a new language, you're putting yourself through college, and you touch the soul of just about every person you meet. How many people walk around spending the last three quarters of their lives complaining about how bad they had it in the first quarter of their lives? You don't complain. You don't blame anyone for anything that happened to you. Sophie, you are only twenty three years old, and you have already made the world a better place than you found it. People like you leave people like me in awe."

Sophie stared at the floor.

"Thank you, Timothy," she said. "I am a very lucky person. The nuns were kind to me. My sister is strong. And I have good friends." She reached out her hand toward him.

Tim looked at her, grasped her hand.

"*Moi aussi.*"

Sophie managed a smile and raised her eyebrows.

Tim let out a long sigh, and then winked.

"Hey, how 'bout a pizza for supper? I'm buying."

Sophie nodded.

"One large onion and pepperoni coming up," he said.

The next morning Tim looked at the photo of Maggie hanging on the wall of his cubicle. She stood on a rock surrounded by the swirling waters of the

Swift River, a few miles down the Kancamagus from Sky Castle. Her arms swung wide, embracing the blues and greens and sparkly reflections of her real life canvas. Her head tipped to the side, Tim could see the end of her ponytail blowing in the wind, releasing dancing strands across her left eye and the corner of her mouth. But the picture did not show what happened a few seconds after he clicked the shutter and set the camera down on their cooler.

Tim had hopped toward Maggie, across the first three of the four standing rocks between them. As he landed on the fourth, his foot slipped. His hands shot up in the air, flailing for balance. Maggie reached to his aid, catching the end of his loose tee shirt. But balance proved to be an elusive state for both of them. The splash signaled their first bath in the icy mountain water.

Tim smiled as he did every time he looked at that picture, remembering Maggie's wide eyes of shock in the cold stream, their klutzy exit of the water, the embrace of cold bodies seeking warmth from each other, and the pulsing giggles of disbelief. He could not think of a better way to start each workday.

Tim opened the workers compensation file sitting in his in-box and reviewed his prior notes on the lined, yellow top sheet. The latest medical report indicated the claimant's disability period was almost double the average for his type of injury. The claimant moved to Maine from Massachusetts just prior to his accident. Tim decided it was time for an independent background check.

He picked up the phone and started to dial the number for O'Hara Investigative Services. He stopped mid-dial, as if in thought, then continued.

"Hey, Pete. It's Tim at Whitfield Casualty in Portland."

"Hi, Timmy," the voice said. "How's life up there in Vacationland?"

"Pretty good," Tim said. "Lobster, blueberries and beautiful women. What's not to love?"

"How about fat, middle-aged guys wearing speedos on Old Orchard Beach?"

"I just close my eyes."

They laughed.

"I have a case for you," Tim said. Tim gave Pete the name, address and other pertinent information on the claimant.

"I need a history and some background on the guy. He's been out way too long."

"No problem. I'll get on this myself. I'm going into the city in a few. I'll see what I can find out at the courthouse."

"That's great," Tim said. He paused. "Pete, I have a personal question for you."

"Sure, Tim," he said. "What's up?"

"I have a friend who needs to know about a guy who was arrested in Pennsylvania by Massachusetts State Police."

"Arrested for what?"

"I'm not exactly sure," Tim said. "My friend says it may have been for fraud or something like that."

"And your friend was one of his victims?" Pete said.

"No," Tim said. "My friend is just trying to track down the guy's daughter. The bad guy's her only known family member. She disappeared a few years ago. My friend wants to send him a letter to see if he can help find her."

"Timmy, be wary, I mean, tell your friend to be wary of what he sends to guys in jail. Especially if it's for fraud. A letter carries a lot of info in it."

"I'll tell him," Tim said. "So where do I look for the info?"

"Tell you what," Pete said. "Since I'll be at the courthouse this morning, I'll check it out for you. Okay?"

"That would be great. Thanks," Tim said. "The guy's name is Frank L. Wood, last known address was 18052 Hillsdale Street, Aldenburg, Pennsylvania. I, uh, we think he was arrested sometime in the past two years or so. I don't know much about him other than he was a con man of sorts."

"Okay," Pete said. "For some reason I seem to remember that Aldenburg is near Lancaster."

"Sorta," Tim said. "It's closer to Reading."

"Okay. I have some friends in that area. They can do a little digging, if we need it."

"Thanks, Pete. You're the best. I will pay for . . ."

"You're not paying for anything," Pete said. "This is all professional courtesy, and no one will know anything about it except you and me."

"Thanks. Next time I'm down, I got the beers."

"Bet your ass you do."

Three hours later, Pete called back.

"Timmy?"

"Yeah, Pete."

"I got you some stuff on the WC guy," Pete said.

"So far he looks clean to me."

"Sounds good. I just had to check."

"The other guy," Pete said. "The one from Pennsylvania."

"Yeah?" Tim said and sat up a little straighter.

"He was arrested as part of a fraud sting," Pete said. "Looks like they were ripping off old lady widows of life insurance payouts. Another guy was arrested at the same time. In Fall River. A guy named Jake Helstrom. They're both doing time. Helstrom's probably the ring leader and got twenty years in Walpole. Wood is a smaller player, a sub-contractor, so to speak. Wood got three to five in Westbrook and will be eligible in less than a year. Looks like he made some type of a deal."

"Jeez," Tim said. "Thanks, Pete."

"Tim," Pete said. "Tell your friend to be wary. Back in the day, my partner and I arrested Helstrom. He's a dangerous prick."

"I'll tell my friend," Tim said. "This helps, Pete. I can't thank you enough."

"The beer will do," Pete said. "And one other thing, I put a couple of probes out there with a friend in Lancaster. Maybe he'll find something more."

"Hey, thanks, Pete," Tim said. "You're the best."

Tim walked up the seven stairs from the sidewalk to the porch of the old converted Victorian. He unlocked his mail box and pulled out the handful of letters and Sophie's *People* magazine. He glanced at the first few envelopes, mumbled a "probably bills" under his breath, and checked out the close-up photo of Jaclyn Smith on the cover of the magazine.

"You're a lucky man, Charlie," he said as he pushed the door open with his shoulder.

"What did you say, Tim?" a male voice said from inside the foyer.

Tim looked up and saw Jeff, who lived in the apartment below his.

"Hey, Jeff," Tim said. "Just telepathetically sending my congratulations to Charlie on his Angels." He held up the magazine.

"Ah, yes," Jeff said. He crooked his head, raised an eyebrow at Tim, and said, "Telepathetically?"

"Yes," Tim said. "It means that I was *telling* him how *pathetically* jealous the rest of us are about his 'Angels.'"

Jeff laughed and reached for the door.

"So says the guy who lives with Sophie."

"We're just apartment-mates," Tim said, starting up the stairs.

"Yeah, right," Jeff said. Then remembering something, he said, "Oh, Tim, I almost forgot."

Jeff held the door. Tim stopped on the third step and turned to face him.

"Some guy was here about an hour ago," Jeff said. "He was on the porch when I came in. He asked me what time you get home, and if I knew where you worked. I told him I barely knew you, didn't know where you worked, and that you worked all types of hours."

"Did he say what he wanted? Or give a name?"

"Neither," Jeff said. "Looked like he was in his early thirties, brown hair, on the scraggly side, mustache, jeans, and a green tee shirt. About my height, five ten-ish. Nothing unusual."

"Can't guess who it was," Tim said. "Thanks, Jeff. Appreciate it."

Tim waved and climbed the stairs to his apartment.

Sophie came in a half hour later. Tim sat before the TV watching the news with a glass of ginger ale.

"Hello, Timothy," Sophie said. "How was your day?"

"The usual," he said. "And yours?"

"Definitely better than yesterday," Sophie said. "Or tomorrow."

Tim looked over at her, his brow wrinkled. "Tomorrow?"

"The funeral," she said. Tim tightened his lips and nodded.

Sophie moved to the sofa where her cat sprawled. *"Allo, mon petit. Comment ca va?"* Sophie sat. The cat moved to her lap, demanding pats.

"What time's the funeral?" Tim said.

"Two o'clock," Sophie said. "At the chapel in the hospital."

"You're going, right?"

"Of course," Sophie said. She stroked her cat and let out a deep breath.

"Did you pick up the mail or was there none?"

"Kitchen table," Tim said. "Under Jaclyn Smith."

"What?"

"Just kidding."

Sophie went to the kitchen, and a minute later, came back with her magazine and a white envelope. She handed the envelope to Tim and returned to the couch, leafing through the magazine.

Tim looked at the sealed envelope. Scrawled across the front was his name, *Timothy Roper* and nothing else. His brow arched. *Odd,* he thought. *This is probably from the guy Jeff saw.* He slipped his thumb under the corner of the flap, slid it across, and pulled out a single sheet of paper.

We want the box. We want no trubble. Do'nt do nuthing stupid or we will tern you in and do other things maybe. I will call you tomorow. Have it.

Tim stared at the note. *What the hell? I have no idea what this guy is talking about. Box? What box?*

"What's wrong, Timothy?" Sophie said. "Everything okay?"

"I don't know," Tim said. "Here, read this." He reached over and handed Sophie the note. She read it.

"What box?" she said.

"Good question," Tim said. "I have no idea."

20

Maggie opened the door in ragged blue jeans and an old Boston University tee-shirt with the collar ripped off. Her hair was pulled back under a Red Sox cap with her ponytail pulled out of the back. She stood barefoot, her clothing, hands and face dotted with spots of different colored paint. She smiled at Tim.

"Sorry, Mags," he said. "I know we agreed to take a breather tonight, but I need to talk to you about something. It shouldn't take long."

"No problem, Timmy. Come in," she said, a look of concern spreading across her face. "What's wrong? You look like you just saw a ghost."

"Not a ghost," he said. "This. It was in my mailbox." He handed her the note, and they each moved to one of the two easy chairs.

Maggie read the note and looked up at Tim.

"What box?" she said.

"That's exactly what I said. I have no idea."

"Who sent it?"

"Beats me. It was inside this." He showed her the envelope. "Any ideas?"

Maggie shrugged.

"Something related to work?"

"I thought of that, but I can't come up with anything that could possibly be related to this. I can't think of anything we do related in any way to a box."

Maggie shook her shoulders a bit.

"Gives me the creeps just thinking about it."

"I thought maybe the prior tenant left a box in the apartment when he moved out," Tim said. "But I remember the landlord had the place professionally cleaned before I moved in. There wasn't a speck of anything there."

"Maybe when we moved in here?" Maggie said. "I can't think of anything."

"Me neither."

"And what is this thing about turning you in? To the cops?" she said. "This is sounding a bit too much like my newspaper note."

"That's why I'm here," Tim said. "Can you think of anyway this could be connected?"

Maggie shook her head, and then stopped.

"How about your trip to Pennsylvania?"

"I can't think of anything related to a box," he said. "The only things I brought back were the pretzels and the mustard. And they were in a bag."

"Maybe he has you confused with someone else?"

"That's about all I can come up with," Tim said. "I'll see what he says tomorrow. I just thought you might think of something I missed."

Maggie shook her head.

"Oh, yeah," Tim said. "I wanted to fill you in on

some other information I got. Totally unrelated to the note thing. Olivia's father is doing time at Westbrook Prison for fraud. He and another guy were trying to rip off old ladies of their dead husband's insurance money. Wood has been in for two years, but he's getting out within a year or so."

"Yuk," she said. "He sounds like a creep."

"Yeah, he is a creep," Tim said. "My gut tells me he's somehow connected to your newspaper note."

"Except he's in prison in Massachusetts and the letter was mailed from Pennsylvania."

"Connected," Tim said. "I didn't say he sent it."

Maggie shrugged her shoulders.

"Okay, I can buy that."

"Well, I should go and let you get back to making Van Gogh envious," Tim said, rising from the chair. "Sorry for the interruption."

"Not a problem, Timmy," she said. "Anytime." She walked him to the door and leaned forward, stretching her head out and up toward him for a kiss.

"No hugs tonight," she said, looking down at her hands and shirt. "My war paint's still wet."

Not long after he sat at his cubicle the next morning, Tim's phone rang. He picked it up on the first ring, expecting the mysterious caller.

"Timmy, Pete," the voice said. "I'm on my way to an all day trial, but I got some more info for you."

"Oh, okay," Tim said, "What's up?"

"My buddy down in PA said there's a bit of a buzz about the Frank Wood house in Aldenburg."

"Really? Like what?"

"Someone broke into it."

"Really? When?"

"Last week sometime," Pete said. "Wednesday, they think."

Tim's palms began to sweat. He controlled the quaver of his voice.

"Really?"

"They think he broke a window in the Wood daughter's old bedroom and stole something from a hiding space under a loose board."

"Do they know what it was he stole?"

"No, but they have a suspect," Pete said. "From Massachusetts. But I don't have any more than that. My buddy's going to make a few more calls. I gotta run. I'll call you tonight, if I get anything more."

"Okay. Thanks, Pete."

Tim hung up the phone. He looked up at the picture of Maggie. But he didn't smile. He thought about his visit to the Wood house on Wednesday. He remembered the broken window. The house looked abandoned and unkempt. *Did anyone see me go there? I didn't see anyone in the area. Oh, crap. The diner. Did my asking questions generate a look at the house? Am I the suspect?*

Tim racked his brain to remember the details of his conversation with A.J. He didn't believe he gave him his name, but he was sure he said he was a claims adjuster. And he did say he was from Massachusetts. *Did I mention Maggie? I don't think so. Olivia? Yes.* An icy stream flowed down Tim's spine. *The box?* Tim pulled the note he received in his mailbox. And read it again. "Do'nt do sumthing stupid or we will tern you in and do other things maybe. Have it." *They will turn me in? To the cops? This guy thinks I broke into the house and stole a box. How would he know where to find me?*

Tim looked at his watch. *Staff meeting in two minutes. "Don't do sumthin stupid." Like what? Go to the police?* Tim grabbed his notebook and headed to the conference room.

At ten minutes of two that afternoon, Tim opened the door of the hospital chapel and looked in. A minister, dressed in a powder blue robe and a coffee-colored stole - hand-embroidered with a peace sign, a fish, and some other symbols of the past decade - stood on the other side of a maple casket. He held his hands folded in front of him, presumably waiting to begin the service.

Two older women in dark dresses and white gloves sat whispering in the front row, occasionally gesturing toward the casket. In the row behind them sat a tall middle-aged woman in a white nurse's uniform, and beside her, dressed in a dark blue dress, with a small bouquet of daisies in her folded hands, sat Sophie.

The minister nodded a solemn welcome to Tim as he quietly shut the door behind him. As Tim turned, he noticed the man standing in the back corner of the chapel, his hands folded in front of him. The man nodded to Tim. *The funeral director.*

Tim slid into the seat beside Sophie. She turned and saw Tim. Her eyes widened.

"Timothy," she whispered. "Why are you here?"

"For this," he said. He reached for her hand and grasped it. "For my friend."

Sophie smiled and squeezed his hand.

The service consisted of a few prayers and a eulogy by the minister so short and generic, Tim thought it could have been said about ninety-nine percent of the population of Maine. The whole thing was over in less than ten minutes. The nurse gave Sophie a hug, Tim a quick nod, and left. The minister spoke with the funeral director. The two older women in the front row turned to Sophie and thanked her for taking care of their friend and neighbor. Sophie walked to the casket and laid her daisies on it. She set her hand on the casket and said a quiet prayer Tim could hardly hear until the end.

"*Au nom du Père, et du Fils, et du Saint-Esprit. Amen.*" She made the sign of the cross.

Tim said, "Amen."

"I wish I knew her better," Sophie said when they got out in the hall. "She was a good woman. I wanted to help her more."

"All you can do is what you can do," Tim said. "You were there when she needed you the most."

Sophie nodded.

"Are you going back to work?" Sophie said.

"Yeah, I got a couple of files I need to review," Tim said. "Sandra's going off to Bangor. I told her I'd cover for her in the morning. You don't look like you're going to work."

"No, I have the rest of the afternoon off," she said. "I think I'm going to do a little shopping and relax."

"Good," Tim said. "You need a break. Do you have time for a quick coffee? I want to fill you in on the note I got."

"Yes," she said. "That is a very curious thing."

At the snack bar in the main lobby, Tim bought two coffees. They sat at a small table in the corner.

"Maggie said she told you all about the newspaper clipping she got and the story about her friend, right?"

"Olivia?" Sophie said. "Yes, she told me when you were in New Jersey last week."

"Well, there's more to the story."

He told her about his trip to Pennsylvania, the details of his visit to Frank Wood's house, and his subsequent conversation at the diner. He told her about the information he got from an investigator, and how it might tie in with yesterday's note.

"I think this guy believes I did the break-in and stole some box or something," Tim said. "I'm nervous about this."

"So what do you need me to do?" Sophie said. "I am willing to help."

"I don't want you to do anything," he said. "I only tell you this so you are aware of what's going on. Be wary in case this blows up into something. Or the guy comes back to the apartment. Okay?"

"I am not worried," she said. "I can take care of myself. And you, as well, if I have to."

"I'm sure you can. But I want you to just keep your eyes open and stay clear of any of this. If the guy calls, play dumb."

"Play dumb? *Moi*?"

21

Tim returned to his office and looked for pink message slips next to his phone. Nothing from either Pete or the mystery man looking for the box. He knew he shouldn't have expected a message from the "boxman," but the note did not identify the writer as the brightest bulb in Portland. He went to the files he had to cover for tomorrow and began his review. He looked up at the clock. Ten minutes of four. He planned to stay until five, then head home and see if the guy called there.

At about quarter to five, the phone rang.

"Hello? This is Tim."

"You have the box?" The voice was low pitched and gravelly.

"Who am I speaking to?" Tim said.

"You're speaking to me," the man said.

"Look, I got your note. What box?"

"The one you stole."

"I didn't steal any box. Where do you think I stole it from?"

"Don't play dumb with me, asshole. You know what one. The one you stole from the house."

"What house?" Tim said, and then regretted it.

"Didn't I just tell you not to play dumb with me?" Boxman said. "You were there. You broke in the window, and you took it. And I want it."

"Okay, okay," Tim said. "I admit I was there. I admit I went to the house. But the window was broken when I got there."

"Bullshit."

"Honest. I was just looking for the owner," Tim said. "I wanted to ask him where I could find his daughter."

"Frank hasn't been there in over two years," Boxman said. "You keep bullshitting me, and you're going to regret it."

"I am telling you I do not have a box or anything else from that house," Tim said. "What was in this box I allegedly stole?"

"It wasn't fucking toys," Boxman said. "It was stuff belonged to Frank. And we want it back, so cut the shit."

Tim's brain raced for something to say. Nothing came.

"Tell you what," Boxman said. "You can keep half the cash. But Frank wants the other stuff back. All of it."

"Listen, Shithead," Tim said. "I don't know what it will take to get it through your so obviously obtuse cranium that I don't have your box or Frank's box or your cash or anything else that you want. How – do – I get – you – to – understand - this?"

Momentary silence on the other end of the line.

"Okay, Mr. Tim," Boxman said. "Perhaps your girlfriend can be more helpful." The phone clicked, then a dial tone.

Tim jumped up and looked at the clock. *Maggie will be walking home from work. Shit.* Tim moved toward the door. As he went past the receptionist's desk, he said, "I gotta run."

Maggie's apartment was eight blocks from his office. He decided it would be faster to hoof it rather than get his car from the garage and drive, especially at this time of day. Tim exited the building and broke into a run. He turned right and headed up the hill toward Congress Street. He considered the route. He calculated where he might be able to cut her off on her way. But she was never on a standard schedule. He decided it was best to go straight to the apartment.

Tim dodged one car when he crossed Franklin Street and almost tripped on a loose sewer grate. He spent an unbearable twenty seconds waiting for a truck to creep past on Washington Ave. He made it to Maggie's apartment, ran up the stairs and rang the bell. Nothing. He pressed the button again and held it. He waited. Still nothing. He banged the heel of his hand against the doorframe and said, "Dammit." He pressed the other three apartment buttons. No response. He stood there, his hands shaking, wondering what to do. He started to turn to survey the street for anybody who might fit the description of Boxman Jeff gave him, but turned back when he heard a buzz from the apartment panel.

"Hello?" A female voice came from the speaker.

Tim recognized it.

"Hello, Mrs. Bergman? This is Tim Roper. Can you beep me in? Did Maggie come home?"

"Hello, Timothy," Mrs. Bergman said. "How are you today?"

""I'm fine, Mrs. Bergman," he said. "Did you see Maggie come home?"

"She left this morning at about eight thirty when I went down to get the paper," Mrs. Bergman said. "She had that big brown briefcase with her."

Mrs. Bergman kept tabs on everything that occurred on the street. Tim rolled his eyes but controlled his anger.

"Has Maggie come home?"

"Not yet," Mrs. Bergman said. "But she will be home very soon."

"Do you know if a man came looking for her?" Tim said.

"No, I don't think so," Mrs. Bergman said. "I didn't see anyone."

"Neither did I," a woman's voice said from behind Tim. He turned and saw Maggie standing at the bottom of the stairs, her oversized leather portfolio hanging from her shoulder along with her pocketbook. She smiled up at Tim.

"What would the man look like?" Mrs. Bergman said through the speaker.

Tim turned back and pressed the speaker button.

"Never mind, Mrs. Bergman. Thank you. Maggie just came home."

"Yes, I know," Mrs. Bergman said. "I saw her coming when she turned the corner."

Tim released the talk button and turned to face

Maggie. He shrugged his shoulders and opened up his arms in a gesture of 'why couldn't she just have told me that?' Maggie cupped her hand over her mouth strangling a laugh.

"Are you okay?" Tim said.

Maggie's brow crinkled.

"Of course, I'm okay," she said. "Why wouldn't I be?"

"Let's go upstairs," Tim said. "We'll talk there."

Maggie's puzzlement faded to concern, but she complied. She unlocked the outside door, and they walked up to the apartment. Tim took the apartment key from her hand, unlocked the door, and went in first.

He surveyed the main room and walked to her bedroom. He peeked into the tiny bathroom. Window closed and locked. The bedroom window looking onto the fire escape was opened, but the screens were intact. Tim walked to the window and peered out. Nothing unusual. He opened Maggie's closet and looked in. It was packed with stuff. No human being could even think of squeezing in there, never mind hide there.

When he turned to walk out the bedroom door, Maggie stood there blocking it.

"Would you mind telling me what you are doing?"

Tim ushered her into the main room

"It's the Boxman," he said. "He called me about a half hour ago."

Maggie sat down on one of the stools.

"Tell me," she said.

Tim told her about the phone calls from both Pete and the Boxman and all that was said. He told her of his fear for her and his sprint here.

"I don't know anything about this guy," Tim said.

"I'm not trying to scare you or anything, but I just don't want to take any chances."

"He sounds a bit on the dumb side, if you ask me," Maggie said.

"Yeah, he does," Tim said. "That's what worries me."

"So what do we do?" Maggie said. "Call the cops?"

"That's what I'm thinking," Tim said.

"But won't that point to you as the suspect for the break-in at Wood's house?" Maggie said.

"Probably," Tim said. "But I did not do it, and I think that would be easy enough to prove."

"Prove what?" Maggie said. "Prove that you are not the guy who went to the library, the high school, and the diner, using a fake name and lying to the people there?"

Tim considered.

"Prove that I did not commit the break-in," Tim said. "There was blood on the window sill, and it was not mine. As for the other things, they are not against the law."

"So what do we tell the police?" Maggie said.

"What else? The truth."

Maggie considered, then nodded agreement.

"I don't think you need to go with me," Tim said. "You're not involved."

"What do you mean I'm not involved?" she said. "All of this started because of me, my insecurities, and my guilty conscience. And am I not the one he threatened?"

Tim was about to nod agreement, when he stopped. His face faded to a grimace.

"Wait a minute," he said. "Why would he think you were my girlfriend? There's nothing in anything I did tying me to you."

"Maybe he's been following you and tracked you here?" Maggie said. "And this was your old address."

"Maybe," Tim said. "But he didn't seem to know much about me. If he found me here in Portland, it would have been through my plate number. And that would be at my new address, not here. I know I didn't mention you or anything about you in Pennsylvania." He paused, thinking.

"Oh crap!" he said. "I bet he thinks Sophie's my girlfriend."

Tim moved to the phone and dialed his home number. While it was ringing, he looked at Maggie, his face pale.

"When I left her after the funeral, she said she was going shopping," Tim said. The phone rang eight times before Tim hung up.

"Shopping can take a long time," Maggie said. "Especially if you go as rarely as she does. Don't panic. Let's go."

They left the apartment and headed up to Congress Street. Within two minutes they found a cab. Ten minutes later, they turned onto Tim's street. Blue lights flashed in front of Tim's apartment building.

"Oh, no," Maggie said, putting her hand up to cover her mouth.

"Pull over and let us out," Tim said to the cabbie. Tim tossed him a twenty and told him to keep the change. The cabbie's eyes widened as he said, "Wow! Thank you, sir."

Maggie and Tim jumped from the cab and ran

toward the police officer standing at the bottom of the stairs in front of the cruiser.

"Is she okay?" Tim said.

"Is who okay?" the cop said.

"Sophie Daigneau," he said. "She's my roommate."

The cop motioned with his head toward the front door of the building.

"Ask her yourself," he said.

Tim and Maggie turned to see Sophie walking through the front door with another cop. Sophie saw Tim and Maggie standing in front of the cruiser. She smiled and waved to them.

"*Allo,*" she said.

Maggie ran up the stairs to Sophie and hugged her. Tim turned to the cop.

"What happened?" he said.

"The suspect apparently tried to attack her," the officer said. "She escaped and flagged us down."

"So the guy got away," Tim said. "Anyone identify him?"

"He didn't get away," the cop said. "We caught him down the street trying get into a stolen car." He gestured with his head to the back seat of the cruiser.

Tim bent and peered through the low sun's glare on the windshield. A stringy-haired man sat in the far corner of the back seat, his hands behind him, cuffed. He looked up at Tim, his face drawn and defeated.

"Will you hold him?" Tim said to the officer.

"Are you kidding?" the officer said. "Attempted rape, car theft and moving stolen property across state lines? I doubt he'll even get bail. He won't be out for a while."

Tim nodded at the cop and smiled.

22

"So what the hell happened?" Tim said after the cops left, and they climbed to the apartment. "Did he hurt you?"

Sophie smiled. "No, he did not hurt me."

"Sophie," Maggie said. "Tell us what happened?"

"I went shopping like I said I would do," Sophie said. "I was walking back to our apartment, and when I turned onto our street, I did what Timothy told me to do - keep my eyes open and be careful."

She looked at Tim and smiled. Tim rolled his eyes and motioned her to keep talking.

"I saw a green car parked on the street a few houses up on the side I was walking, across from our place," she said. "The license plates were blue and yellow, not white and black. I never saw plates like that parked near here. When I got closer, I saw that they were from Pennsylvania. I saw a man's head sitting in the front seat.

"I looked around to see if anyone else was around.

I saw a woman clipping flowers along the fence in front of that pink house, two houses up from us," Sophie said and pointed to her left. "I did not know her, but I turned and made like I did. I waved and crossed the street before I got to the car."

"Good move, Sophie," Tim said.

"When I reached her," Sophie said, "I stood facing her with the car behind me. I introduced myself. The woman stood and told me her name was Deborah. I told her the man in the green car was a mental patient from where I worked – I showed her my hospital ID – and that he had made sexual advances on me. I was afraid he wanted to attack me."

Maggie dropped her jaw and looked at Tim.

"I asked Deborah to call the police for me," Sophie said. "She walked into her house as I waved to her. I took a few more steps toward our house, and then I dropped my bag. On purpose. I bent over and picked up the stuff to delay. Then I started home again."

"You kept going?" Tim said. "Why didn't you just go in the house with Deborah?"

Maggie said, "Sophie, what were you thinking?"

Sophie got serious.

"I was thinking I did not want to scare this guy away, so he could come back again another day. I wanted to get rid of him. I do not want a pig like that to worry me or my friends ever again."

"So then what happened?" Maggie said.

"Just before I got to the house, a car went by in the opposite direction. I did not know the driver, but I waved when it went by so I could turn and see behind me without being noticeable. The man in the green car stood waiting to cross the street after the car passed.

"When I got to the top of our porch stairs, I checked for the mail and fumbled in my purse for the keys. I did not want to unlock the door, so he could push me in the hall where no one could see us."

Maggie looked over at Tim with a look of both wonder and admiration for Sophie's guts.

"Yes," Tim said to Maggie. "She is totally insane."

Sophie smiled.

"I heard him come up the stairs and turned to face him," Sophie said. "He did not appear to have a weapon. He probably thought this tiny little girl in a funeral dress with a shopping bag would be easy to intimidate."

"He said to me, 'I got a message for your boyfriend.'" Sophie said, mimicking the low, hoarse voice of her foe. "I looked at him and said, '*Quoi?*' He looked at me like I was speaking in tongues. He said, 'I said I got a message for your boyfriend.' I said, '*Excusez-moi. Je ne parle pas Anglais.*'

I kept a steady stream of French going. It confused him. He did not know what to do. I turned my back to him and made like I was reaching for the doorknob. He grabbed my left arm and pulled me back, swinging me around. In my right hand was my canvas shopping bag, which had some heavy things in it I bought. I swung it as hard as I could at the side of his head."

"You are out of your mind." Tim said. "He could have killed you."

Sophie smiled and went on.

"He fell down so I kicked him as hard as I could in...*le glande sexuelle*. Then I ran down the stairs and started yelling as loud as I could - in English, of course - just so I would confuse him even more. But he was not able to get up. He could not find his breath."

"You kicked him in the crotch?" Tim said.

Sophie nodded.

"I agree with Tim. You truly are out of your mind," Maggie said. "But I am totally impressed."

Sophie laughed.

"Deborah was back outside, and I ran to her. Deborah witnessed the whole thing and said she called the police. We saw the bad man limping across the street to his car. When he got there, he glared over at me. '*Cochon!*' I yelled at him. I saw him pat his pockets looking for something. At first I thought it was a gun or something, and I started to get scared. But he got into the car and disappeared down on the seat.

"When the cruiser arrived two seconds later, Deborah and I pointed to the green car. The officers went over to it, with their guns pulled out, and arrested him.

"When I came back to the house to get my purse and my shopping bag, I saw the man's car keys lying on the porch, just under the edge of the railing. I gave them to the police for evidence."

"Sophie, when I told you to be aware, lie low, and play dumb, did I tell you this is what I had in mind?" Tim said.

"Did I not tell you I would have difficulty playing dumb?" she said with a big smile.

Maggie laughed, walked to Sophie and hugged her. She spoke to her loud enough for Tim to hear.

"I'm so glad Tim lives with someone who can protect him. He needs a good bodyguard."

Tim gave them both a sour look.

"I think I'm doomed to always find the strangest,

most nutty women around." The two women turned to Tim, side by side, big grins on their faces.

"Just call us 'Timmy's Angels,'" Maggie said. Sophie raised her arms as if flexing her muscles.

Tim shook his head and threw his hands up.

"I give up," he said, then added, "and I bet Charlie doesn't have to make his own coffee."

Tim picked up the carafe from the coffee machine, walked to the sink, and emptied the remains from the morning's brew. He filled the carafe with fresh water and poured it into the machine. He reached for the can from the shelf above the stove.

"Do not drink that," Sophie said. "I have something better - imported from Canada - and suitable for an occasion like this. In my bag."

She pointed at the bag on the counter next to Tim.

Tim opened the bag and looked in. He smiled. He stuck his hand in, pulled out a can of Sophie's favorite Hasbean coffee, and held it up with his left hand. His right hand swept across the front of him and stopped, pointing at the can. He looked at the two women, turned the can in his hand, and revealed a large dent in its side caused by the Boxman's head. With his best TV commercial voice he said, "When we say our coffee packs a punch, we mean it."

The next morning Tim received a call from Pete O'Hara.

"Good news," Pete said.

"Don't tell me," Tim said. "You found our mysterious workers comp claimant running an underground wrestling operation?"

"Not that exciting," Pete said. "Your friend is off the hook in the B&E case in Pennsylvania."

"Really?" Tim said. "You don't even know who my friend is."

"Is he a woman?"

"No."

"I didn't think so," Pete said. "The burglar was female. She left blood droplets on the window she went in. They can tell a person's sex from blood."

"Okay," Tim said. "They have any leads?"

"I don't think so," Pete said. "Although my buddy did say she probably knew what she was looking for. She pulled back the corner of a carpet in a bedroom and removed some fake floorboards to a hiding place. Nothing else was out of place. She knew where to look for whatever she found."

"Maybe she was the guy's daughter?" Tim said.

"Could be, I guess," Pete said. "Maybe the guy's wife came back. Didn't you, or maybe it was Carl, who said the wife took off some time ago?"

"Yeah, that's what I heard, but I also heard she got killed in a car accident." Tim said. "Who's Carl?"

"My buddy in PA."

"Oh, okay," Tim said. "Pete, I can't thank you enough for this. I'm coming down in a week or so. How 'bout we go to the Hilltop? My treat."

"Just tell me when," Pete said. "Ciao."

23

She pulled into the entrance and stopped at the gate. She told the uniformed guard her business, awaited his okay, got it, and drove in. She pulled into a parking spot, shut off her engine and stared through the windshield at the tall brick walls with coils of barbed wire on top. The dark-haired woman walked to the main entrance of the prison.

Two conflicting thoughts went through her brain - she felt relief Frank Wood lived in a place like this, but she feared the reality that she, too, may soon live in a similar place. She came here two months ago, saying she was a writer researching a book on financial con games. She told Frank he was smart. She told him he was unique. She played to his ego. She batted her eyes. He believed her.

After checking in as a visitor - with all that goes with verifying her identity - she sat in the waiting area for almost forty-five minutes. She heard her name called and followed her escort to the booth. She sat down and looked through the glass panel to the prisoner's entrance door. A few minutes later, Frank Wood entered the room and was escorted to the seat across from her.

Frank was about five feet nine, with a graying crew cut of brown hair. His rheumy, hazel eyes and thick, hairy ears formed the top line of a pock-marked face. A flat nose and thin lipped mouth topped sagging jowls. The dark-haired woman felt the same up-push of bile she tasted when she last saw him.

"Well, well, well," Frank said. His wide grin did nothing to improve his face. "If it ain't the pretty little writer come back to see ol' Frank. You bringing me a copy of the book to sign?"

"Uh, no," she said. "Not done yet."

"So ya just couldn't live without me, heh?" he said. "Bet ya can't wait 'til I'm out. You and me, a little party, perfect?"

He laughed at his joke. She stared at him, her face steady with just a slight upturn at the corner of her mouth.

"Frank, even if something that repugnantly disgusting had the slightest chance of possibility," she said. "I doubt you will even be able to get it up."

Frank laughed.

"Don't underestimate ol' Frank. I'm a powerhouse when I want to be, and I've been in here two years, two years saving it all up for you. I'll be out this time next year."

"Frank, you won't be out before I'm a grand-mother," she said.

Frank looked at her, his grin falling a bit.

"What are you talking about?" he said, a tone implying his feeling she was dumber than dumb.

She looked at him, her mouth curving up to a smile.

"Do you know a guy named William Shannon?"

Frank's face dropped again, the lines on his forehead deepening.

"That piece of shit? Yeah, I know who he was," Frank said. "And I emphasize the word 'was.' He sucked up the big one in the river." This caused the ripple of a smile to cross his face.

"How did you know him?" she said.

"I never met him, but he and his bitch-wife tried to frame me for killing my daughter, but of course, they couldn't, because I didn't."

Frank sat back and folded his arms across his chest, the smile on his face celebrated his outwitting of this woman.

"The truth is, Frank," the dark-haired woman said. "William Shannon and his bitch-wife knew you didn't kill Olivia. You killed her mother."

Frank's face dropped again.

"That bitch moved out on me when our girl was little. She didn't love our daughter like I did. I had to bring her up on my own."

"I think we both know that she didn't love your daughter anything like you did." The dark-haired woman stared eye-to-eye with Frank.

"You don't know jack shit," he said. "And what's it to you anyway? None of that shit is about money fraud, and ain't that what you said your book is about?"

"No, it isn't," she said. "My story is about you killing Olivia's mother."

Frank's cheeks flushed. His anger became visible. The woman looked through the glass toward the guard standing just outside the door. The guard cast an inquiring look. She gave him a slight shake of her head and lifted her palm in a symbolic "I'm okay." The guard nodded.

"You been listening to that Shannon prick and that Hammond bitch-wife of his," Frank said. "None of it is true, and no one can prove nothin'."

"Hammond?" the dark-haired woman said, her look somewhat puzzled. "Margaret Hammond?"

"That bitch talked my Olivia into running away in high school," Frank said, almost spitting the words. "She was Shannon's girlfriend, and the two of them stole my Olivia from me. But that bitch got what was coming to her when her prick of a husband died in the river. She can rot in hell now, and I told her that."

"You spoke with Margaret Hammond? And she told you she married William Shannon?"

"I didn't talk to her," he said. "But I had something sent to her tellin' her that. She was Shannon's girlfriend. I figured she's the one that married the asshole, then took off. I tracked her down. That bitch-wife will get what she deserved."

The dark-haired woman sat staring at Frank, considering her next words. Frank looked away, focused on bringing his breathing and anger under control.

"Frank," she said. "What would you say if I told you William Shannon dug up papers that show your late wife did not leave you because she had nowhere to go, no way to get there, and no money to help her?"

"I would say Shannon was an idiot," Frank said with a sarcastic laugh. "My wife had her own car. She had jewelry and probably sold it for money. I bet the bitch had some asshole boyfriend she was screwing and

ran off with him."

She stared at him, a smile emerging from her tightened lips.

"What would you say if I told you your late wife's car was sold to a salvage yard in Scranton a week after she disappeared?"

"Maybe that's where she ran off to?" Frank said, the volume and timbre of his voice rising.

"What if the guy who dropped off the car and got the fifty dollar salvage fee was paid by check? And coincidently, he happened to have the same name as your brother, Thomas W. Wood?"

Frank looked at her without saying anything. The woman looked past him at the guard, who held up two fingers. Two minutes left. She nodded.

"What would you say if I told you I held your wife's wedding ring and diamond pendant in the palm of my hand two days ago? She never sold them."

Frank's eyes widened, his top lip curled, his breaths quickened, his fists clenched.

"And Frank," she said. "You did know your late wife kept a diary, right?"

Frank cocked his head and eyed the woman.

"What if I told you she didn't take it with her?" she said. "What if it was filled with writings about you and how you abused her, and how she suspected you were harming your daughter?"

Frank's eyes spit hatred at the woman. His breathing became rapid, but he said nothing.

"No comment?" she said. "Well, would you make any comments, if I told you I read that diary two days ago?"

Frank stared at her, his eyes widened.

"Or maybe you would like to comment on a certain patch of ground along a mass of brambles a few hundred yards behind your house? You remember it, Frank? Isn't that where your wife 'ran off to?' It seems late wife wasn't the only one in your family who saw things and wrote them down."

Frank stood up and slammed his hand on the table just as the guard opened the door to return him to his cell.

"Watch yourself, Wood," the guard said, which stopped Frank. He continued his glare at the woman.

"I know what you're thinking, Frank," the dark-haired woman said. *"You're thinking I'm a bitch, right? Well, I am a bitch. In fact, I'm Bill Shannon's bitch-wife. I never changed my last name. Margaret Hammond never married Bill Shannon. She had nothing to do with any of this. I married Bill Shannon. I was Olivia's English teacher."*

The guard took Frank's arm to lead him toward the door. Frank pulled his arm away and leaned forward, both arms on the table.

"You fucking bitch," he screamed. *"You will regret this."*

The guard grabbed Frank's right arm and twisted it up behind him.

Sarah Bodden smiled and stared, unflinching.

"Oh, one more little thing," Sarah said, as the guard moved Frank out the door. *"All that stuff I just mentioned? I sent all of it to the FBI yesterday morning."* She smiled. *"Now you can rot in hell."*

24

Tim's phone buzzed once indicating the call was from the receptionist. He lifted the handset.

"Yeah, Andrea?"

"There's a woman here to see you," the receptionist said.

"Did she say who she was?"

"She says she's with the FBI."

"The FBI?" Tim said. "I'll be right there."

As he walked to the lobby, his thoughts went to the Wood house in Pennsylvania. *Oh, crap. What have I gotten myself into?* He could see down the corridor into the glass walled reception area. Standing there in a dark blue business suit, with a briefcase hanging from her left hand, was a tall, elegant looking woman, perhaps in her mid-thirties, with long, straight brown hair. When he entered the lobby, she turned to him.

"Hi," Tim said. "I'm Tim Roper. Can I help you?"

She reached out her hand. "I'm Special Agent Gretchen McGill." She showed him her FBI ID.

"Is there something I can help you with?" Tim said. He caught a glance at Andrea staring wide-eyed at the pair, taking it all in.

"Is there someplace we can talk?" the agent said.

Tim fumbled a bit. "Um...sure." He looked over at Andrea. "Anyone using B?"

Andrea shook her head.

"This way," Tim said, and the agent followed him through the door to the nearby conference room. They entered, and Tim shut the door.

"Can I get you a cup of coffee or anything?" Tim said.

"No," she said. "I'm good."

"So what can I do for you, Madam Special Agent?" Tim said. "Am I under arrest or something?"

The Agent looked at him.

"You will be if you call me 'Madam Special Agent' again." She smiled. "Just call me Gretchen."

"Okay, Gretchen," Tim said, relaxing a bit. "How can I help you?"

"I work out of the Portland office and have been asked to conduct a few interviews related to the disappearance of a young woman in Pennsylvania."

"Olivia Wood, right?" Tim said. "She disappeared almost ten years ago."

"Yes," Gretchen said. "Did you know her?"

"No," Tim said.

"How did you know her name?" she said.

"My ex-girlfriend went to high school with her and talked about her."

"That would be Margaret Hammond?"

"Yes."

"What did you talk about?"

Tim made the decision neither he nor Maggie was guilty of anything. His best course of action was to be honest.

"We talked about how circumstances led to a confrontation between them in high school."

"What kind of a confrontation?"

"I wasn't there, and Maggie was remembering something that happened ten years ago like you said. You should ask her."

"By Maggie, you are referring to Ms. Hammond, correct?"

Tim nodded.

"I need to know what Maggie said to you."

"She said that Olivia accused her of spreading rumors about her in the high school," Tim said.

"What kind of rumors?"

"That she was pregnant."

"Who was pregnant? Olivia or Maggie?"

"Olivia, of course," Tim said. "You really should be asking Maggie these questions, not me."

"Please," she said. "Just answer the questions, and this will be easier."

Tim let out a deep breath and nodded.

"You'll torture me, if I refuse to answer, won't you?"

"Probably not," she said. "I haven't tortured anyone in weeks. Not physically, at least."

Tim smiled.

"So, Olivia was pregnant?" she continued.

"According to Maggie, yes."

"How did it end?" she said. "According to Ms. Hammond, of course."

"The pregnancy?"

"No, sorry. The confrontation."

"Olivia stomped out, and Maggie never saw her again."

"Why were you at the Wood home on Wednesday, June twenty-second?"

"Jeez," he said. "You guys don't miss anything." He took a breath. "I was down in that area on a business trip and decided to see if I could find Olivia's father. I didn't know he was in prison at that time."

"How did you find out he was in prison?"

"The cook at the diner in Aldenburg."

She tipped her head, her brow furrowed.

"The cook?"

"Yeah, A.J." Tim said. "I asked him if he knew Frank."

"Okay," she said. "We'll get back to that in a minute." She wrote something down on her notepad and continued.

"When you were at the house, did you see anyone else there?"

"No," Tim said. "I did notice one of the windows was broken and some wooden milk crates were stacked up in front of it."

"Did you enter or attempt to enter the house?"

"No."

"Did you remove anything from the property?"

"No."

"How long were you there?"

"Altogether, about seven to ten minutes."

"Where did you go after you left the property?"

"I went to a diner called A.J.'s in Aldenburg Center."

"What happened there?"

"I ate and had a short conversation with A.J.," Tim said. "That's when I asked him what he knew about Frank Wood. He said Frank was a scumbag and was arrested by cops from Massachusetts."

"Did anyone mention Olivia?"

"Yes," Tim said. "I asked A.J. if Wood had a daughter, and he told me that her name was Olivia. He said he heard she killed herself."

"Did he say anything else about her?"

"Nothing I can remember."

"Did you talk to anyone else about either Frank or Olivia Wood?"

"Nope," Tim said then added. "I did ask the waitress if she ever heard of Wood, but she said she was new to the area and didn't know him."

"What was her name?"

"I don't know," Tim said. "She was a tall blonde who likes to chew gum when she talks."

Special Agent McGill smiled.

"Have you ever met Frank Wood?" she said.

"No."

"You have a roommate, correct?"

"An apartment-mate, yes," he said.

"She is not American, correct?"

"Correct," Tim said. "Why do you need to know that?"

Agent McGill looked at him and said, "We're almost done. Please answer the question."

"Yes, she's from Montreal," Tim said. "Her name is Sophia Daigneau."

"She was attacked in front of your apartment yesterday. Is that true?"

"Yes."

"Do you know who did it?"

"I think Sophie said his name was Tom."

"Had you ever met or seen him before?"

"Nope," Tim said, paused, and then added, "But I believe I spoke with him on the phone earlier in the day."

"About what?"

"He thinks I stole something from Frank Wood's house when I was there."

"How did he know you were there?"

"I don't know," he said. "I guess someone got my plate number."

"What did he think you stole?"

"A box."

"What kind of box, and what did it have in it?"

"I haven't a clue," Tim said. "Although he did say I could have half the money in the box, but none of the other stuff."

"Did he say what the other stuff was?"

"Nope."

"Did he threaten you?"

"Yes. He also threatened 'my girlfriend.' I ran to Maggie...uh, Margaret Hammond's apartment thinking it was her. After I got there, Maggie and I began to think he thought Sophie was the girlfriend he meant, because I live with her, uh, share an apartment with her. We got to my apartment just after the cops arrested him."

"Is there anything else you want to add?"

"Not that I can think of," Tim said. "Oh, wait. There is. The guy who was arrested for attacking Sophie left a note in my mailbox the day before the attack. That's when he said he wanted the box."

"Do you still have the note?"

"Not here," Tim said. "It's at home."

"After we're done here, I want you to go with me to your apartment and get it for me. It won't take long."

"No problem."

"One more thing," she said. "Have you ever met anyone named Sarah Bodden?"

"No. But Maggie told me she was her high school teacher."

"Did she say anything else about her?"

"Not really. She said all the kids loved her. She said Miss Bodden was going to help Olivia."

Special Agent McGill closed her notebook.

"That will do it here, Tim," she said. "We can chat a bit more on our way to your apartment. Thanks for your help."

"That's it? Am I in trouble for anything?"

"Did you do something wrong?"

"No."

"Then you're fine," she said. "Just next time stay away from abandoned houses with banners tacked on the front that say, 'No Trespassing,' okay?"

Tim crossed his heart and raised his right hand. "Madam Special Agent Gretchen, I promise."

Tim returned to the office about a half hour later. Andrea stared at him, not knowing what to say.

"No," he said. "I was not arrested."

"Oh, no, no," she said. "I didn't think that. I just thought...um...uh..."

"It's okay," Tim said with a chuckle. "Any messages?"

"On your desk," the young receptionist said.

"Thanks," Tim said. He started to walk into the office, then stopped, and turned back to her and rubbed his right hand around his left wrist.

"Boy, those handcuffs were one size too small. But the lock was easy to pick."

Andrea stared at him. He turned and walked towards his desk, suppressing his laughter.

In his cube he sat down and checked his messages. He stood and turned to walk to the kitchen for a cup of coffee. Jack, Sandra, and Dean - one of the other supervisors - stood looking at him.

"What's up?" Tim said.

"You need to settle a bet," Dean said.

"A bet?" Tim said.

"On the FBI visitor," Jack said.

"Dean bet she came here about a workers comp case," Sandra said, rolled her eyes and pretended to suppress a chuckle.

"I bet she was hitting on you to be your next girlfriend," said Jack. "She just stopped by to visit. You meet her at The Skipper's Key?"

"I bet you are under investigation for some sinister crime," Sandra said, she glanced side to side at the other two, as if she were about to be announced the winner.

"You what?" Tim said. "Sandra, why would you think that?" His mouth opened in shock.

She gave him a smile and raised her hands palms out in front of her, hunched up her shoulders, and dipped her head a little to the left. "It's possible."

Tim looked at each of them in mock shock. He looked at Dean.

"No, this was not related to a case," he said.

"Tol'ja," Sandra said to Dean.

Tim looked at Sandra. "And I am not under investigation for some sinister crime."

Sandra scowled and banged her fist on an imaginary table in front of her. Tim shook his head.

"Pay up," Jack said, reaching his hand palm up toward the other two.

"And while Special Agent McGill is an attractive and personable woman, she is not my next girlfriend," Tim said letting out a sigh. "I am a witness in a mugging case she's investigating."

"The FBI is investigating a mugging case?" Jack said.

"The bad guy lives out of state." Jack and Dean turned and headed for their respective offices, shaking their heads.

Sandra walked alongside Tim as he went to the kitchen.

"I can't believe you bet money I was a criminal," he said.

"I didn't think you were a criminal," Sandra said. "I was just playing the odds."

"The odds?"

"Yes, I played the long shot" she said. "For my dollar bet, my payoff was the biggest. They thought I was crazy and an easy target. First, I said I wouldn't make the bet without 4 to 1 odds. I'd win eight bucks on a two dollar bet. Second, it would be very exciting when the FBI comes in and takes you away in cuffs. I've never seen that before. Third, can you imagine the talk in the lunch room for the next six months?"

She raised her brows in anticipated delight.

Tim looked at her and shook his head. "I can't believe you are saying this."

"And fourth," she said. "I'm next in line for your job."

"That's it," Tim said. "Your review's coming up. Wait 'til I write that one. You'll be begging for a job pouring coffee at a donut shop."

Sandra flashed him a big smile.

"I'm not worried," she said. "You love me, and you know it." She took a right turn before the kitchen and headed to her cube. She raised her fingers above her shoulders as she walked away, wiggling them in a wave.

Tim walked into the kitchen shaking his head. He laughed as he poured coffee from the pot.

***

The blue Crown Vic turned off Route 27 onto the long, tree-lined driveway leading to the expansive brick home. The driveway split into a circular parking area surrounding a small, round garden centered by a stone patio with two park benches facing each other.

"Nice little cottage," the man in the passenger's seat said.

"Welcome to Newborough," the driver said. He pulled the car to the right and parked behind the blue Honda.

"Looks like she's home."

They walked to the front door and rang the bell. A few moments later, the door opened. An attractive thirty-something woman, with medium length dark brown hair, a gray business suit, and a smile greeted them.

"Come in, gentlemen," she said. "I'm Sarah Bodden. I've been expecting you."

Both men raised their hands to flash their ID cards.

"I'm Special Agent John Bartman of the FBI Boston Office," the tall one said. "This is Special Agent David Wilson."

Sarah continued to smile and swept her arm up to encourage them to enter.

"Are you here to arrest me?" Sarah said.

"That depends," Special Agent Wilson said.

"On what?" she said.

"On whether you are willing to come with us to Boston," Special Agent Bartman said. "We need to talk."

"Of course, I'll go with you," she said. "I packed a bag." She pointed to a suitcase sitting on a chair near the front door. "Do you want to check it for weapons or drugs or a metal file or anything like that?"

Special Agent Wilson smiled slightly and said. "That won't be necessary." He walked to the suitcase and picked it up.

"You have children," Bartman said.

"They're in school right now," she said. "My sister lives here with me. She knows what's going on and will take care of them. Just let me tell her I'm leaving."

She walked to the bottom of the staircase at the other end of the corridor and yelled up.

"Kat! They're here, and I have to go."

"Okay," a muffled female voice responded. "Hold on a minute."

Sarah looked at the two agents and shrugged.

"*My kid sister's just in from her morning swim. God forbid she appears before men without make up and dry hair.*"

The men smiled and nodded.

"*We have time,*" *said Bartman.*

A short woman appeared at the top of the landing, standing so she was only partially visible by the two men. She wore a long pink robe she held tight around her. Her hair was wrapped in a turbanized bath towel, the loose end of which hung down the side of her face.

"*Don't worry,*" *she said to Sarah.* "*I'll pick up the boys like I always do. I'll tell them you're off on another of your business trips. We'll be fine.*"

"*Okay, Kat,*" *Sarah said.* "*Wish me luck.*"

"*You know I always do,*" *Kat said.*

Sarah and her escorts left for Boston.

25

"Hey, Timmy," Maggie said when he answered the phone. "How was your day?"

"Probably a lot like yours," he said.

"I doubt it," she said. "Guess who came to talk to me today?"

"The FBI?"

"Ah, you, too?"

"Yup," he said. "Tall brunette named Gretchen."

"Same."

"You turn me in?"

"No, but I thought of it."

"For what?"

"Bad jokes."

"Ugh. I was worried about that."

"You should be," Maggie said. "So what did she ask you?"

"About my little journey to Pennsylvania and whether or not I went into the Wood estate," Tim said. "I told her the truth on everything."

"Me, too," Maggie said.

"Why did she want to talk to you?" Tim said. "You weren't directly involved in the note or the attack on Sophie."

"No, but I think this is bigger than that," she said. "I think they had more on Boxman than we know. They asked me questions about my relationship with Olivia in high school."

"Maybe they are investigating the disappearance of Olivia," Tim said. "Otherwise, I don't know why she would be asking me questions about Sarah. And I think it's odd she called her Sarah Bodden rather than Sarah Shannon."

"Yes, she did the same with me," Maggie said. "I asked her if she talked to Sarah. I told her I'd like to get in touch with her and say 'Hi.' She didn't answer me."

"I was thinking," Tim said. "Pete told me the blood of the person who broke into the Wood's house was a woman. You think it could be Sarah?"

"I can't think of any reason why she would do that."

"It just seems weird to me," Tim said. "What would William Shannon's death, his body being found in a river, Sarah Bodden - aka Sarah Shannon – possibly involved with Olivia Wood's disappearance and/or suicide, Frank Wood in prison for some type of scam, the B&E of his house, and the mysterious box have in common?"

"Maybe Billy was the father of Olivia's baby?" Maggie said with a touch of resignation in her voice. "Maybe Olivia had the baby, and there's a grandchild out there somewhere who just came to everyone's attention?"

"Yeah, maybe," Tim said. "Maybe that mysterious box contained a birth certificate or something like that. Hey, I wonder if Olivia hid it somewhere in the house, and it said that Shannon was the father. Shannon married Bodden. Bodden has money. Maybe Frank came up with a way of extorting money out of them?"

Maggie thought for a few moments.

"Could be."

"Maybe Shannon's death created an inheritance situation, since the kid's mother is also dead. Maybe dead. The grandfather - that being Frank - makes a case for part of the Shannon/Bodden estate going to the kid, and bingo, he's in the moola. Bodden decides she's not giving the guy a cut, especially since the only connection is her dead husband. Sound reasonable?"

"Yeah," Maggie said. "That sounds like a plausible theory. With holes, of course."

"What holes?"

"First, where has the baby been for the past eight or nine years?"

"With the aunt in Colorado or some other relative."

"Okay," she said. "Second, how does Sarah Bodden know to look under a carpet and floor board in Frank's house?"

"Olivia told her that's where she hid the papers," Tim said.

"Olivia was not all that pregnant when she disappeared," Maggie said. "Do you think she'd have the baby, sneak back to the house of her father whom she seemed to hate, and hide the most important things her baby had? And then run back to Sarah, who she believed ratted her out?"

"Good points," said Tim. "But maybe they're

explainable. Maybe not. And I guess we'd have to figure out why Bodden would even know to go looking for those things."

"And don't they read all letters prisoners send from jail?" Maggie said.

"Yeah, I think so," Tim said. "He obviously has at least one accomplice. Of course, Boxman's as dumb as a stump. There's gotta be at least one more person out there not doing time."

"Third," Maggie said. "You told me your investigation of Shannon's apartment made it look and sound like he lived alone. If he and Bodden were divorced, would there still be a direct line to the Bodden money from Billy to Olivia's kid? Assuming there actually is a kid."

"That's a good question, Mags," Tim said. "And I do not have any answers. We're missing something."

"You know, Timmy," Maggie said after a few moments to think. "This all started with me feeling guilty because I believed I drove Olivia to kill herself. Now I'm feeling guilty, because I've let myself become distracted from my earlier guilt by worrying more about trying to solve this mystery. I'm feeling guilty because I have competing guilts. Does that make any sense? And am I a total psychological mess?"

"I'll take the fifth."

"Scotch or gin?"

"Scotch," Tim said. "These are all good questions we need answers for. I think we can do two things. We can let the FBI do their jobs and mind our own business. This option has merit, of course. The FBI has greater information and access to even more, connections to all the characters, unlimited resources, and they carry handcuffs and guns. And they actually know what they are doing. The downside is that we may never know what we want to know."

"What's the second option?" Maggie said.

"We can continue our 'Hardy Boys Meet Nancy Drew' adventure and find your old English teacher on our own. We risk getting beat up, arrested or shot. But we might find out what went on."

"The first option makes sense," Maggie said. "It's rational, logical, cheaper and safer for both of us."

"I agree," Tim said. "The second option is irrational, illogical and dumb." Silence hung across the phone line for a good ten seconds. Tim spoke first.

"So, Nancy," Tim said. "Where do you think we should start?"

"Boston."

26

"You have the right to remain silent," the tall FBI Special Agent said. "Anything you say can and will be used against you in a court of law. You have the right to an attorney. If you cannot afford an attorney, one will be provided for you. Do you understand the rights I have just read to you?"

"Yes."

"With these rights in mind, do you wish to speak with us?"

"Yes."

"Please state your name and address for the record."

"Sarah E. Bodden," she said. "523 Cooper Road, Newborough, Massachusetts."

"And you also understand we are recording this conversation?"

"Yes, I do."

"Thank you, Ms. Bodden," Special Agent Bartman said. "Can you tell me where you were on the night of

Saturday, June 18, 1977?"

"Please call me Sarah," she said. "I was in Aldenburg, Pennsylvania."

"Did you visit the home of Frank L. Wood at 18052 Hillside Street in Aldenburg, Sarah?"

"Yes," Sarah said. "I did."

"Was anyone else with you?"

"No."

"Was anyone on the property or in the house when you arrived there?"

"No."

"Sarah," he said. "What did you see when you arrived?"

"The house was dark. It was obvious no one lived there for some time."

"Did you have free access to the building?"

"No," Sarah said. "There was a sign on the front door that said 'No Trespassing.' I think it also said the property was owned by the Commonwealth of Pennsylvania."

"Did you enter the house?"

"Yes, I did," she said. "I pried open a bedroom window in the back corner of the house. I stacked some old crates I found next to the garage and entered through that window."

"Sarah, you do understand that you broke the law when you did that."

"I do."

"What was your reason for breaking into the house?"

"I wanted to see if Olivia left some information in her secret hiding place there about her disappearance, and where she might have gone."

"By Olivia, you are referring to Frank Wood's daughter, Olivia Wood. Is that correct?"

"Yes," Sarah said. "She was my student at Cummington High School about nine years ago."

"What did you find?"

"I found a cigar box in her hidden spot."

"What was in the container?"

"Some jewelry, some old photographs, and a diary."

"Photographs of what?" Special Agent Wilson said.

"Some were photos of a young girl of about 4 or 5-years-old posing with a woman," Sarah said. "I assumed it was Olivia and her mother. It looked like Olivia might have looked when she was young. There were a couple other pictures of the women. One was a close-up of her face. She had two black eyes. One eye was swollen shut. The other photo showed a close up of what looked like a woman's abdomen. It was cut and badly bruised."

"Was there anything else on the photos?"

"On the back of the photos showing the injuries were written the names of doctors and a date."

"Were they the same date?"

"No," Sarah said. "Different dates. Different months and years."

"What kind of jewelry?" Bartman said.

"The jewelry I sent to the FBI," she said. "A diamond necklace, a gold wedding ring, and a diamond ring, like an engagement ring."

"The diary," Bartman said. "Was that the same book you sent to us?"

"Yes," Sarah said. "It was Olivia's mother's diary."

"Did you read it?"

"Yes, I did," she said. "What I read caused me to send everything to the FBI."

"Did you send everything you found in the container?"

"Yes."

The two Special Agents looked at each other. Bartman nodded to Wilson.

Wilson said, "How did you know about this 'secret hiding place' of Olivia's?"

"My late husband told me."

"Your late husband is William Shannon, is that correct?"

"Yes."

"And how would he know?"

"Olivia told him."

"Is not Olivia dead?" Wilson said. "When did she tell him?"

"She told him about nine years ago when she was in high school."

"Nine years ago?" Wilson said. "She told him nine years ago, and you just decided that this would be a good time to break into her old house and have a little treasure hunt?"

"I told you," Sarah said. "I thought I might find something that might say where she disappeared to."

"Yeah, okay," Wilson said. "But why would she tell her teacher about the secret hiding place in her home? You don't think that sounds a bit strange?"

"Yes, it probably does sound strange to someone like you," Sarah said an edge coming to her voice. "But Bill and I are teachers."

Wilson rolled his eyes.

"Olivia was in my English class," she began. "Bill was my student teacher at the time, and because I missed six weeks of school as the result of a car accident, Bill took over the class.

"Olivia had natural writing talent. One of the essays Olivia passed in was ostensibly about the murder of her dog, but there was something about it that didn't settle right with Bill. It was a bit too creepy for a fifteen year old. He told me he approached Olivia about the essay, and she kind of blew him off. Her next essay was about killing herself, and all the alarms went off in Bill's head. He approached Olivia and offered to schedule one-on-one meetings, overtly focused on helping Olivia with her writing.

"And she just told him she had a secret hiding place?" Wilson said.

"Excuse me, but would you rather I make up an easy explanation you can understand or tell you the truth regardless of its complexity?" Sarah said.

"Why don't we all just relax a bit," Bartman said. He looked at Wilson who put up his hands, indicating he'll cool his bad cop routine. Then Bartman looked at Sarah who nodded assent.

Sarah continued.

"You almost have to know Bill to understand how his brain works. He had this incredible ability to 'read between the lines' of what people say or write. He could actually understand not only what their words said, but what their hearts said."

Special Agent Wilson rolled his eyes. Sarah ignored him and focused on Bartman.

"Bill deduced that the dog murder essay was really about Olivia's mother getting killed. In the essay, she *mentioned this secret hiding place where she hid her dead dog's collar. In the essay she said this hiding place 'held all her secrets and all her dreams.'"* Sarah raised her hands signaling the quotation marks. *"That's how he knew she had a hiding place."*

Sarah paused and took a deep breath.

"Of course, right after that, the pregnancy issue with Olivia popped up, and all hell broke loose. Rumors had it she moved in with an aunt in Colorado. No one at the school ever saw her again. But I believe you all know about that part."

"She never showed up in Colorado," Bartman said.

"She didn't?" Sarah said. *"I hoped that's where she went. She said that's where she was going...Oh my God! Do you think her father killed her, too?"* Sarah's hand came up over her mouth, and she closed her eyes.

"That's not our issue here," Wilson said. *"So when did this revelation about this secret hiding spot suddenly come to your husband nine years later?"*

"A couple of months ago, I think." Sarah said, still shaking her head.

"Just out of the blue?" Special Agent Bartman said.

"No," Sarah said. *"We heard the rumors Olivia killed herself. Bill apparently still had Olivia's essays from all those years. He reread the one about the suicide.*

"The essay said something like 'all her secrets, her dreams, and her terrors, sat cringing in a corner of her bedroom.' She described it in a more poetic way, but that's the translation as Bill described it to me. The essay said that 'someday the truth will rise up through the floor and unleash its love and wrath through the sword of justice.' Those are probably not the exact

words, but they're as close as I remember."

Sarah looked to the two agents for understanding.

"Don't you see the connection in the two stories?" she said. "Olivia's secrets and dreams in a hiding place in one essay, then again, her secrets and dreams in the corner of her bedroom in the other essay? Rise through the floor? You don't see it? She was telling us where to look."

Sarah lowered her head to her hands and slowly shook it.

"Okay," Bartman said. "You still have the essays?"

"No," Sarah said. "I don't know what Bill did with them."

"So you and your husband decided that you would just go to this house, break in, and wield the sword of justice?" Special Agent Wilson said.

"No," Sarah said. "But we talked about it."

"Why would you want to do that?" Bartman said.

"We wanted to bring peace to Olivia."

"She's dead," Wilson said. "What difference would it make?"

Sarah stared at him, holding back the venom she felt for him.

"We would not know if it would make a difference until we knew what was hidden," Sarah said. "And I would like to point out that we would not be sitting here having this discussion if the contents of that box were not discovered."

"We would not be sitting here having this discussion if you didn't break into a private home, clearly marked with No Trespassing signs, and steal the box," said Wilson.

"I owed Olivia a debt and this was my way of

paying it to her."

"And what debt was that?" Bartman said.

"I was responsible for word of her pregnancy getting out to the school," Sarah said. "I made a mistake, and it could have caused her to kill herself." Sarah closed her eyes, lowered her head, and sniffled.

Bartman looked at Wilson who rolled his eyes and sat back into the chair. Bartman went to the credenza, swung open a door, and retrieved a box of tissues. He set them on the table next to Sarah.

"I think we could all use a break," he said. "Sarah, the Ladies' room is out this door and to your right. It's the second door on your left."

Sarah stood up.

"Thank you," she said, picked up her purse and left the room.

"What do you think?" Bartman said to Wilson.

"She could be playing us," Wilson said. "But she's definitely one of those hippy dippy types. All that 'lalala' and poetic shit. But I don't know." He shook his head.

"I think I'd give her the benefit of the doubt right now," Bartman said. "But let's see what develops. Do we charge her?"

"With what?" Wilson said. "Breaking and entering? That's Pennsylvania's problem, assuming they even give a shit."

"Transporting stolen property across state lines? Conspiracy?" Bartman said.

"I don't know. Let's keep her talking for a while and see what develops," Wilson said. "I will say one thing. She's as frigging smart as she is pretty."

27

Tim left early for Boston on Tuesday morning - the day after July 4th - trying to avoid the swarms of people leaving Maine and New Hampshire after their holiday weekend. He crossed the high arch of the Piscataqua Bridge connecting Kittery, ME and Portsmouth, NH. The low eastern sun bathed Portsmouth in the thick honey of a sweet New England summer, reflecting off the early ventures of city cars and the towering derricks of a working waterfront.

Tim looked down at a large tanker anchored close to the bridge. He marveled at the strength and grandeur of these vessels seen close up and thought about the films and photos he'd seen of those same ships being tossed about through ocean storms like toy ducks in a two-year-old's bath. He pondered the power of nature and the resolve of the men who overcome it. He needed some of that resolve.

Fifteen minutes later he passed through the

Hampton toll booth and headed straight into Boston.

The Boston office of his company sat in Center Plaza across from City Hall on Tremont Street. From the sixth floor window of the conference room he used as his temporary office, he could look out on the broad plaza of City Hall and the one-year-old Faneuil Hall Marketplace. Beyond the Marketplace flowed the combined discharge of the Charles and Mystic Rivers on its way to Boston Harbor. From his perch, Tim could see to East Boston and Logan International Airport.

He finished his case work by 12:30 and called Pete about meeting him for dinner - Tim's treat, of course. They agreed to a 6:00 meet-up. He thought about walking down to Faneuil Hall Marketplace for a quick bite and to explore the shops and pushcarts for some trinket to bring back for Maggie. But as he stood to leave, he noticed the telephone on the sideboard, and next to it, the oversized Boston phonebook.

He opened the book to the middle of the B-names and ran his finger down the page until he came to the first entry of the name "Bodden." Anthony lived in East Boston. He thought about what he knew of Sarah and decided she probably wasn't an East Boston native. In all he found fifteen entries. None listed an Adrian or Sarah. He eliminated eight of the others based on neighborhood and started calling the other seven.

"Hello?"

"Hi. Is Sarah there?" he said.

"Sarah?" the voice said. "Sarah who?"

"Sarah Bodden. This is a friend of hers from college."

"Sorry. I don't know anyone named Sarah." Hang up.

"Hi. Can I speak to Sarah Bodden, please?"

"You got the wrong number." Hang up.

"I'm sorry the number you have dialed in not in service."

"Hello. Is Sarah Bodden there?"

"I don't know no Sarah?" Hang up.

"Hello, is this Sarah Bodden?"

"Don't I wish," the woman said. Tim sat up straighter.

"Oh, you know her?" Tim said. He looked down at the address in the phone book. Brighton.

"Actually," the woman said. "I really don't *know* her, but I do know *of* her. I think she's somehow related to my husband. But I think she came from the better side of the tracks."

"I think I'm probably from the same side of the tracks as your husband," Tim said. "But I did work with her in Pennsylvania a few years ago. I'm in Boston on a business trip and knew she was from Boston. I'm going through phone numbers trying to find her just to say 'Hello.'"

"I believe Sarah is the daughter of Andrew Bodden. He owns – or used to own – Dynamore Tools in Natick. He passed about ten, twelve years ago. I saw it in the paper. They had a picture of Sarah at the funeral. She looked so sad and so beautiful. I felt bad for her."

"Do you know where she lives?" Tim asked.

"I'm not sure, but I think her parents lived out in the Framingham or Worcester area. Probably some big house with lots of land. Her father also raised horses, if I remember the obituary correctly."

"Okay," Tim said. "Thanks. You have been very helpful. If I find Sarah, I'll tell her you said. 'Hi.'"

The woman laughed. "Yeah," she said. "Tell her I'm her long lost aunt."

"I'll do that. Thanks, again." Tim hung up.

He went to the sideboard and opened the doors looking for a Boston Metro West phone book. He didn't find one there. He dialed the operator.

"Yes, hi. Can I please have the number for Sarah Bodden in Framingham?"

After a moment, "Sorry, sir, we have no Sarah Bodden listed for Framingham."

"Maybe she doesn't live in Framingham, but I know it's real close to Framingham. You must have a listing in the area. Do you mind checking for me?"

"One minute, sir." A few moments passed. "Sorry," she said. "I only have one Bodden out that way and that is an unlisted number in Newborough. Sorry, sir."

"That's okay. Thanks." He hung up.

Newborough. If I remember correctly, it's definitely on the upscale side. Tim picked up his briefcase and left the conference room. He walked to one of the adjusters, asked where they kept their Cole's Directory. Two minutes later, he had an address.

Tim stopped at the reception area and told the receptionist he was going to take the rest of the afternoon off and see a little of Boston. He said he'd check back for messages later in the afternoon.

It took him about forty-five minutes to get his car from the parking garage and get out on the Mass Pike past Route 128. He knew where Newborough was. He'd been there a few times on claims when he worked in Salem. He left the Pike at the Framingham exit and headed southwest. Twenty minutes later, he crossed into Newborough. He followed the signs to the center of town and found the street he was looking for.

The property was more gentlemen's farm than anything else. An old New England stone wall ran along the street with a wire fence on top, tall enough to contain the two horses munching grass in the field. He turned up the driveway and pulled into the circular parking area, stopping behind a blue Honda with a Penn State sticker on the back window.

He walked to the door and rang the bell. He waited half a minute and rang again. Five seconds later the door opened and a young woman about Tim's age with short, curly blonde hair stood looking at him.

"Yes?" she said.

"Hi," he said. "My name's Tim Roper. Are you Sarah Bodden?"

"No," the woman said. "She's my sister. Sarah's not here right now. Why do you want her?" The woman eyed him and then looked past him to his car before making a quick scan of the driveway.

"I just trying to track down someone," Tim said, his guard going up a little bit. "I think Sarah may know the person."

"What person?" the woman said. Her eyes darted back to the driveway, and then stared up at Tim.

Tim didn't think the claims adjuster looking for a witness act would work here. He changed course and steered toward the truth.

"Someone she had as a student about nine years ago in Pennsylvania," Tim said. "Her name is Olivia

Wood."

The woman took a half step back. Her eyes narrowed, holding a stare on Tim, while her head lifted and tipped slightly to the right.

"She's dead," the woman said.

"Olivia's dead?" Tim said. "Are you sure?"

"That's what we heard," the woman said.

"Do you know how she died?"

"I think you should talk to Sarah." The young woman started to close the door.

"No, wait, wait," Tim said, putting his hand in the door. "Please, when do you think she'll be home?" The woman eased the door back open.

"I don't know. She's on a business trip."

"A business trip?" Tim said. "I thought she was a teacher."

"It's summer vacation," the woman said. "She's also a writer."

"A writer?" Tim said. "Wow, I didn't know that. What's she writing?"

"A book about a man who killed his wife," she said.

"A mystery," he said. "Nothing like a good mystery novel."

"Nothing like it," she said.

Tim heard movement behind him and turned to see two young boys running past the bottom of the stairs. The smaller boy chased the older boy with a small armload of tomatoes. He threw one at the older boy as he ran by. Both were laughing.

The woman shook her head and stepped out past Tim onto the porch next to him.

"Toby," she called. "Stop that right now."

The two boys continued the chase.

"Brian," she said. "If you want a ride to Cub Scouts you better listen to me." She shook her head as they rounded the house. "Boys."

"That could have been me not that long ago," Tim said. "They your kids?"

She hesitated a moment and pushed herself back into suspicious mode.

"They're Sarah's," she said.

"Oh, really," Tim said. "You take care of them when she's away?"

The woman nodded, but said nothing.

"How long is she gone for?" Tim said.

The woman shrugged her shoulders.

"Can you give me her phone number, so I can call her when she gets back?" Tim said.

"Sarah is very clear about not giving out our number to anyone. Sorry."

The boys came running around from the other side of the house. Tim smiled to himself. The woman shook her head and closed her eyes for a moment.

"I'm telling you, Brian," she yelled. "If you two don't cut out this tomato business, Auntie Kat will not be driving *anyone* to scouts. And when your mother sees what you did to her garden, she's going to lock you in your rooms and throw away the keys!"

The boys changed course and headed toward the barn. She shook her head again and looked at Tim.

"Auntie Cat?" Tim said.

"Short for Katherine," she said. "Look, I've got to go referee those two. Sorry you missed Sarah."

She stepped out, pulled the door closed behind her, and moved by Tim. Tim stepped back a step and started to follow her.

"One more thing," he said. The woman stopped, sighed and turned.

"Could you ask Sarah to call me when she gets back?" Tim pulled a pen and one of his business cards from his pocket. He held the card in his palm and wrote his name and home phone number on the back. He flipped it over and scribbled a wavy cross out on the front. "This isn't business related. I wrote my home phone."

Kat took the card and looked at it.

"You're from Maine?"

"Yeah," Tim said. "But I was born and raised not far from here. In Worcester."

Kat nodded blank faced.

"I'll see she gets this, but I don't guarantee she'll call. She has a lot on her mind."

Tim nodded, gave her a quick goodbye wave, and moved to his car. He needed Sarah to call. On an impulse, he turned and looked over his car at Kat, who was walking away.

"I almost forgot," he said. "Margaret Hammond sends Sarah her condolences. She said Bill was a good man."

Kat stopped walking and stood still.

"I'll tell her," she said without turning. A moment later she resumed her walk toward the barn.

Tim got in the car and headed back to Boston.

28

"So where's Newborough?" Maggie said.

"Southwest of Framingham," Tim said. "Sort of halfway between Boston and Worcester. Small town. Big Money."

Maggie nodded. "You said her sister had no idea when she'd be back?"

"No," Tim said. "It did seem a bit odd. If she were on a business trip, wouldn't you think it would be more defined than 'I don't know when she'll be back'?"

"Wouldn't you think she'd be home by the week end?" Maggie said. "Then again, maybe she's at a trade show or something. Don't those sometimes include weekends?"

"Not the weekend after the Fourth of July," Tim said. "They don't usually do trade shows this time of year. Everyone's on vacation."

"Maybe she's back in Pennsylvania? You know, settling some things about Billy's death."

"Doubt it," Tim said. "Wherever she went, she

probably flew. Or rode with someone else. Her car was parked in the driveway."

"How'd you know it was her car?"

"It was a blue 1976 Honda Accord," Tim said. "She's listed as the owner and primary operator."

"And you know this because . . .?"

"Because claims adjusters can find out these things with a plate number. It's part of our job. Want the VIN number?"

Maggie shook her head.

"You guys make me nervous," she said.

"Hey, you used to be one of us," Tim said. "Remember, that's how you found me."

Maggie rolled her eyes.

"So what if she doesn't call you?"

"It's Wednesday. If I don't hear anything by Saturday night, maybe I'll go back down Sunday," he said. "See if I can catch her home. Want to come? I'm thinking of making a trip down to Worcester anyway."

"Definitely," Maggie said. "I'd like to see Miss Bodden myself."

"Good. We'll leave early Sunday," Tim said. "My mother's having a cookout that afternoon. We can eat there."

"Is that why you're going to Worcester?" Maggie said.

"Not exactly. I need to pick up something from my mother's house."

Maggie looked at him with some puzzlement, and then her face changed to a big grin.

"You're going to get the bass fiddle?" she said.

"You were right. It needs to be played."

Maggie went to Tim and put her arms around him

and hugged him.

"I think your father is smiling right now."

"Yeah, well, nobody's heard me play it yet. It's been twenty years since the last time I played it. And then, I was only seven."

"You'll be great," Maggie said.

"Hey, Timbo," Ray said, as Tim walked up to the bar. "Welcome to another wild Friday night at The Key. The usual?"

"Yup," Tim said. "Along with a very weak tequila sunrise and a glass of red wine."

Ray looked past Tim and saw Maggie and Sophie stopped and talking with Didi. Ray shook his head.

"I don't know how you do it," he said, putting the glass of stout in front of Tim. "Most guys would sell their souls to walk in with one of those two. And you walk in with both."

"It's my looks and my charm that does it, Ray," Tim said. "Plus I pay them."

"Really?" Ray said. "How much?"

"Not enough. But don't tell them I said that," he said with a feigned worried look over his left shoulder. "Truth is they only bring me along for show. It's you they really want."

"Now that sounds more believable," Ray said.

Maggie and Sophie came to the bar and sat on a stool with Maggie between Sophie and Tim. Ray placed the wine in front of Sophie and the tequila in front of Maggie.

"How's it going, Sophie?" he said. "Maggie, glad to see you back in form."

"Describe form," she said.

Ray got a couple of beers for some guys at the other end of the bar and came back.

"You guys want a menu?" he said.

"We're going to get a table when one's available," said Maggie. "Didi's on it."

Ray nodded. On the TV, the Sox were playing the Brewers in Milwaukee. The game wouldn't start for another hour because of the time difference. They sat, sipped their drinks and chatted with Ray and some of the regulars sitting or standing on the other side of Tim. Fifteen minutes later, Didi escorted them to an open booth table. Tim sat alone on one side, the women on the other.

Tim ordered another stout. When Didi brought it back, they all ordered the Fish & Chip Special from the chalkboard. Didi went to the kitchen. Sophie leaned forward over the table.

"Don't look," she said. "But see that guy at the bar in the blue shirt sitting two stools up from where I was sitting?"

"How can I see him, if I don't look?" Tim said.

"Don't turn until I tell you to," Sophie said. "Maggie, you see him. Do you know who he is?"

"Never saw him before," she said.

"I think he was sitting in a car on our street this afternoon," Sophie said. "When I was walking home, I stopped and chatted with Deborah. She pointed him out to me and said he'd been parked at the end of the block for about forty minutes."

"My God, you've got blood lust," Tim said. "Why didn't you just beat him up then and there, like you did the last guy who parked on our street?"

"I'm serious," Sophie said. "And I'm pretty sure he's the same guy I saw this afternoon. I was going to get his license plate number, but he was backed up too close to the car behind him."

"Hang on," Tim said. "I'm going to take a look." Despite Sophie's muffled protest, he slid out of the booth.

"Don't worry," he said. Tim winked, and then turned and walked toward the man. The man glanced at Tim and turned his look towards Ray. He held up his glass, and nodded he needed a refill.

Tim walked by him and went into the Men's room at the far end of the bar.

When Tim came out a minute later he walked past the man and stopped just behind the man's right shoulder, focusing up on the TV, watching the pregame comments of Don Zimmer, the Red Sox manager.

"Who's pitching tonight?" Tim said, his face not moving from the screen.

"Reggie Cleveland," the man said. "Against Slaton."

"Good. I like our chances," Tim said, smiled, looked at him, and turned to walk. "Thanks."

At the booth Tim sat down and said to Sophie, "I never saw him before."

Sophie nodded.

"Do you remember what kind of car he drove?" Tim said.

"A tan one," Sophie said.

"Can you give me a little more to work with?" Tim said. "Was it a Chrysler? A Chevy? A Ford? You know, something with a little more detail?"

"I do not know cars," she said. "It had one of those

shield things on it."

"Shield things?" Tim said.

"Like a shield with two little square wings coming out of the side?" Sophie said.

"Where was this shield thing?" Tim said. "On the hood? The trunk?"

"The back," Sophie said.

"Wait a minute," Maggie said. She reached into her pocketbook and pulled out a pen. She grabbed a napkin out of the dispenser and drew an outline of a car logo. She held it up to Sophie.

"Something like this?"

"Yes," Sophie said. "Shaped like that."

Maggie slid the napkin to Tim.

"Chevrolet," he said. He slid the napkin back to Maggie. "Do you mind signing this for me? It will be worth a lot of money someday when your paintings hang in the Louvre."

Maggie took it back and signed it. Instead of Tim, she gave the napkin to Sophie.

"She deserves the money more than you do. She's your bodyguard." Sophie and Maggie laughed. Tim shook his head.

Didi showed up with their dinners. After they had everything sorted out, Sophie glanced over at the bar.

"He's gone," she said.

Tim and Maggie both looked over and saw a woman on the mystery man's stool. They surveyed the pub and saw no sign of the other guy.

"He's gone now," Maggie said. "Probably just a coincidence, anyway."

Sophie didn't respond, but nodded in tentative agreement with Maggie.

"Let's just keep our eyes open," Tim said. "But it's probably just a coincidence."

The Sox beat the Brewers seven to three. Sophie and Tim walked Maggie the three blocks to her apartment, escorted her upstairs, and stayed for a cup of instant coffee.

Maggie showed Sophie her close-to-done painting of the spot on the Kancamagus. Tim felt the bittersweet taste of regret rising from the pit of his gut, but he let his heart and his brain push it back to insignificance. He loved Maggie and believed she loved him. Only that mattered.

A half hour after they arrived, Maggie exchanged hugs with her two guests and bade them goodnight. Tim and Sophie walked to Tim's car and headed home. Neither of them noticed the tan Chevy Nova, with the man sitting in the front seat, parked a half block away from Maggie's apartment.

29

"Hello?"

"It's me."

"What do you have for me, Gus?"

"I think he's clean."

"Why do you say that?"

"I think he's just the boyfriend."

"You 'think?'"

"There's another female. Canadian. Redhead. Very pretty. The guy lives with her, but I think it's just a roommate thing. Nothing else."

"How do you know that?"

"The three of them hang out together at a bar not far from the Hammond woman's apartment. He and Hammond lived together for a couple of years, but she broke it off around seven, eight months ago. No one I talked to seems to know the details. Guys in his local hangout say he's still in love with Hammond. Most think he wants to get her back. She is pretty hot."

"So you don't think he's working her."

"Nah. I watched him a bit at the bar. He's definitely all goo-goo eyes. I get the impression he's the classic boy-next-door type. Friendly, polite, do-gooder. Neighbor says he's always helpful and considerate. No record."

"A regular boy scout, huh?"

"Sounds it."

"Got the addresses?"

"Yup." He read the addresses out loud.

"Okay, Gus. I'll take it from here. Send me the bill."

"Will do."

"And thanks."

"No problem. You got my number. Any time."

***

Tim lay in bed thinking about how he'd spend the day. He wanted to hang out in the apartment in case Sarah Bodden called. He and Maggie agreed to take in an early evening movie. The question at the moment was which of the new movies to see. Maggie voted for *Annie Hall*, while Tim favored *Star Wars*. Tim knew it would be *Annie Hall*, but his mind worked to come up with arguments that might convince Maggie the other way.

He heard the apartment door close and looked at the clock. 9:00. Sophie off to work. He pulled off the sheet and got up. Hot day coming. The air conditioned theatre would be a welcomed relief later in the day. No need to throw on his terrycloth robe. Sophie was gone. He walked to the kitchen in his boxers, poured coffee from the half full pot Sophie made, and sat down to read the paper she'd retrieved from the porch.

Apparently, very little was happening in the world, at least according to the scarcity of news beyond Portland. He pulled out the local section. Nothing happening in Portland either, but then nothing usually does. He read the sports page about last night's Sox victory over the Brewers, learned nothing that he didn't already know, and put down the paper. He rose, emptied the coffee pot into his cup, and moved to the living room.

He thought about this little adventure he and Maggie had been on. *Let's see. Maggie's been drunk in an alley. I almost got arrested. Sophie came close to getting mugged. Two of us have been threatened and interrogated by the FBI. We've learned nothing that explains the newspaper note to Maggie or makes her feel any better about her run in with Olivia. Sam Spade, I'm not.* Tim laughed at himself and ran the palms of his hands through his hair. *But on the other hand, Maggie and I may have found a path back together.*

He smiled.

"And worth every second," he said aloud.

The front door buzzed. Tim rose from the chair, went to the speaker and pressed the talk button.

"Hello?"

"Tim, this is Gretchen McGill," the voice said. "If you have a few minutes, I'd like to speak to you."

"Um, sure," he said. "Can you give me a minute? I just got up."

Tim heard a little chuckle through the speaker.

"By all means," she said. "Put on some pants."

"Will do," he said. "Come on up."

He pressed the buzzer and moved to his bedroom. He pulled on a pair of jeans and grabbed a clean tee-shirt from his bureau drawer. He looked in the mirror running his fingers through his hair to make it look semi-presentable. He returned to the living room and opened the door.

Special Agent McGill stood in the door, her brown hair pulled back in a ponytail, a smile on her face. She wore jeans, a beige pullover top, and sandals. Tim took a step back in surprise.

"Whoa," he said. "Are you undercover or something?" She laughed. He motioned her to enter. "Please have a seat. Can I make a pot of coffee?"

"No, thank you," she said. "I don't have much time. I just dropped my daughter off for her dance class and need to pick her up in twenty minutes."

Tim nodded and sat in the chair across from her.

"What do you need?" he said.

"Nothing. This is totally unofficial. I just wanted to put you and Sophia at ease," she said. "And Margaret, as well. Is Sophia here?" She looked toward one of the bedroom doors.

"She's at work," Tim said.

Gretchen nodded.

"I don't think you have to worry about the man who sent you that note and attacked Sophia," she said. "He has a long list of issues with the law. I doubt he'll be out of jail for a long time. He's been shipped off to Pennsylvania."

Tim nodded his head.

"And don't worry," she said. "None of his issues were all that violent, except for his attack on Sophia. He's really just a stooge for a couple of guys who are doing time, as well."

"Is one of them Frank Wood?" Tim said.

Gretchen did not respond verbally, but she did smile while spreading her hands like she didn't know anything. Tim got her message.

"I'll tell Sophie and Maggie," he said. "They'll feel better."

Gretchen nodded and stood to leave.

"You and Sophia may get a call sometime in the future to be witnesses, if he goes to trial on the assault charge, but that looks unlikely at this point. There's enough on him in Pennsylvania. If Sophia doesn't push the assault charge here, that'll be the end of it."

Tim nodded, stood, and followed her to the door.

"Did you get any information on Sarah Bodden?" Tim said.

Gretchen turned and gave him a just-be-thankful-I-told-you-what-I-did kind of look.

"Sorry," Tim said. "Thought I'd just give it a shot."

Gretchen offered her hand. Tim shook it. He watched her as she walked to the staircase and turned to go down them. She looked back at Tim.

"You should marry that woman," she said.

"Which one?" Tim said and smiled.

"Margaret, of course," she said. "You couldn't handle Sophia. She could kick your ass."

30

Tim sat in his comfy chair reading *The Adventures of Huckleberry Finn*. He heard the kitchen screen door open, and then slam shut. He looked up at the clock. A little after three.

"*Bonjour, Sophia,*" he said.

"Hello, Timothy."

He heard her set her pocketbook on the table and open the refrigerator. He heard the hiss of a soda bottle open. She came in and sat in the other chair.

"She call?" Sophie said.

"No. I doubt she will," Tim said. "How was work?"

"Quiet, actually," she said. "A welcome break."

"I have some good news for you," he said. "My FBI friend stopped by. She said the guy whose ass you kicked has been sent back to Pennsylvania. He has an extensive rap sheet, and he won't be out of prison for a long time."

"Rap sheet?"

"Criminal record," Tim said. "He won't be stalking us anymore."

"That's good," Sophie said. "He was a scummybag, as you say."

Tim chuckled.

"So what are you doing tonight?" Tim said. "Studying?"

"As a matter of fact," she said. "I have a date."

"A date?" Tim said. "That nursing student friend of yours?" He emphasized *nursing student*.

"No," she said. "Do you remember the police officer who took my statement after I was so viciously attacked by the scummybag?"

"You're dating a cop?" Tim said. "Is that even legal?"

"Of course, it's legal," she said. "You don't think police officers have a social life?"

"Yeah, but can they actually date someone they meet on the job?"

"Why not?" Sophie said. "I wasn't the bad guy."

"There must be rules about dating witnesses," Tim said. "It just doesn't seem right."

"And how did you and Maggie meet?"

"At work."

"And were there rules against that sort of thing?"

Tim hesitated. "Well, yes," he said. "But that was different."

"Oh, yes," Sophie said. "That was different because it was you."

Tim twisted his face and bobbed his shoulders back and forth like he was trying to simultaneously squirm out of a trap and come up with a snappy retort.

"And besides," she said. "Paul is a very good man. And I think he likes me."

"He must be brave, too," Tim said. "He saw what you did to Boxman."

"It might give him pause someday," she said.

"Where are you going?" Tim asked.

"The movies," she said. "He asked me to go to see *Annie Hall*. I told him I'd rather see *Star Wars*. He said we would go there instead."

Tim stared at Sophie.

"You made that up, didn't you?" he said.

"*Moi?*" she said. "No, of course not." She turned and moved toward her room. "If it's okay with you, I'd like to have the bathroom for a while. I need a bath."

"No problem," Tim said. "I'm going to hang out here and read for an hour or so. Then I'm going to Maggie's for five."

Not long after Sophia went to take her bath, the phone rang. Tim picked up the handset.

"Hello?"

"Is this Tim Roper?" the woman caller said.

"Yup."

"This is Sarah Bodden," she said. "My sister told me you wanted to speak with me?"

"Uh, yeah," he said. "Um, thanks for calling. Sorry, you took me by surprise."

"What is it you want of me?" she said.

"I want to talk with you about Olivia Wood. But not on the phone."

"Why?"

"It's a long story," Tim said. "I'd like to drive down

and talk with you. I'll be in your area tomorrow."

"How about we meet right now?" she said.

"Right now?"

"I'm in a phone booth on Congress Street about two blocks from your apartment."

"You are?"

"There's a diner across the street," she said. "Meet me there."

Tim hung up and slipped on his sneakers. He considered calling Maggie, but decided against it.

"Sophie," he said through the closed bathroom door. "I'm going out for a walk. Enjoy the movie, if I don't see you."

On Congress Street, he passed the blue Accord, parked at a meter, with its Massachusetts plates and Penn State sticker in the rear window. He crossed the street, walked up the steps, and entered the diner. He scanned the handful of occupied tables and stopped at the attractive brunette sitting in the far corner booth. *I know why the guys at Cummington liked their teacher,* he thought. They stared at each other for a moment and she nodded acknowledgement.

Tim slid into the seat across from her.

"Miss Bodden?" he said.

"Sarah," she said. She reached across and offered her hand. "Nice to meet you, Tim."

"You, too." Tim finally had the moment he'd been waiting for, and he felt himself unable to think of what to say. "Did you come all the way up here just to talk to me?"

"No," she said. "I have another reason. Just thought

I'd kill two birds with one stone."

Tim nodded.

"So how is Margaret?" Sarah said.

"She's good," Tim said. "She told me some very nice things about you."

"And some not so nice things, as well?"

Tim smiled and shrugged.

"Maggie's got a lot on her mind right now," Tim said.

"And that has to do with Olivia?" Sarah said.

"Some of it." Tim said. "And your late husband."

Sarah nodded and looked down. The waitress came over, and both Sarah and Tim ordered a coffee.

"I know she and Bill had a relationship before he came to Cummington," she said. "It was just as well it ended when it did. It would have been a mistake for them to stay together."

"Because he was destined to be with you instead?" Tim said.

"You don't understand," she said, shaking her head. "Bill would never marry Margaret."

Tim's lips tightened and his eyes stared into Sarah's.

"Are you kidding?" he said. "Maggie is perfect."

Sarah paused for a moment, and she dropped her eyes and shook her head.

"You don't understand," she said. "Bill was ill. He knew he carried a disease that was going to kill him." She looked up at Tim. "And it did."

"He drowned in a river," Tim said.

"No," she said. "He was fishing and fell into the river when his heart stopped working."

Tim did not respond. He looked at Sarah, saw the

red eyes, and turned away.

"When Bill was sixteen, his doctor told him he would not likely make it to thirty years old," Sarah said. "His condition was genetic. It killed his mother's father. The coroner believes it killed him. Heart failure is listed as his cause of death, not drowning. I believe that is accurate."

"I'm sorry," Tim said. "I'm sorry for your loss, and I'm sorry I spoke to you that way."

"Don't worry about it," she said. "I understand."

Tim nodded a thanks.

"So what is the issue Margaret has concerning Olivia?" Sarah said

"Maggie recently heard that Olivia killed herself," Tim said. "She blames herself for being part of the reason why Olivia did it."

Sarah's brow wrinkled, and she cocked her head.

"Why would she think that?" Sarah said.

"You don't know?" Tim said. "Olivia blamed Maggie for broadcasting her pregnancy to the school."

Sarah's expression soured. She lifted her right elbow to the table and rested her forehead in her palm, her thumb and fingers massaging her temples.

"Oh, shit," she said.

Tim looked at her, not sure how to respond. Sarah looked up.

"Olivia did not blame Margaret for anything," Sarah said. "It was my idea."

"Your idea?"

"I mean my fault."

"I'm not sure I understand," Tim said.

"I think we need to include Margaret in this conversation," Sarah said.

"I can call her and have her meet us here," Tim said.

"Can we just go to her apartment?" Sarah said. "I think it will make things a lot easier if we all talked in private."

Sarah dropped a ten dollar bill on the table, and Tim followed her to the car.

Tim pressed the button next to Maggie's name. A few seconds later Maggie's voice came through the speaker.

"Hello."

"Hi, Mags. I know I'm early. You free?"

"Sorta. Just painting," she said. "C'mon up." The door buzzed.

"Maggie, I have someone with me."

"Who?"

"Your English teacher." After a long pause, the door buzzed again.

Tim led Sarah up the two flights of stairs to Maggie's landing. The door was open a crack. Tim put his hand on the door, looked back at Sarah, and nodded. He led her into the apartment.

Maggie stood at the sink washing her hands. She picked up a hand towel and began drying them as she turned and looked directly at Sarah Bodden. Maggie's face had a few streaks and smudges of green paint.

"Hi, Miss Bodden," she said and walked toward her an offered her hand.

"Hi, Margaret," Sarah said. "It's great to see you. And please call me Sarah."

"Only, if you call me Maggie."

"It's a deal, Maggie," Sarah said.

Maggie turned to Tim and said, "You're just full of surprises."

"I didn't actually plan this," he said.

"I surprised him," Sarah said.

Maggie nodded and looked at Sarah.

"Can I get you something to drink?" she said. "Coffee? Beer? Ginger ale?"

"I'll have a beer," Tim said. Maggie smirked and shook her head.

"A ginger ale would be good," Sarah said. "I have a long drive ahead."

"I got it," Tim said. Tim walked to the refrigerator and retrieved the beer and ginger ale. He looked at Maggie.

"You?"

"I'm good," Maggie said.

Maggie offered Sarah a seat in one of the stuffed chairs and left the green one for Tim. She sat on the cobbler's bench facing them. Sarah broke the ice.

"So tell me, Maggie," Sarah said. "How was Boston University?"

Maggie told her how much she liked BU and how living in Boston was such a great thing. Sarah asked her about her job and the move to Portland. But the conversation had not gone far before Tim decided it was time to address the elephant in the room.

"Sarah told me William Shannon didn't drown in the river," Tim said, interrupting Maggie. "A congenital heart disorder killed him."

Maggie looked at Tim, and then turned to Sarah.

"That's true," Sarah said. "There was nothing sinister about his death."

Sarah went on to tell Maggie what she told Tim in the diner.

"Bill Shannon could not allow his relationship with you go on, because he knew it couldn't go on. He felt guilty, because he knew he was going to hurt you. He told me he cared a lot about you."

"Billy told you that?" Maggie said. "Why would he tell you that? You were his wife?"

"Not really," Sarah said. Before she could say anything else, Maggie interrupted.

"Not really? He married you. You had kids together. Not really?"

Sarah raised her hand in front of her.

"It's not as simple as it sounds," Sarah said. "Why don't I just start at the beginning, and I'll tell you what I know about Bill and about Olivia. Okay?"

Tim looked at Maggie and raised his brows, looking for her agreement.

Maggie nodded

"You have the floor," Tim said to Sarah.

"Okay," Sarah said, looking at Maggie. "Let's start back at school when you told me about Olivia. She was pregnant and needed help."

Sarah took a deep breath.

"I already knew that before you told me. Bill told me about his meetings with Olivia and their confrontation in the auditorium you overheard. He told me he believed Olivia was very troubled. Like you, he believed she needed help." She paused. "And he told me about your relationship with him over the prior summer."

Maggie dropped her head for a moment, then looked up and nodded.

"He suggested I approach Olivia and see what I could do to help her," Sarah said. "The next morning, when you met me and told me your story, I had already heard almost the same thing from Bill.

"Olivia was in my last period class that afternoon, and as she was leaving, I stopped her and asked if she would help me carry something to my car. Remember that I was on crutches at the time.

"When we got to the car, I told her what I knew about her predicament. She reacted with anger, but I calmed her down by convincing her I could help her, if she would trust me. We sat in the car and talked for almost two hours. She told me about her father and how he physically abused her as he had abused her mother when Olivia was younger. She believed that if her father found out she was pregnant, he'd kill her. Literally. She said she needed to get away from Cummington and get an abortion. She refused to tell me who got her pregnant." Sarah stopped, looked at Maggie, and said, "But I know for a fact, it was not Bill Shannon."

Maggie did not respond.

"My brother, Adrian was a psychiatrist and professor at Dartmouth College. He lived in our parent's summer place in Vermont. I offered Olivia the opportunity to move there. I told her we would do this secretly with the only people knowing this being Olivia, Bill, me, and Adrian. Her father would never know what happened to her and would never suspect me. He'd think she just ran away.

"My offer was conditional on two promises from Olivia. First, she had to agree to become Adrian's patient and undergo his counseling. And second, she had to agree not to have her baby aborted for at least three weeks and spend that time thinking about her options. If she decided to abort, we'd help her. If not, we would help her through her pregnancy. I told her I would get up to Vermont as frequently as I could.

"Olivia responded immediately to the idea. She said she would do whatever it took to make this happen. She just needed to get away from her father. We worked out a plan," Sarah said. She took a sip of her ginger ale and let out a deep sigh. "Maybe we could have done a better job, if we took more time and planned better, but my gut was yelling at me to do something quickly.

"I told Olivia not to bring any of her stuff with her to school the next day. She had to pretend it was no different than any other day. Then I told her she needed to let people know publically it was her intention to leave Cummington. We did not want anyone to go looking for her."

Sarah looked at Maggie, her face lined.

"I told her to confront you in the hallway at school and make sure people heard she was going to take off. Olivia and I went over what she would say to you, not only to convince onlookers, but to convince you she was angry."

Sarah dropped her head.

"I'm really sorry, Margaret. We needed you to feel guilty for her leaving. We needed to put some of the focus on you, so that if you were asked what you knew, you would be convincing. People had to think Olivia left on her own accord. That was my idea, and I never thought about the heartbreak it might cause you. Please forgive me."

Maggie eyes welled, but she held her stare at Sarah and did not speak.

"Maggie went through hell because of that," Tim said, anger rising in him. "She did not deserve that."

"I agree with you, Tim," Sarah said. "I am sorry. And to be fair, Bill told me something similar after he heard what happened. But I convinced him absolute secrecy had to be maintained, not only because her father was psychotic, but because we were actually committing a federal crime. Olivia was only fifteen, and we were taking her to a different state. And abortions were illegal in 1968.

"Olivia, too, felt badly about putting you on the spot. She said you were the only person to approach her, with any offer to help, at any time during her year and a half at Cummington. I wish she had the chance to tell you that."

Maggie closed her eyes and opened them.

"So Olivia really is dead?" she said.

Sarah paused, let out a deep breath.

"Yes. Olivia is dead."

"Suicide?" said Maggie.

"Yes. Olivia made the decision to end her life," Sarah said and held up her empty glass. "I think I need a glass of water."

Sarah started to stand to get her own, but Maggie stood up and raised her hand.

"No, I'll get it, "Maggie said. "There's plenty of ginger ale?"

Sarah nodded. Maggie walked to the kitchen, got some ice, and started filling the glass.

"Adrian and Olivia got along fine. I believe his counseling convinced Olivia to have the baby rather than an abortion. She decided she would give the baby up for adoption."

"What about her father?" Tim said. "He didn't think it odd that she just disappeared?"

"I thought the same thing at first," Sarah said. "But he's the one who told the principal she went off to his sister's place in Colorado. I don't think he wanted anyone looking too closely at him."

Tim nodded, looked over at Maggie, and then back at Sarah.

"I resigned as a teacher in Cummington as soon as school got out. I moved to Vermont with Adrian and Olivia. A few weeks later Olivia gave birth to a baby boy. We checked her into a hospital in Battleboro under an assumed name and paid for everything in cash. She named the boy Brian. I thought she really took to him, and I believed all was fine and figured both Olivia and Brian would stay with us indefinitely. I put a great deal of effort into making her feel welcome."

"Brian?" Tim said, remembering his discussion with Sarah's sister.

"Yes," Sarah said. "That Brian."

I got a job teaching not far from where we lived. All was well until November. I came home one day and found a note and a screaming baby. The note was from Olivia. She said she had to leave. She said she was going to be a bad mother and could not inflict herself on Brian. She said she was heading west to live on a commune – or something like that. You know how things were back then.

"I was distressed and saddened. Sure, I was relieved she left Brian with us. I loved that kid so much. I hired a private detective to see if he could track her down, but after a month and a hefty bill, he found nothing.

"I wasn't sure what to do about Brian. I wanted to keep him, but I was afraid at some point someone would ask questions. I finally decided to let the local police know of his presence. I told them a young woman knocked on our door one day looking for help. She had a newborn boy with her. She told us her name was 'Aquarius.' She stayed with us for a couple of weeks. She never told us her real name. One morning I got up, and she was gone. I told the police she left her baby.

"We said we'd get a nanny to take care of the baby while I was at work or until Aquarius came back for him. Our family was well known in the area. And we had connections. We had no trouble getting Child Services to agree. That's when we asked my sister Katherine to move up from Newborough and become the boy's nanny for a couple of months."

Sarah stopped talking and reached for a tissue from the box on the cobbler's bench. Tim could see the wetness in her eyes. He looked over at Maggie and saw the same thing.

"So the boy I saw at your house in Newborough is Olivia's son?" he said.

"No," Sarah said. "Brian was Olivia's biological son. But he is my son."

"You adopted him?" Maggie said.

"Bill and I adopted him, yes," Sarah said. "Brian is the reason Bill and I got married."

"Tim said there was another boy named Toby," Maggie said. "Is he your natural son? And Billy's?"

Sarah looked at Maggie and shook her head.

"Bill and I shared something in common beyond a love of literature and children," Sarah said. "Our inability to reproduce ourselves. He didn't want to pass his genes on to a child. I couldn't. "

Maggie's jaw dropped, her eyes widened, and her forehead wrinkled. Tim spoke first.

"I don't think Maggie and I understand."

"Bill had the bad heart," Sarah said. "I'm simply infertile. My doctor diagnosed it when I was seventeen and asked for a prescription for the pill. One of the tests he ran on me showed some abnormalities. Further tests showed I cannot bear children. Ever."

Sarah paused, dropped her head, and looked at Maggie.

"Toby was adopted two years after Brian," Sarah said. "His mother was another young teenager in trouble. Adrian ran into a lot of them because of his job."

Tim looked at Sarah and nodded his head.

"Sounds like Brian and Toby got really lucky," he said.

"I agree," Maggie said. She smiled at Sarah and reached across the table and waited for Sarah to take her hand. Maggie squeezed it lightly and let go.

Tim saw the tear well in Sarah's eye.

"Thank you both," Sarah said. She took a deep breath.

"I worried a lot about Olivia after she left. I worried about Brian. I worried that her father might track us down and come looking for his grandson. Six or seven months after she left, I began to think I had to do something to prevent that from happening. I spoke to my lawyer about adopting Brian. He said I would have to prove the mother had abandoned her baby. He didn't think that in itself would be a problem. But he did say being a twenty-seven year old single woman would be a problem.

"Bill and I talked about it and decided to get married. We did it solely for Brian. We knew it wouldn't be forever." Sarah paused, drew a deep breath, and exhaled. "And I admit, we did it for me. I loved that boy. I loved Bill, too, but we were not lovers."

Sarah stopped and inhaled.

"About six months after that, I received a letter from Olivia, postmarked in Los Angeles. It was a suicide note. I hired a lawyer from LA who checked it out. He got us a death certificate. She took a bottle full of pills."

All three sat silent. Sarah stared at the floor. Maggie looked up toward the skylight, watching the late afternoon rays bouncing through the glass. Tim stared at Maggie.

"You never heard from Olivia's father?" Tim said.

"I didn't, but Bill did," she said. "But that really wasn't about the adoption. I don't believe he knows anything about Olivia's baby. But Bill became curious about both Olivia's disappearance and her mother's disappearance. Frank heard about some inquiries Bill made and called him a number of times. Frank made some threats, but nothing ever happened."

"Maggie," said Tim. "You should show Sarah the newspaper note."

"I'll get it." Maggie went to her bedroom and returned with the envelope and letter. She handed it to Sarah.

Sarah unfolded the newspaper article and skimmed down the text. She stared at the written note at the bottom. She closed her eyes.

"'Got your wish. Now rot in hell.' Do you have any idea who wrote that?" Tim asked.

"Yes," Sarah said. She lifted her head and looked straight at Maggie. "I did."

Maggie looked like she just got hit with a two by four.

"You sent that to Maggie?" Tim said. "Why would you do something as mean as that?" Tim could feel the anger building in his chest.

"I said I wrote it," Sarah said. "But I did not send it to Margaret. I sent it to Frank Wood."

"Frank Wood?" Maggie said.

"I told you Frank knew Bill was suspicious about the death of Olivia's mother," Sarah said. "He sent some mean things to Bill and made some veiled threats. When Bill died, I wanted to punch Frank. I know he didn't know Bill and I were married. I wanted it to stay that way. But I had this burst of anger because of Bill's death. I pulled the article from the paper, wrote the note on it, and sent it to him - anonymously.

"In some ways it was stupid and made little sense. But at the time I also thought of it as a way to let Wood know that Bill was dead, end the trail to Bill, and perhaps ultimately, to Brian. I also swore I would continue Bill's efforts to find a way to keep Frank in prison for the rest of his life. I just learned last week that Frank had the note resent to Maggie."

"How do you know that?" Tim said.

"Frank told me," Sarah said.

31

"A month or so before he died, Bill was convinced Frank murdered his wife when Olivia was eight or nine years old," Sarah said. "Bill's mind is...was... incredible. He read a number of Olivia's high school essays and somehow deciphered suggestions Frank killed his wife. He was also convinced Olivia stashed away evidence of the murder somewhere in her house. Since Frank didn't appear to know me or recognize my name, we came up with an idea.

"I pretended I was writing a book on mail fraud and sent him a letter in prison saying I read the transcripts of his case. I had to use my real name to get into the prison, but Frank apparently didn't recognize it as Olivia's teacher, and agreed to listen to my pitch. I told him I was impressed by some of the creative techniques he used, and I would like to interview him for my book. I played to his ego. He agreed to the meeting. I spent an hour interviewing him in prison. I didn't get too much related to what we really wanted to know, but I got a good feel for his nature and how he operates. He is pure slime. I came from that interview convinced Bill was right about him."

"And you broke into his house," Tim said.

"Yes," Sarah said. "A few weeks ago, I broke into his home and followed Bill's instructions on where I might find the evidence Olivia hid. I found the box where he said it would be."

Tim looked at Maggie.

"She's the one," he said and turned to face Sarah. "I went to the house after you and saw the broken window. How's your cut?"

Sarah looked surprised. She lifted her skirt to expose a healing laceration on the back of her left calf.

"Someone got my plates, and the cops thought I broke in," Tim said. Tim told her about their encounter with the Boxman.

"That would be Tommy, Jr." Sarah said. "His father is Frank's brother and is somewhere in hiding. Or dead. No one's seen or heard from him since Frank went away."

Sarah looked at Tim, shook her head and smiled.

"Sorry, Tim," she said

"It was my own fault for sneaking in there," said Tim. "So did the cops catch up with you?"

"I caught up with them," Sarah said. "I sent all the stuff I found to the FBI. Frank isn't getting out of prison for a very long time."

"You sure?"

"Absolutely," she said. "The box I found in Olivia's room contained some personal items Olivia's mother would have taken with her if she took off. They included some jewelry and photographs, but more importantly, her mother's diary.

"Bill had collected some newspaper articles about a financial scam operation in Pennsylvania and Massachusetts, where some con men were hitting on old people. He also had copies of bogus contracts an 'almost victim' had received from someone matching Frank's description. Bill took the contracts to a handwriting expert who matched the handwriting to the signature on a permission slip Frank signed for a field trip to a play Olivia went on with her class in high school. And how he did it, I don't know, but Bill collected receipts for some pawned jewelry, he believed matched the description he read about in the newspaper clippings.

"But there was something else. Bill believed Olivia knew a great deal about what happened to her mother. He believed she suppressed it almost to the point where she couldn't consciously remember what she knew. He believed Olivia revealed some of this in her writings. That was how he figured out where the hiding place was. That was how he began to be suspicious that Frank murdered his wife. A few weeks before he died, Bill took a walk through the woods behind Frank's house, and based on one of Olivia's essays, he believed he found the spot where Frank killed her. He told me this on the phone, but he died before I could get down there, and we could go over and find where he buried her."

Sarah took a sip of water and a deep breath.

"And then I got another idea. I decided to make last week's appointment to go back to see Frank in prison one more time. Frank controlled himself pretty well, until I told him what we found – the diary, the jewelry, the receipts. When he finally lost it and started yelling at me, I brought up the spot Bill identified as the burial site. He exploded, and I knew Bill was right. The FBI found Katherine Wood's body buried there two days ago."

Tim and Maggie sat and absorbed what Sarah said.

"Wow." Tim said. "Remind me not to ever cross you."

Sarah smiled.

"It was really Bill who figured it all out. I was just the executioner."

"That's what I mean," Tim said.

"So how did my name come up in this, and why did Frank send the newspaper article to me?" Maggie said.

Sarah looked at Maggie and nodded.

"For some reason Frank thought you married Bill and were part of the conspiracy to frame him for the murder," she said. "He told me he sent you something and told you to 'rot in hell.' I believe he had Tommy, Jr. resend this article to you. From Reading."

"How would they know where to send it?" Maggie said.

"Did you attend your fifth high school reunion?" Sarah said. "Have you had any correspondence with the school in the past few years? If that information is at the school, people can get it. Even people as dumb as Tommy, Jr."

Tim looked at Maggie, shrugged his shoulders, and smiled.

"But relax, Margaret," Sarah said. "Frank now knows you had nothing to do with any of it. I set him straight and took full credit. Or fault, depending on how you look at it. I couldn't help but brag."

Maggie looked like she was still processing what she learned.

Tim watched her, turned to Sarah, and said, "Thank you for telling us this. It helps us sort through a lot of pieces. I do appreciate it."

"I started all this," Sarah said. "I ended it. I'm sorry for whatever difficulties we may have caused you. I should have come to you after Olivia died and told you that you were not responsible. I'm sorry."

Sarah stood and walked over to Maggie. Maggie got up from the stool, and the two embraced.

"Margaret," Sarah said. "You need to know Olivia spoke very well of you. She said you were one of the few people at the school who talked to her as a friend wanting to help her. You have nothing to feel guilty about."

"Thank you, Sarah," Maggie said. "Thank you for coming here and telling us all this."

Sarah released Maggie and embraced Tim.

"Thanks, Sarah," Tim said. "I appreciate this."

"Thank you both for understanding," Sarah said. She looked at her watch. "I need to run. I want to tuck my boys in. It's a long drive back."

Sarah walked to the door and opened it to leave. She hesitated and turned.

"One more thing, Margaret," Sarah said. "As your English teacher, I would like to make one more comment."

Maggie looked at her having no idea what she was going to say.

"I never got the chance to tell you," Sarah said.

"Outstanding Rosalind!"

Maggie laughed and curtsied thanks in her best Elizabethan manner.

After Sarah left, Maggie and Tim sat in the chairs, each with a beer in hand. For a while, little was said as they absorbed what Sarah had just told them.

"Well, what do you think?" Tim said and took a sip of beer.

"She answered a lot of my questions," Maggie said. "I wish she had better news about Olivia."

"Sarah is quite the woman," Tim said.

"That she is," Maggie said. "I wasn't lying when I described her to you, was I?"

"So how do you feel about all this?" Tim said. "Is there anything related to all of this still needing resolution?"

"No, I don't think so. I think I'm okay," Maggie said. "Well, at least until Patty calls me with something else."

"I think I need another beer," Tim said and walked to the refrigerator.

"Don't worry," she said "I think we can close down our detective bureau."

Tim smiled and raised his beer in salute.

"You need one?" he said.

"No. I'm good," Maggie said.

"Typical you," he said. "Always bragging,"

Maggie stuck her tongue out at him.

"So are we still on for the movies after we grab a bite to eat?" Tim said.

"Absolutely," she said. "But I'd rather not go to

Annie Hall. I'd rather do *Star Wars.*"

Tim looked at her in disbelief.

"Fine with me," he said. "Where's the paper? I'll check out the show time."

"Second show starts at 8:15," she said. "I told Sophie we'd meet Paul and her at 8:00."

Tim stared at her and shook his head.

"Ray's right. I can't handle both of you."

32

The black Ford Pickup truck passed through the Portland toll booth and headed south on I-95. Tim drove. Maggie rode shotgun.

"I feel like I'm driving a tank compared to my VW," Tim said. "It was great of Ray to lend me this to pick up the bass."

"You're going to need to replace your car with something bigger when you join a band, and travel all over New England playing beautiful music with all your groupies following you around," Maggie said. "I just hope you remember us little people."

"I think you may be a little ahead of yourself," he said. "The last time I played my father's bass was in 1957. As for you little people, just write your name in my trusty notebook, so I'll remember to send you tickets when I play in the next Woodstock."

"Front row, right?" she said.

"I'll try," he said. She gave him a light elbow jab.

"I know where you can get a good deal on a pick-up like this," Maggie said. "Jill's Aunt Sue is selling off her late husband's truck. It's a Cheyenne or something like that."

"That's a Chevy," Tim said. "When I get famous, I'll consider it."

They rode with the windows wide open. The radio blared Creedence. The canvas top over the truck's bed flapped in the passing wind, sounding like a flock of pigeons descending on a spilled popcorn bag on Boston Common. The sun warmed Tim's left arm and glinted an occasional reflected beam off his watch toward his sunglassed eyes.

Tim looked over at Maggie. She sat up straight on the bench seat of the truck, but its deep cab allowed her to kick off her sandals and rest her bare feet against the dash. Tim smiled at her toes moving in time to *Down on the Corner*. He followed her thin calves up to the smooth turn of her knees. Stray threads of her cutoff jeans and the sleeves of her beige, V-necked pink top danced on the air coming in through the window. Her right hand surfed the passing waves of sixty-mile-per-hour air.

Tim looked at the profile of her face with its splotch of green sunlight on her cheek, filtered through her round, white-rimmed sunglasses. Her straight nose and focused eyes looked forward, down the highway, toward new destinations. He saw the corners of her mouth curled upward, relaxed in the delicate smile he hadn't seen in a long time. *She really is the perfect woman.*

Since yesterday's meeting with Sarah Bodden, Tim

saw the quiet settling of peace in Maggie. She cried a few times after Sarah left, but not the cruel tears of guilt and regret. Maggie cried for Olivia. She cried for the sadness and despair that poor girl endured in her short life.

Maggie turned her head toward him.

"In my next life I want to be Princess Leia," Maggie said.

"You want to be Princess Leia?" Tim said. "Where did that come from?"

"I was just thinking," she said. "Princess Leia is young and beautiful. She fights for goodness and helping the down-trodden. The guys fawn all over her. What's not to love?"

"Maybe the near death experience she has about every five minutes?" Tim said. "Maybe her fights with scary creatures from other worlds?"

"But she can protect herself with her lightsaber," Maggie said.

"Princess Leia doesn't use a lightsaber," Tim said.

"Not yet. But she will when they make a sequel."

"Do you ever notice all those little strokes of paint on your face and body after one of your all day painting sessions?" Tim said. "And you're only wielding a small paint brush. Imagine what you would do to yourself swinging a lightsaber?"

"I can learn," she said. "And I bet Sophie would be good at it. She could teach me."

"You're out of your mind," Tim said. "You realize that, right?"

"Yes, I do," she said. "And today it feels great to get out of my mind." Maggie reached her left arm toward Tim. He clasped her hand and felt her energy flowing into him. Maggie turned her head forward, closed her eyes, and returned to her mind. The smile never left her face.

They went through the southeast corner of New Hampshire into Massachusetts. The traffic was light.

"Tim," Maggie said. "Do you think Sarah lied to me?"

Tim looked at her and said, "Lied to you? About what?"

"About Olivia understanding that I was trying to help her. About Olivia liking me. About Olivia forgiving me."

"Why would she lie about that?" Tim said.

"To make me feel better," Maggie said.

"I doubt it," Tim said. "She drove all the way up to Portland to talk to you. I think she had guilt about putting you as the bad guy in this drama. The attack on you in the hallway was staged by Sarah. She put you in jeopardy by letting Olivia's father think you were the one helping Olivia disappear, that you were the one working with Shannon to expose Wood as the killer of Olivia's mother."

"Yeah, but Sarah didn't know that was what he thought until the end," Maggie said.

"Maybe," Tim said. "But I doubt anything Sarah told us yesterday was a lie."

But even as he said it, Tim knew the words leaving his lips might be a lie. He, too, had doubts about Sarah Bodden. He wasn't sure where those doubts came from. He didn't know what part of what she said might be her lie. Or lies.

Sarah tied up everything in too neat a bundle. She was smart and clever, no matter how you looked at it.

She convinced Maggie back in high school that she was hearing about Olivia for the first time. She conned Frank Wood into believing she was a journalist writing a book about him. She probably conned William Shannon into being the front man for the investigation of Olivia's mother. She managed to avoid arrest for breaking and entering by the local police department, and it sounds like she managed to do the same thing with the FBI. Sarah is a good actress. And things fit together a bit too neatly. Somewhere buried deep inside, her story might hold "The Big Lie," that one piece of the puzzle, that when you fit it in place, the rest of the pieces finally make sense.

Tim thought about that missing piece. He asked himself questions. Why is it that Sarah is always the authority on causes of death? Olivia's mother's murder? Shannon's death by natural causes while fishing? Olivia's suicide? Brother Adrian's cancer? She said Olivia never said who her baby's father was. Maybe it *was* Shannon. Was Sarah jealous and manipulated events to her own favor? Why does she seem to always be living somewhere different? Sarah said she and Shannon agreed never to produce children of their own. Then he remembered something Mary Louise told them in that library in Vermont. *Oh my God.*

"Whatcha thinkin'" Maggie said.

"I was thinking about work," he said. "I have a case going to trial tomorrow."

"Don't think work," Maggie said. "Think sunshine and blue skies. Think peace and love and happiness. Think about me with a lightsaber."

Tim laughed. "I don't believe I've ever seen anyone

this happy while driving to Worcester."

"It's not where I'm going," she said. "It's why I'm going. And who I'm going with."

"Ditto," Tim said.

The sign said the Worcester exit was coming up in ten miles. Tim had to make a decision. He looked at Maggie and her smile. He thought about her lying unconscious on the ground next to that dumpster, an emotional mess. He thought about Maggie's tears and her story of Olivia and Billy Shannon and the guilt she carried. He knew what he had to do. He knew doing it was at risk. But he needed to stop the lie.

"Maggie," he said. "You hungry?"

Maggie looked at him. "Yes, I'm hungry, but I thought we were going to a cookout at your Mom's house."

"That's not until three o'clock," Tim said. "I can't wait that long. When I went to Sarah's house, I went by this new diner. I mentioned it to her sister when I was there, and she said it was great. They use pure Vermont syrup and serve buckwheat pancakes, which, as you know, are my all-time favorites. C'mon. You know you're hungry."

"I wouldn't want to stand between you and your buckwheats," she said.

"I'll even give you a bonus," Tim said as casually as he could manage. "I'll do a drive-by of the Bodden estate. You'll be impressed."

"Okay," Maggie said. "Let's go."

I do not want to say anything to Maggie. I do not want her worrying. I have about twenty minutes to come up with a good reason to stop in and talk to Sarah.

Ten minutes later Tim took the exit for Newborough. The summer bloom painted the homes and farms along their path with the yellows, pinks, reds and greens of New England in July. The few fields of corn they passed were shorter than the tall stalks he maneuvered through in Berks County. They passed a rocky pasture containing five basking Jersey cows.

The stone wall and wire fence framing the Bodden's paddock rose from the woods and ran along the road. Tim saw the house and its long driveway beyond the paddock. He was about to point out the house to Maggie and utter his excuse for dropping in on Sarah, when something far greater caught his eye. He pulled over onto the wide, grassy space between the road and the wall.

"Why are you stopping?" Maggie said and looked at Tim.

Tim pointed past her. Maggie turned and saw three people walking a saddled horse towards a worn, grassy circle in the middle of the paddock about seventy five yards from them.

"The taller boy is Brian," he said.

Maggie looked over at Olivia's child. He wore grey shorts and a blue and white polo shirt. His brown hair blew in the soft breeze as he walked. He held the horse's lead.

His brother Toby sat atop the horse, his hands holding both the reins and the front of the English saddle. His green T-shirt and white shorts belied the formality of the dark riding helmet on his head.

"The blonde woman walking next to Brian is Sarah's sister, Kat."

Maggie watched Brian lead the horse into the circle

and hand the reins to his aunt. He stepped back out of the circle as his aunt attached a longer lead to the harness. She moved to the middle of the circle and appeared to give instructions to Toby. The horse began a slow circle around her.

Maggie's eyes stayed on Brian, the back of her head to Tim. Brian stepped closer to them as he moved out of the path of the walking horse. He picked up a stick lying in the grass and threw it flying through the air at some unknown target. As he finished his throw, he caught sight of the parked truck on the other side of the wall. He walked a few yards toward it, then stopped, surveying it. He couldn't see the two in the truck through its tinted windows, but Maggie could see him and enough of his face to see the round cheeks and wide forehead he inherited from Olivia.

Tim heard the sniffle.

"He even looks like her," Maggie said. "I wish to God she could see him."

"I'm sure she does," Tim said.

Something else caught Brian's attention, and he bounded off toward the cluster of trees between the paddock and the driveway. Maggie smiled to herself at his short attention span and watched him pull himself up to the lower branch of a maple tree. He began to climb. Maggie looked back at Toby and Kat. Kat was lifting Toby from the horse, and Maggie saw Toby pointing over her head to Brian in the tree.

"He's telling on his brother," Maggie said with a smile.

"Remind you of someone?" Tim said.

"Yes," Maggie said. "I'm surprised my brother still talks to me."

Kat turned, saw Brian, and called to him. He ignored her. Kat handed the lead to Toby. The horse munched on the grass.

Maggie watched Kat walk toward Brian's perch. She watched Kat's arm gestures pointing down and smiled to herself as Brian ignored his aunt. Kat shook her head in frustration and ran her hand up, pushing the curly, golden locks off her face.

Tim heard the sharp intake of Maggie's breath and knew he was right. Maggie turned to look at him, her eyes wide, her mouth open.

"Oh, my God." she said.

Tim said nothing. He knew.

Maggie turned back to the window. Olivia stood beneath the tree, her hands on her waist, her head looking up scolding her son. Brian climbed down the tree. When he got to the bottom, Olivia lifted her hand in front of him and waved her index finger in his face, scolding him. Like a mother would. Brian hung his head. Maggie saw him shaking his head up and down, like he was agreeing to whatever she was saying. They turned and walked toward the horse.

Maggie saw Olivia put her left hand up around Brain's shoulder, first to guide him away from the trees, but then she squeezed him close to her. Brain's arm reached around the waist of the woman he calls his aunt, and squeezed himself to her. They reached Toby and the horse. Olivia took the lead and helped Brian climb up on the horse. Brian rode it around the circle.

Maggie watched them for ten minutes or so without saying a word. Tim remained quiet in the driver's seat.

"When did you know?" Maggie said.

"I figured it out on the way down."

Maggie turned in the seat and faced him. She wrinkled her brow and tipped her head.

"You figured it out on the way down?"

"Actually, you told me," Tim said. "When you were telling me I needed to buy a pick-up truck from Jill's Aunt Sue."

"What are you talking about?" Maggie said.

"You pronounced her name as, 'Ant' Sue, like the bug, not 'Ahhnt' Sue, like we who are born and raised in New England would say," Tim said.

"That's how I talk," she said. "You've been listening to me talk like that for four years. Actually, most of the country says, 'ant.'"

"But not people born and raised in New England," he said. "Not people like me or Sarah Bodden...or Sarah Bodden's sister. When I was here talking to Kat, she told Brian, if he didn't behave, 'Anty' Kat would not drive him to Cub Scouts. Its significance didn't register with me at the time – I'm so used to listening to you - but when you said it this morning, I remembered thinking she sounded like she was 'anti-cat,' you know, someone who hates cats."

"And that made you leap to the conclusion that Kat was Olivia?" Maggie said.

"It planted the seed that Kat was not from around here," Tim said. "I've had something spinning through my brain since Sarah went home yesterday. The Ant Kat thing somehow broke through it." He paused. "Remember our conversation with Mary Louise in Densmore?"

"Yes."

"Mary Louise said Adrian and Sarah were the only Bodden children," Tim said.

Maggie said. "I don't remember that."

"I do. In any case, it no longer matters," he said. "Olivia is alive. You see her. Sarah lied to us, no, she lied to you. She owed you more than that. She showed up in Portland, because she didn't want us to show up down here. She didn't want you running into Olivia. We should go to the house now and tell her we know."

Maggie turned toward the window and watched Brian, now riding at a slow trot. She saw his body bouncing in the saddle, his hair flopping up and down with each stride. Even from this distance, Maggie could see the growing smile of his face as he settled into the saddle, gaining control of the horse.

Maggie watched Olivia holding the long lead, her look never leaving her son, guiding him forward, encouraging him in ways Olivia never knew when she was his age. Maggie watched the animated language of Olivia's body matching the growing smiles of accomplishment on her face. Maggie turned back toward Tim, the streak of tears ending at her upturned smile.

"Sarah did not lie to me. Maybe she walked a narrow line, but everything she told us yesterday she said to protect Olivia. Frank can never know. Sarah told me Olivia was dead. Olivia *is* dead. Olivia died eight or nine years ago, when she resurrected herself as Katherine."

Maggie stopped, thought for a moment and said with a growing smile, "And didn't Sarah say *Katherine* was Olivia's mother's name?" Maggie shook her head, her hand reaching up to the corner of her eye. She breathed deeply.

"Maybe I played my small part in this. But Sarah

Bodden accomplished all that I asked her to do nine years ago. And she accomplished a great deal more. Sarah saved Olivia when they created Kat. Sarah Bodden owes me no apologies."

Maggie looked back out her window.

"In an odd sort of way, Sarah also helped me find my new life, Timmy." She turned back to face him. "And you, my love, are the best part of it."

Maggie leaned over and kissed him.

"So drive on, Sweet Prince," she said. "Our part in this play is done."

THE END

ABOUT THE AUTHOR

Ken Amidon was born and raised around
Worcester, Massachusetts
and southeastern Pennsylvania.
He graduated from the
University of Massachusetts at Amherst.

Ken lives with his wife Suellen in a small town
in Central Massachusetts.

18641429R00164

Made in the USA
Lexington, KY
16 November 2012